BEAUTIFUL
DISTRACTION

J. C. REED

BEAUTIFUL DISTRACTION

Copyright © 2016 J.C. Reed

All rights reserved.

Cover art by Larissa Klein

Editing by Shannon Wolfman

Inline Editing by Therin Knite

ISBN: 1522897909
ISBN-13: 978-1522897903

BEAUTIFUL
DISTRACTION

Kellan Boyd always gets what he wants—except that one infuriating city girl who bumped into his new chick magnet sports car, dared to call him a jerk, and basically threw his pity check in his face.

Fast forward three months later. When Ava Cross suddenly knocks on his door in the middle of a storm, soaking wet and in dire need of help, he's determined to settle old scores and finally get her between the sheets where she belongs.

Ava knows Kellan is a complex man with a dark past and a wild reputation he can't deny. Forced to stay, Ava begins a desperate search for the truth about the one man she wants to despise and quickly discovers that the passion she feels for him isn't just deep…it's dangerous to her heart.

Kellan is a beautiful distraction. When the traps of her own weakness stand in the way, Ava is faced with one choice only: peel off the layers of a man who's a wild cowboy at heart.

DEDICATION

This book is for those who never give up dreaming and believing in love. Here's to new beginnings, second chances, hot cowboys, enjoying a night under the stars, and to living in the moment.

PROLOGUE

"AVA, WHERE ARE you?"

I grimace, not in the least surprised by the high pitch of my coworker 's voice. Carol Evans is at her wit's end, and I can't blame her. Being the assistant to the editor-in-chief is one shit-ass job. Tanya Bollok, TB, or The Bitch, as we like to call her at work, is the devil incarnated. Because of her endless demands, impossible requests for perfection, and mile-high expectations that would kill anyone's private life, everyone fears her.

I scowl. "Obviously not at the office."

"No shit." I can sense the obligatory roll of her eyes. "I already know that because I looked for you everywhere."

"You have? Is this about my article?" I wince at the phone and hasten my steps. "Look, I'll have it done by Monday. TB won't even notice."

"Trust me, she will. I need it by midnight."

I let out a laugh. "You can't be serious."

The dead silence on the other end confirms the worst.

We have a tight deadline. I get it. But the print run is Monday two a.m. No article needs to hit the editor-in-chief's desk before Sunday night.

Try to explain that to TB.

God forbid you actually try to have a life or friends outside of the office.

And God forbid you leave said office as early as six p.m. on a Friday night, which is what I've done for the first time in my career, and now it comes back to bite me.

I don't know why I let my best friend Mandy talk me into driving her to Club 69 on a Friday evening, but as usual, after a five-minute tirade about how she was too late to call for a taxi and she had to be at work *that instant*, I caved in and took the one-hour drive upon me to help her out.

I shouldn't have. Because now I'm going to be in a shitload of trouble with my boss.

I groan again. "TB won't even be back until Sunday."

"So we all thought," Carol says. "She took an early flight. I expect her back within the hour."

"What?" I didn't mean to shout. Several people turn their heads to regard me. Waving my hand, I mouth, "I'm fine. Haven't been mugged or anything," and tune back to the conversation.

"You're lucky I was here to intercept her call or else you would've been the fifth she fired this month."

"She can't fire me." Not in the least because I'm great at what I do, but TB has never been the reasonable type and I'm not one to take my chances. "Okay. I'm coming." Cradling the phone between my shoulder blade and my chin, I scurry to my car, fishing for the keys in my bag while guessing how long it'll take me to get back to the office. A glance at my watch tells me it won't be before ten p.m. Great. I'll be spending another unpaid Friday night staring at a computer screen with TB breathing down my neck.

I open the car door and throw in my bag,

suppressing the urge to remind Carol that everyone's entitled to an evening off every once in a while. But what would be the point in arguing with her when it's not her fault?

"What if she arrives before you?" Carol asks.

"Tell her I'm sick."

"I thought you said your grandmother died. That's what Jay said you told him when you left early."

I cringe. "Yeah, that too."

"Ava, you can't die twice."

"Meaning what?"

"Meaning you already told the same lie last year, so keep your lies straight."

Actually, that was only a half-lie because Grandma *was* sick and TB wouldn't let me fly home until I came up with the dying part. Thank God, Grandma lived. But TB even had me show her the hospital bill.

"Yeah. Remind me to make a list." I let out a nervous laugh as I'm rounding the car to get into the driver's seat.

"I'll try to steer her off of you, but no guarantees. Can you be back in half?" Carol asks.

"What? Half an hour?" Yeah, if I learn how to fly. "Sure," I say chirpily.

My gaze brushes over the busy street and the long line of people trying to get into Club 69 as I push the key into the ignition and start the engine. I throw the car into reverse and try to wriggle my way out of the congested parking lot. I scoot my car forward a scant three feet in line, my eyes focused on the busy street. As I'm about to exit the parking lot, a car approaches mine.

I don't know my way around cars, but I'm pretty sure it's a red Lamborghini.

Shiny, and brand new, and expensive as shit.

And it honks impatiently.

Probably some rich guy who'll wave his wallet into the bouncer's face to get into the club.

Another entitled jerk who thinks he owns the world.

The guy honks again.

"Asshole," I half-shout.

"Excuse me?" Carol says.

"Not you. I'm talking to the guy behind me." I groan and glance in the rear-view mirror. "If TB arrives before me, tell her I'll be back as soon as I can. And I have every intention of working through the night."

Which I usually do anyway. Coffee's my best friend. Sleep's the enemy. If I could live off one and get rid of the other, TB would probably hug me.

"Try to get here ASAP."

"I'm on my way." I hang up and throw my phone onto the passenger seat, my glance shooting back to the red car. As I try to move forward, my engine dies.

Another impatient honk—drawn out and annoying the living hell out of me.

Seriously?

Arrogant bastard. Can't he wait for two frigging seconds?

What is it with people and Club 69? Just the mere possibility of seeing the it-band Mile High greeting the crowd has everyone, including my best friend Mandy, out of their minds.

Right then he holds his hand out of the window and waves at me, motioning for me to move ahead.

"Thanks, jerk!" I gesture at him through the open window and then press hard on the gas at the same moment the red Lamborghini moves forward, whipping around me.

The crash is inevitable, the sound of scratching metal making my heart drop into my lap.

Fucking hell!

Why would he give me a heads up to move and then do the same?

And who the fuck drives like a maniac, heedless of the usual traffic around Club 69, or the fact that it's Friday night and the streets are bound to be busy?

My blood's boiling in my veins, the thick liquid thrumming in my ears.

I kill the engine and jump out of the car, leaving the door ajar.

"What the hell did you think you were doing?" My voice is a choked mixture of rage and exasperation.

Maybe the owner of this quarter-million-dollar chick magnet has the fluffy bank account to have their car repaired, but I sure as hell will have to live with the dents forever. I'll probably have to skimp on food for a month to save the money for new headlights.

"I could ask you the same thing." The low grumble of a male voice reaches me through the open window before the door's thrown open and out jumps a male in his late twenties.

I take a sharp breath. Then another, my heart skipping beats.

Wow.

He's hot. And certainly not in an earthy, imperfect way.

He looks like a god.

His hair, dark and shiny, frames an attractive face with a straight nose, chiseled chin and the most stunning eyes I have ever seen. The expensive, light blue dress shirt can't hide his broad shoulders or the fact that he's probably sporting a six-pack beneath it. The sleeves are rolled up, revealing strong, tan arms and capable hands that don't look like they're stuck to a computer keyboard all day.

He works out...probably a lot.

He steps closer, and I can make out the color of his irises. In the dim light, his eyes shimmer in the dark crystal green shade of a beautiful, untouched lake.

Standing at six-foot-two, he oozes confidence and money.

And something else.

Sex.

The word invades my mind, and for a moment that's all I can think about.

Hot, steamy, wild, rough sex. The kind of sex that has you gripping at the sheets as wave after wave of orgasm rolls over you.

I'm not cheap, but I'm not a saint either. I appreciate a hot guy when I see one. And this one tops the charts. And judging from the long line of women glancing at him, like bees swarming around an exotic flower, I know I'm not the only one having those kind of thoughts.

But not even a hot guy can distract me from the situation at hand.

I examine the damage to my car.

My car's headlight is broken, while his car looks intact.

"There's a scratch." His voice is deep and low. His sexy accent sends a delicious tingle down my spine as I stare at my car in the knowledge it'll cost me way too much to get it repaired—money I don't have.

"You call that a scratch? Can you—" I turn sharply to face him and stop midsentence, expecting him to be inspecting my car.

Instead, he's leaning over *his* car. "You're right. It's more of a chip." Hot Guy points to a small nick, which I swear could just as well be a smudge of dirt, and trails a finger over it, his face drawn in worry. "This is going to be expensive."

I scoff, feeling angry.

"You're talking about a chip? Have you seen my car?"

He glances at it fleetingly before his eyes return to me. "That old thing? I'm surprised you can still drive it."

My jaw drops as I'm rendered speechless.

My beloved Ford might have been previously owned, twice—at least I hope the car dealer told me the truth—but it's been with me through more ups and downs than any human being in my life.

I feel strangely nostalgic toward my beloved Ford, and tears begin to sting the corners of my eyes.

Yes, it's just a car and a battered one at that, but I can't let a guy get away with hurting the one thing that I worked my ass off saving up for—the most valuable thing I own, even though it probably costs less than his polished pair of dress shoes.

"Why are we talking about your car?" I ask. "You can hardly see the damage."

"Do you realize how much my Lamborghini's worth?" Mr. Expensive Shirt says, raising a perfect brow, reading my thoughts.

I can't believe it.

"Jerk!" I yell. "Arrogant prick. I don't know how much your damn car's worth, and I don't care because it's *your* fault." I spit out the last two words, oblivious to the fact that I probably look like a madwoman the way I stab my finger into his chest. He doesn't even seem to register it as his gaze travels down the front of my snug top and tight jeans, which I threw on in haste.

"Did you just call me a 'jerk' and a 'prick'?"

Oh, that voice. Deep and hoarse and penetrating, carrying the slightest hint of amusement. It instantly sends a pleasant chill through me. I can almost feel it vibrating between my legs. My skin prickles from the expression he gives me as he scans my body.

I'm suddenly aware of the fact that I look like a hot mess: my brown hair's all tangled, and I'm hardly wearing any makeup. I couldn't stand out more among the Club 69 crowd of long, oiled-up legs and short skirts. Had I known I'd be having a close encounter with Mr. Sex On Legs, I might have even made an effort.

"Yes, I did," I spit out. "Because it's your fault."

"My fault?" He turns his head to me, his gorgeous face drawn in surprise. "*You* gave me the signal to go ahead."

"I did what?" Frowning, I let out a sarcastic laugh. "No, you gave *me* the signal to go ahead."

He shakes his head. "I most certainly didn't."

Is he suffering from some neurodegenerative disease?

I stare at him, open-mouthed, then mimic his wave. "This is the go-ahead sign to move."

"No, it means you drive like an eighty-year-old, and I don't have all day to watch you amble around." His eyes meet mine, his gaze challenging.

His features are relaxed; his mouth is slightly open as he stares me down in amusement. I don't know why, but I get the distinct feeling he's enjoying the situation.

Well, I'm not amused.

"I wasn't ambling. I was waiting to get in line and you tried to overtake me," I state the obvious.

"You stopped," Hot Guy points out. "That means you gave me the all-clear."

My mouth opens and closes, which probably looks like I'm a panting fish out of water. At last, I shake my head in disbelief. "Are you for real? I stopped to check if a car was coming."

"So you say." His lips twitch. "Let's face it. You were distracted by that phone glued to your ear, chatting as if I had all the time in the world." He steps forward. "Has no one ever told you that talking on a phone while driving can cost lives?"

I want to remark that I wasn't driving while I was on the phone, but I refrain from it, because he's right. "This is hardly a highway."

"It's still called dangerous driving," the guy says.

For a few seconds, all I can do is stare at him. My pulse quickens and my breathing sounds just a little louder than it should. Knots begin to form in my abdomen as I stare at his perfect teeth and his perfect lips.

God dammit.

He screams sex on legs.

The kind of guy you take home to let him fuck your brains out, and then you discard the next day because there's no way in hell a guy like him settles for anything less than a harem.

He also screams incurable, arrogant bastard.

Everything he's said so far tells me he's a big-ass jerk.

I don't know why the thought that his dick's probably had more mileage than a porn star's pops into my head. But it does, and it reminds me that I'm very angry.

Fuming mad.

He hit my car...I remember. I can't afford any repairs. On top of that, I shouldn't be thinking about sex, especially not with Mr. Arrogant who's more concerned with his stupid car than with the damage he's caused to mine.

"It's just a scratch," I point out. "Nothing a good paint job won't solve."

"Look." He sighs. His hot, sexy breath hits my face as he turns to me. "I get it. You don't have the money to pay for the damage. You probably don't even have insurance, and I wouldn't wait for a check anyway, but damn, I just had it flown in from Italy. Don't you have eyes, woman?"

I gape at his audacity.

He's the one driving like a moron, and he's still trying to blame *me* for *his* shortcomings?

And what kind of accent is that?

A slight drawl, rather subdued, as though he's trying to hide it.

No one's ever made me hot and bothered by just *talking* to me, and it's not even dirty talk.

I can't help closing my eyes for a moment, enjoying the onset of sexual tension. When I open them barely a second later, I find him staring at me, his tongue tracing his lower lip.

And is that the slightest hint of a smile I glimpse on his lips?

It can't be because that would imply he's—

Laughing at me.

I cringe.

"Jerk," I mutter.

"Really? Do you know who I am?" he asks, completely oblivious to my growing annoyance with him.

My brows shoot up. "Should I? I don't think so...unless you've done something worth remembering, like saving the world or—"

I gesture with my hand, trying hard to think of something that could prove my point. Truth is, I most certainly *wouldn't* forget him if I knew who he was because he's anything but forgettable.

His grin turns into laughter. I stare at him, confused.

I just insulted his expensive ass.

Why the fuck is he laughing?

"Trust me, if I *did* something, you wouldn't be asking. You'd definitely be feeling it for days to come." His green gaze shimmers, challenging me. "I might be a jerk, but I'm the kind of jerk who always lets the woman come first. And not just once."

My eyes widen. "What?"

Sensing my confusion, he continues, "Either way, I'm okay with settling this incident privately."

"How do you propose we do it?"

"I know a few ways." His lips crack open into a smile.

My jaw drops. Is he hitting on me? Can't be because—

"What?" I croak, my voice suddenly hoarse and my body on fire. My nipples strain against the thin fabric of my top, and most certainly not because of the cool NYC air.

Oh, the traitors!

Mr. Sex On Legs licks his lips slowly and deliberately, his gaze seemingly glued to my heaving chest. He doesn't even *try* to hide the fact that he's eye-fucking my breasts. Hell, in his dirty mind, I'm probably eagle-spread on his bed with him on top of me.

"I'm sorry. I don't follow." I shake my head, trying to make sense of his words. "What are you talking about?"

"You can repay the damage by going out with me tonight," he says. "After which we can head over to my place."

I blink once, twice. My mouth parts ever so slightly. My labored breath barely makes it past my suddenly parched lips.

Fuck, that's hot!

Oh, I want that.

I haven't been with anyone in more than a year. It's been so long I wouldn't be surprised to find cobwebs down there.

If I were into one-night stands, he'd be perfect. Hot, arrogant, the kind who wouldn't even think about asking for your number, let alone call you after you'd done the dirty deed.

But there's no way in hell I'd hook up with someone who's so obvious and obnoxious about it.

Somewhere in the background, I can hear my phone ringing, reminding me that time is of the essence.

"Is that your boyfriend calling?" He grins. "You seem to be ignoring him."

"That's none of your business."

"No boyfriend, then." His arrogance is monumental. You can probably see it from outer space. And it irritates the hell out of me. "So, what do you say? In case you didn't get it, I asked—"

"I heard you loud and clear, and the answer's no."

"No?" His brows shoot up in surprise.

"No."

"You sure?" He peels his gaze off my breasts, albeit unwillingly, and finally settles on my face.

I cross my arms over my chest and regard him coolly. "Has your flavor of the day stood you up and now you're in desperate need of a replacement hookup? I'm no replacement fuck, ever. There's definitely not going to be any coming. And I'm not a hooker. I'm not offering up my body to pay for the damage to your car."

"I figured that much. At least let me buy you a drink, and we'll take it from there." His gaze sweeps over me again in that deliberate, tantalizing way. "You owe me."

In spite of his harmless words, I can feel what

he's thinking.

"Owe you?" I laugh. "Why are you like this? You don't even know me."

"In my line of work, I don't have time to waste, especially not when I like what I see." He peers behind him. I follow his line of sight to the long queue in front of the club.

What is it that he does?

Is he a pimp?

A drug lord?

I'm fascinated and curious as hell.

I almost take the bait and ask, but bite my tongue to stop myself before I do.

"Sorry, I think I'll pass. You're not my type." I take a step back to put some distance between us. A pang of disappointment flashes across his face, but he seems to get the message.

"I'm everybody's type," he says. "You just have to realize it."

I have no doubt about that, but I keep my stony expression in place, proud that I've just rejected the hottest guy I've ever seen. Later, in the loneliness and privacy of my four walls, I'll probably feel differently.

His flirty expression seems to change before my eyes.

Yeah, he definitely got the memo.

His gaze travels the length of my Ford, assessing it with what I assume are knowing eyes. Without waiting for my reply, he pulls his wallet out of his back pocket and begins writing a check that he goes on to squeeze into my hand. I peer at the sum he's just agreed to pay, and my mouth goes dry.

Holy cow.

That's a lot of money.

My Ford's not worth that much.

"This should cover your repairs, though my advice is to buy a new car."

My gaze jumps from the stark white piece of paper to his smug expression and then back to the check. I thought I was angry before, but it was nothing compared to what I'm feeling now.

The lump sum he's offering is enough to cover the cost of a new car.

My heart pumps so hard, it might just be about to burst out of my chest...and not in a good way.

I'm humiliated...and furious.

Not because his gesture implies that the accident was all his fault and he's basically in my debt. I'm furious because the smugness in his expression tells me he's convinced of the exact opposite.

He feels sorry for me, and his generous check is

basically a handout.

A pity check.

The audacity!

Is that the reason why he hit on me in the first place? Because he thought I might be poor and impressed by his flashy car and clothes, and consequently eager to spread my legs for him just because he's *privileged*?

"What do you think? Is this enough?" he prompts impatiently.

Ignoring his questions, I smile sweetly and step closer.

The plan is to look straight into his eyes and tell him where he can shove his check. But instead, I find myself having to tilt my head back to look all the way up into a pair of sinfully green eyes the color of deep, dark forests and haunted meadows. Somehow, my frosty stance doesn't look as confident and significant as I had planned it to be.

In fact, his height intimidates me and I almost choke on my words.

"Keep it. I don't want your money," I push out through gritted teeth. "And there's no way I'd ever sleep with you. Not today. Not tomorrow. Not ever. Got it?"

With shaky fingers, I throw his check at him,

careful not to touch him in any way.

His brows rise. Slowly, his smile dies on his lips.

"I'm not demanding that you—"

I'm no longer listening as I turn my back to him and jump into my car, then slam the door shut.

I avoid looking at him as I start the engine, but I can feel his gaze on me, and it's burning my skin. My insides are on fire, even though my anger seems to have evaporated into the balmy night.

Without looking back, I speed past him. I don't live in his world, so I know I'll never see him again. But that doesn't make his eyes easily forgotten, nor does the knowledge dull the delicious throb between my legs.

The fact still remains: he was a jerk.

Some arrogant bastard I'll never see again.

I'd rather eat his check before I accept a handout from a stranger with the sick fantasy of settling it in private—in his bed.

CHAPTER ONE

Three months later

A bitch of a hurricane is brewing up. It's been all over the news for the past few days. I was too wrapped up in my research for my new article to watch TV or read the headlines, but Mandy has no excuse for dragging me along on this road trip through Montana with dark clouds gathering above our heads.

Okay, maybe she has a reason...in the form of two tickets to see Mile High—the hottest indie band in the world. Too bad the concert's taking place in Montana, which is probably the reason why it isn't sold out. I mean, would you drive across half the country to see a pretentious bunch of delusional idiots dry humping the air and lip synching the life out of some auto tune while believing they're the incarnation of Mozart?

Yeah, me neither.

But Mandy's a fan.

Apparently, the fact that they're wearing black carnival masks (and not much else) and no one knows their real identities makes them even hotter— or so Mandy says. She doesn't just have the band's entire repertoire, which I swear consists of all of five songs that seem to run on replay across all stations nationwide (you can't escape them anywhere); she's actually not even ashamed to admit she's into them.

Talk about turning into a groupie and reliving her teens.

Imagine my dismay when my car license registration won two concert tickets in a big radio swoop. I don't want to sound ungrateful, but out of all the great prizes (think a new iPhone and a makeover with a celebrity hairstylist), I had the misfortune to win the tickets when I'm probably the only female in the world who wouldn't know who they were if it weren't for Mandy's eclectic taste in music.

The moment I won the tickets, someone must have also bashed me over the head because I was stupid enough to tell Mandy about the win *and* reveal that I was considering selling them on eBay. Mandy almost blew a gasket and basically dragged me into the car to head for Madison Creek.

The fight was lost before it even began.

Which is why I'm here—God knows where—with the enthusiasm of a turtle at the outlook of putting my poor ears through the torture that's about to befall Montana.

Poor Montana, too.

Forget the band.

Fortunately, the tickets come with a 'one-week all expenses paid hotel stay for two.' That's the only upside of my prize, at least in my opinion, and the main reason I agreed to keep it.

I desperately need the one-week vacation before the boring work routine engulfs me once again.

I've no idea where we are, only that we're hours away from New York City, when I unplug Mandy's iPhone in favor of some local radio station's playlist of Sheryl Crow and David McGray songs. We're halfway through the second song when the news comes through.

"Storm Janet is picking up speed as she makes

her way across western Montana. Residents are advised to stay indoors as severe, rare storm force winds with heavy rain are expected across some parts of..." Mandy switches off the radio.

Suddenly the gray clouds gain an ominous new meaning and my throat chokes up.

"A hurricane? Are you fucking kidding me?" I yell at Mandy, who's speeding along an unpaved country road, past green pastures and untouched nature.

"Relax. It's just a bit of wind, Ava," Mandy says. "Besides, we're almost there. Relax and enjoy the scenery."

Relax?

I cringe and bite my tongue hard so I won't say something I may come to regret later. Mandy isn't exactly irresponsible; she's just *easygoing*, to put it mildly.

Maybe even a bit reckless, which is what I usually adore about her.

When I met her in kindergarten, we found our friendship based on opposites:

I loved to collect coins and shells; she amassed clothes for her impressive doll collection.

I collected novels; she collected the phone numbers of hot guys.

Today, I'm a journalist; she's an environmentalist

lawyer working for a non-profit organization and needs to work as a club hostess on the side to make ends meet.

I'm a worrier; she reminds me of the positive things in life.

While I have a list for everything, including the contents of my wardrobe, she would get bored halfway through *writing* a list and always ridicules me for being overly conscientious, which she lovingly calls obsessive-compulsive.

"You should have told me we'd be facing bad weather. We could have waited until tomorrow. We didn't have to depart today." I shoot her a venomous look, even though she can't see me because her eyes are fixed on the road, one hand on the steering wheel, the other resting on her thigh.

"And risk missing a day in a free five-star hotel? Maybe." She shrugs. "But the thing is, if I had told you just how bad the weather might be, you wouldn't have trudged along to see Mile High. We've wanted this for ages."

As in, *she's* wanted this for ages and sort of insisted that I come along.

I set my jaw and let her continue her little monologue.

A heavy gust of wind rocks the car. I wiggle in my

seat nervously. "Are you sure the hurricane's not heading our way?"

"Relax," Mandy repeats. I swear she's turning into a walking mantra. "Hurricanes can only form over water. Montana is far too inland to be hit by one. "

"Why were storm force winds mentioned then? What is this if not a hurricane?"

Mandy casts me a short side-glance. "A little storm or hurricane won't stop us from having the adventure of a lifetime. For all we know, it might not even hit Montana. They said so on TV. We both know the weather newscast tends to be a little overdramatic."

There, she just said the word.

Oh, my frigging God.

The wind howls louder, the trees whip back and forth in a wild frenzy, and the car trembles with the force coming sideways. Mandy tries not to show it, but I can see the whites on her knuckles as she holds on tightly to the wheel, forcing the car to stay on course.

I try to calm my thumping heart, but it's hard. Hurricanes are unpredictable. Mandy might even be right about the last part, but I don't want to be outside, in the middle of frigging nowhere, to find out. I sigh and slump into the passenger seat, keeping my eyes focused on the road ahead, praying we'll reach our destination soon—a hotel near Madison Creek.

The tickets couldn't have come at a more fortunate time. Mandy had been a fan for ages. She had also been talking about looking forward to a last adventure together. With my career as a journalist really taking off, Mandy figured we might as well see more of the world before we end up stuck behind a desk in an air-conditioned office in stuffy New York City. Not that I don't like NYC; I've lived there my whole life and couldn't imagine living anywhere else in the world. But lately, it's been oppressing...filled with people and memories I want to push into the proverbial filing cabinet deep inside my brain.

That was the only reason why I agreed to trudge along.

"This kind of wind rarely lasts more than an hour," Mandy says, resuming the conversation.

"I hope so," I mutter and close my eyes, slumping deeper into my seat. "So, where are we *exactly*?" I ask for the umpteenth time.

"It's a road trip, Ava. The beauty of it is that you *don't* know where you are," she says dryly, leaving the rest open to interpretation.

I watch her in thought.

Her lips are pressed together, and her grip on the steering wheel has tightened.

"Basically, you have no idea where we are," I say matter-of-factly.

She shrugs. "You're wrong."

"I'm so not wrong."

I wouldn't be surprised to find out she hasn't thought about a stopover to get dinner either.

I should have known better than to leave the planning details to her. Now, with thick rainclouds roiling and twisting over our heads, and the wind picking up in speed, I can only hope the satnav will guide us safely to the nearest town.

I groan audibly to communicate my displeasure. "You said you were taking a shortcut, but this shortcut is taking longer than the estimated time to arrival. How do you explain that?"

"Fine. If you *must* know." Mandy shoots me a disapproving look. "We sort of got a bit off track, but don't worry, we'll get there eventually."

I sit up, suddenly alert. "What do you mean by 'off track'?"

Warily, I peer at the satnav, which is a palm-sized black device attached to the windshield, its screen turned to Mandy. Given that neither I nor Mandy are particularly adept at reading road maps, the whole purpose of buying the thing was to get us from A to B without the need for a map. I realize it's been at least two hours since we last stopped at a petrol station. It's been even more than that since we last drove past a city.

With a strong sense of foreboding in the pit of my stomach, I turn the screen toward me and realize in horror that all it shows is a country road surrounded by a huge patch of green and a message stating 'no service available at this time.' There's no street name, no information on the nearest highway, no sign of a petrol station or motel. Wherever we are, it's not on the freaking map.

Shit!

We probably left civilization behind a few hours ago.

"We're off the grid," I say, mortified, as I stare at the screen. "Mandy!"

"It's not a big deal." She shrugs again.

"How can you say it's not a big deal? We're lost."

"We're not lost," Mandy protests feebly. We've been friends for ages, which is why I know she's lying. She catches my glance. "As soon as the storm calms down, the satnav will start working again. I'm pretty sure we're headed in the right direction anyway."

"How do you know?"

"Call it my gut feeling."

"Is this the same gut feeling that almost got me expelled from school after you suggested we paint the walls red as a means of protest against the lousy food?"

Mandy remains quiet, so I ask the most obvious question in a voice that can barely contain my anger, "How did this happen?"

"I took a shortcut." Her words come so low I'm not sure it wasn't just the howling wind gathering around the car that spoke to me.

"What?"

"I said I took a shortcut!" she yells at me. Then she adds quietly, "Or so I thought. And then the damn thing failed—" she points at the satnav "—probably because I forgot to update the software."

"This is so typical of you." I open the glove compartment to pull out the roadmap, but all I find are cans of soda and several packs of Twinkies. "Where's the map?" I ask, even though I know the answer.

"I didn't think we'd need it." Mandy shrugs and stares ahead at the darkening road.

I laugh from the waves of hysteria collecting at

the back of my throat.

Why would anyone *ever* take a shortcut in the middle of nowhere and consciously decide against packing a map? Then again, this is Mandy. Given that I've known her all my life, I have no one to blame but myself.

"There goes my backup plan," I mumble.

"It wasn't really that much of a backup plan anyway, given that neither of us has ever found her way around with the help of a map," Mandy says, not really helping.

"But still. You should have known better."

"What about you?" Mandy prompts. "You could have thought about packing one instead of obsessing over your non-existent love life." The accusation is palpable in her voice. She's trying to blame it all on me.

"I'm not even going there because I wasn't obsessing. I spent the last few months working my ass off. You know how hard I had to work to get where I am now."

"Where?" she asks innocently. "We both know that by 'work' you mean you were secretly obsessing about the fact that you shouldn't have brushed off the guy who hit on you at Club 69."

Oh, for crying out loud.

She's trying to divert attention from her mistakes by annoying the living shit out of me.

I roll my eyes. "Get us out of here before we end up completely lost and living in a self-made wooden hut. I'm not learning how to set traps and collect berries to keep your sorry ass alive."

"If this helps, I did pick up how to make a fire when I was a Girl Scout."

I grin at her. "Yeah, your fire will be of immense help when we're trapped in a storm."

"Check the cell," Mandy says, her face brightening at the idea.

"And call who if we don't even know where we are?"

"The police, obviously. They could track us."

Intentionally, I don't praise her as I retrieve my cell phone and then stare at the no signal sign. "Dammit. No bars."

Which isn't much of a surprise.

We *are* in the middle of nowhere. There's no doubt about it because ninety-nine percent of mainland USA has cell phone coverage, which is about everywhere. Mandy has just managed to find the remaining one percent, and she didn't even have to put a lot of effort into it.

"No signal," I say needlessly and drop my cell

phone back into my handbag, which I then toss it onto the back seat amid Mandy's toiletry case, several shoeboxes, and countless fashion magazines, all of which she picked up during our petrol station stopover. For the money, she could have bought at least two roadmaps. The thought manages to make me even crankier.

CHAPTER TWO

WE REMAIN SILENT for a long time. At some point, I consider asking her to drive back to the gas station, but then decide against it. For one, she's taken so many turns that I doubt she'd find her way back before the rain begins cascading down on us. And second, the gas station is at least a two-hour drive away. If the weather's playing along, we have three or four hours to find a motel before dusk falls.

"I could turn around," Mandy suggests, jolting me out of my thoughts.

"No. Just keep going. The road's bound to take us *somewhere*." I open my eyes and scan the sky, worried. The gathering clouds dim the light, bathing the deserted road in semi-darkness. It's only four p.m., but it feels as though nighttime is about to fall. As the car rolls on, the first drops of rain begin to splatter against the windshield.

Within minutes, the drizzle turns into a raging downpour and the road begins to resemble a huge puddle of water. The engine is roaring and the tires keep slipping on the muddy ground. The visibility's so bad Mandy slows down the car and leans forward in her seat, fighting to see through the foggy glass.

"Should we stop and wait this one out?" Mandy asks.

"No. Don't stop," I yell to make myself audible through the noise of the splattering rain. "I fear if we stop, the tires will get stuck in the mud and no one will ever find us out here. No one can possibly survive on Twinkies and soda forever."

"You're right." Mandy hits the accelerator, and the engine thunders in protest. "We're almost there," she says for the umpteenth time, casting another nervous glance at me.

I squint my eyes to make out the road, but it's too late to make out the dark silhouette to our right.

"Tree!" I shout.

Instead of swinging left, to the other site of the road, Mandy turns the wheel sharply to the right, the unexpected impact of hitting unpaved, muddy earth pushing me against my seatbelt as we barely escape a collision with a tree.

Thunder echoes in the distance, once, twice, when I realize it's not thunder but the spluttering sound of a dying engine.

The car cogs several times...and then stops abruptly.

"That was close." Mandy leans over the steering wheel, panting.

"Yeah. You could say that."

She turns the key in the ignition, but nothing happens. She tries again. Still nothing.

Double shit.

This isn't good at all.

"Ava?" The panic in her voice is palpable.

"We'll be fine," I lie, even though I know better than to make false promises. More than likely, we'll have to spend the night in the car, huddled together for warmth in the hope that the rain will stop at some point.

I make a mental note to be mad at her for the rest of our lives.

I peer out the passenger window into the dark. The sky has turned black, and the torrential rain makes it impossible to see more than a few feet ahead.

Except for a road sign consisting of a wood panel that appears to have cattle carved on it, I have no idea where we are.

"Great. Just great," I whisper.

We'll freeze to death.

The thought is so scary I shiver against the coarse fabric of my jacket and barely dare to look out the window into the pitch black.

Mandy shoots me another nervous look and tries to start the engine a few more times, without any success.

This is it.

Now we're really stuck.

"It was worth a shot," Mandy says, raising her chin defiantly.

I stare at her in disbelief. "Who the fuck tries to turn around on an unpaved road with apocalyptic rain pounding on us?"

"At least I'm not sitting on my ass doing nothing."

Mandy can never shut up. If we continue like this,

we'll be at it all day and night. Someone has to take the high road—and as usual, that someone is me.

I bite my lip hard to keep back a snarky remark and decide to change the subject.

"Did you pack an umbrella?" I ask.

"Yes." Mandy peers at me warily as she draws out the word. "Why?"

"There's no point in us both sitting around and waiting for a car to drive past because that might never happen, so I'm going to find someone who can help us." I draw a sharp breath and exhale it slowly as I ponder over my decision. It's a risky one, but what other choice do we have? "I'll go back to the road and take the first shift waiting. Let's hope someone else decides to 'take a shortcut.'" I don't mean to infuse a hint of bitchiness in my voice, but I can't help it. "We're in deep shit. The sooner you realize this, the greater our chance to make it out before we freeze to death or a hurricane hits us."

"Are you crazy?" Mandy asks. "You'll get lost out there. We'll wait out the storm."

I raise my hand to stop her protest. "Where's the umbrella?"

For a few seconds, she just stares at me in a silent battle of the wills. When her shoulders slump slightly and she looks away, I know I've won. She squeezes between the seats and rummages through the stuff scattered haphazardly on the back seat, then hands me a tiny umbrella—the kind that you usually carry around in your oversized handbag; the kind that couldn't keep you dry from a drizzle, let alone the downpour outside. But the end is pointed and sharp. It'll definitely do.

"You can't use that thing out there," she says. "The wind's too strong."

"I know. I'm taking it with me in case a wild animal attacks me and I need protection."

"A wild animal in Montana? What are you scared of? A cow?" Mandy lets out a snort. I give her an evil glance that's supposed to shut her up—but doesn't. "Yeah, you'll poke it to death with that thing."

"Do you have a better idea?"

Now she's silent.

A flashlight would be extremely helpful, but that's something Mandy would never think of packing, so I'll have to make do without one of those.

"I'll be back in an hour. Wish me luck that I find someone," I say and jump out of the car before she can protest.

"Be careful!" Mandy shouts after me.

I nod my head, even though she probably can't see it, and wrap my jacket tighter around me.

The rain soaks my clothes almost instantly, and a cold sensation creeps up on me before I've even taken a few steps. I suppress the urge to open the umbrella, knowing it wouldn't help much against the freezing wind that makes walking difficult.

Big drops of water are cascading down my face and into my eyes. I blink against what seems like a bottomless well pouring down on me and spin in a slow circle as I try to regain any sense of orientation. The road is barely wider than a path, with what looks like fields to either side, but that's about all I can see. The headlights are illuminating the ditch we hit, but did we spin to the left or to the right? I can't remember, and any tire tracks have already been washed away by the water. Basically, I have no idea which direction we came from, and the pitch black isn't helping. The main road could be anywhere.

Dammit.

Suddenly, my emergency plan doesn't seem so appealing after all.

We can't be too far from the main road, so I decide to make it a brisk ten-minute walk and then turn around and head the other way.

"I can do this," I mutter to myself in a weak attempt at a pep talk and start walking down the path. After only a few paces, I realize the ground conditions make it harder than I anticipated. The slippery mud around my shoes and jeans weighs me down, and my pulse begins to race from the effort of lifting my knees up high. It seems as though I've walked for miles, which can't be because I still see the headlights of our car shining in the distance.

My groan is swallowed by the relentless rain.

That's when I see the light in the distance. It looks like the beam of a flashlight. I should be getting back to Mandy to tell her about it, but I fear if I return to the car, whoever's holding it might disappear and I'll never find out whether rescue awaits us at the other end of it.

"Help," I scream, but the light ahead doesn't shift.

As I head closer, I realize it's not a flashlight but a bulb hanging from a string, which stirs in the wind, and there's a whole house behind it. The pain from plodding around in knee-deep mud forgotten, I quicken my pace and reach the porch in a heartbeat, then slam my palms against the doorframe so hard the sound could wake the dead.

Thump.

My fist hammers harder against the wood.

"Hey! We're stuck out here and need help," I yell, just in case my thudding is mistaken for an oncoming hurricane.

The few seconds that pass seem like an eternity. Eventually, a bolt slides. The door is pried open, and I find myself staring at the six-foot-two figure of a guy.

My jaw drops open.

He seems oddly familiar.

His hair's dark and curled at the tips; his strong jaw is shadowed, as though he forgot to shave this morning, the dark stubble accentuating his full lips. He's wearing nothing but tight jeans with the upper button undone, but that's not what makes it impossible to pry my eyes off of his half-clad body to meet his questioning gaze. It's his familiar face, the green eyes that are now narrowed in surprise.

"You!" he states. His voice, deep and sexy, sends a shudder down my spine. Something about his tone rings a bell. Where do I know that accent from?

It takes me a few seconds before the penny drops.

My heart skids to a halt as I swear all heat is draining from my body.

Holy. Pearls.

It can't be. And yet, I know it's *him*. Or someone who looks just like him: the rich guy with the expensive car who offered me a handout in exchange for some implied fun between the sheets. The one I brushed off.

What are the odds?

Even though he's dressed more casually and his hair is a bit longer—past the need for a cut, and styled in a casual mess that demands you run your fingers through it—I see the resemblance straight away. My gaze brushes over his chest.

The same muscular build.

The same features and hard body, all shrouded in a layer of mystery, that have been haunting my dreams ever since he bumped his Lamborghini into my Ford and then offered me a shitload of money because he felt sorry for me.

Club 69.

That's where we met three months ago.

And that certainly explains his palpable disdain for me.

He can't take rejection.

For the first two weeks, I couldn't get him out of my mind. I even started skipping through the gossip pages of various magazines in case he might be someone rich and famous.

Needless to say, I didn't find his picture, so I forced myself to push him out of my system—Mandy made that part almost impossible.

Of all the places in the world, I had to meet him

here—in the middle of nowhere, with no escape route.

Shit. Shit. Shit.

I stare at him, my body frozen in shock. I'm so stunned, for a moment I'm rendered speechless as we continue to eye each other.

Meeting him here, in the middle of nowhere, feels surreal.

His chest—all hard muscles—is clearly defined and emphasized by the light bulb dangling over my head. A black snake tattoo adorns his left arm, which is stretched against the doorframe, as though to block my way, while the other is clutching at the door, as though ready to slam it in my face. I look up into eyes the color of storms and realize that's exactly what he's considering doing.

"This is private property. You're trespassing." His voice is raw and gritty, with a strong accent. No 'How can I help you?'; no 'Please come in.'; not even 'Hi, how are you? Hey, I remember you. You look great, by the way.'

I stare at him, dumbfounded, until I remember that Mr. Expensive Shirt has no manners.

He demonstrated it before, and he's doing it again. My hands ball into fists, and for a split second, I consider turning around and heading elsewhere. If only he weren't the only person around. I can't afford to offend him. Not when he's the only person who can help us.

I grit my teeth and force myself to take slow, measured breaths.

"I need help," I whisper, my voice slightly hoarse.

"Say again?"

"Our car's stuck down the road," I say and point behind me in a broad circle because suddenly I can't remember which direction I came from.

His shrug is almost unnoticeable as he regards me in silence. I open my mouth to explain my situation, when he leans against the doorframe, his posture hostile.

"What do you want?"

"Isn't that obvious? A hurricane's coming," I say slowly in case he missed the countless weather and safety alerts. Or the pitch-black sky on an otherwise fine afternoon.

"There are no hurricanes in Montana. Only storms." He eyes me with a frown, as though he suspects me of making up some bullshit excuse to get inside his home and then burgle him. Yeah, I watch the movies.

"This storm's the reason we're in trouble," I mutter. His gaze travels to my umbrella. I hide it behind my back before he utters a snarky remark and I won't be able to hold my tongue, after which he'll most definitely kick me to the curb.

"In trouble?" He sounds unconvinced.

Seriously?

"We got lost and need help." Maybe even a hot cup of coffee, which I don't mention because, judging from the deep frown lodged on his stunning face, he doesn't strike me as the welcoming type.

"The next town's just a few miles down the road. Just take two right turns. You can't miss it."

I look at him incredulously. He can't possibly have said what I just heard, and yet his stony expression speaks volumes. The muscles in his biceps flex, which is probably a sign that he's about to slam the door in my face.

For real.

He can't do that; he's our only chance at surviving the night.

"Wait," I say before he closes the door.

"What now?" he asks.

I inch forward and plant my foot right next to the doorframe so the door won't close if he shuts it, and moisten my lips, suddenly aware of the wet strings of hair covering half of my face. I can't blame him for not wanting to help when I probably look suspicious as hell.

"Look." I grant him a tentative smile. "I had no idea you lived here."

His brows furrow and his expression darkens, but he says nothing.

"Honestly, I had no idea," I add. "If I had known, I wouldn't have knocked, but we need help. We really do. My friend, Mandy and I—" I make sure to emphasize Mandy's name in the hope he'll be more inclined to help once he realizes my traveling companion is female "—we've been driving for hours. We don't know our way around this place, and our phone's not working. Worst of all, the car's stuck in the mud, and we have no idea where we are. Is there any way we could use your phone to call for help?"

"Lines are down."

Socially inept *and* not a man of many words. What a fine combination.

I cringe inside, but force myself to smile again. I really don't want to ask for what he should have offered five minutes ago, and yet I have no choice.

A strong wind tears at my hair, whipping wet strands of it against my face. The gust is so strong I tumble forward and almost stumble into him.

"Would you mind if we stayed for a few hours,

just until the storm's over?" I ask.

His stare turns a few degrees colder, if that's even possible. Holding my breath, I almost expect him to say no and turn on his heels, but to my surprise, he just nods and opens the door a little bit wider, though not enough for me to squeeze through.

"How long are we talking about exactly?"

"Three hours max," I say.

"All right," he says after a pause. "But only under one condition: you don't bring any suitcases. And you take off your shoes. I just had this place cleaned. Three hours. Not more. Are we clear?"

I want to point out that those are more than one condition, but now isn't the time for petty mindedness. So I nod quickly before he changes his mind.

"Get your friend. I'll switch on the lights," he says. "And you better hurry. You're letting in the cold."

"What about—" *the car*, I want to ask, but he's already disappeared inside, closing the door in my face and leaving me to figure out the rest.

CHAPTER THREE

FRIGGIN' UNBELIEVABLE.

Out of all the places Mandy could have taken me, she's just managed to find the one place with the one guy I hoped to never see again. Judging from the way he acted, almost kicking me off his property, he was pissed.

Like, really pissed.

Like I-had-no-sex pissed.

I don't know if he remembers me, but if he does, he's most certainly someone who doesn't take rejection well. Either that, or the repair bill for the chip on his car was higher than he expected.

Big deal!

My poor Ford's still not professionally fixed.

I roll my eyes and hurry back to the car, my pulse quickening with—fear? No! Anticipation? Maybe. Sexual tension at the prospect of seeing him again? *What? What!* So not true. (Okay, maybe a bit.)

Whatever it is, I know I'll have to confront him, break the ice, so to speak, and explain why I didn't take him up on his offer. Maybe then he'll find his lost hospitality and offer me a steaming cup of coffee—God, I'd kill for one, metaphorically speaking. I'm pretty sure after a mature conversation and getting to know him a little better, this fantasy attraction of mine will dissolve into thin air.

The attraction I've been feeling over these past three months, six days, and six hours has been just that—a mere fantasy.

Obviously, that's not something I'd ever admit to anyone's face.

Nor the fact that, in my mind, I got to know his body surprisingly well whenever I took out my vibrator.

With the rain cascading down on me, I stop and

groan, unsure how to deal with the baffling discovery that we've just met again.

In real life, he looks even hotter than in my daydreams. The sexy tattoo snaking down his arm and chest even gives him a dangerous flair. There's a blurred line between daydreaming about some fantasy guy with a fast car and a dirty mouth, and the nightmare of a guy who thinks he rocks every woman's world. Until now, I sort of managed to push the latter to the back of my mind. Now no longer.

The dream, I could handle.

The nightmare...not so much.

Because as sexy as he is in real life, he's most certainly not all sugar and glitter.

In the distance, the faint lights of my car remind me that obsessing over don't-even-know-his-name isn't a priority right now. Mandy and I need to find shelter for the night...and that in three hours before Mr. Hot Guy throws us out.

Mandy must have switched on the lights, or maybe they were on all this time.

I can't remember with the icy wind piercing through my clothes.

Tightening my grip around my umbrella and shielding my eyes from the dirt flying through the air, I dash for the car. Once or twice, the wind trips me and I almost take a tumble, but I eventually reach it. The moment Mandy spies me, she opens the door and totters out.

"God, Ava. I thought you'd never come back!" she yells against the howling wind as she crosses the distance between us. Her expression instantly changes as she catches my expression. "You didn't find someone, did you? God, I knew it. We're going to be trapped in a storm."

I shake my head. "No, I found someone, all right."

"You did?" Her expression relaxes, and then she hugs me, letting out a laugh of relief. "I was so worried about you. Where is he? I hope he's bringing help because the bags are way too heavy for us."

"I highly doubt that."

Her arms drop. "Why? Is he old?"

"No, he isn't old. He's..." How can I possibly put my feelings into words that Mandy will understand?

Sexy. Arrogant. Hostile. And probably a recluse.

"What?" Mandy prompts.

"Weird?" I suggest and switch off the lights. Before I can stop her, Mandy's heaving her suitcase out of the trunk. I just shake my head and lock up the car. There's no point in arguing with her. The darn thing's heavy as hell, and even more soaked. I can either help her or waste a few hours watching her drag the thing after her. Helping her lift it, I pull her after me. "Let's go. He's waiting, and I'm scared he might just change his mind."

Mandy plants her feet into the ground, forcing me to face her. "Wait. What do you mean by weird? Like axe-wielding-in-the-hallway weird? Did you see blood splatters? Did you smell decay?"

"Just weird." I tug at her arm again, but Mandy stands frozen to the spot. There's no way I'll get her to move without an answer. I sigh. "He doesn't seem to like visitors, but he's agreed to let us stay for three hours, until the storm's over. Don't expect him to be hospitable."

"He must really be a loner, living out here, not liking guests," Mandy says and finally moves from the spot.

"Hmm." I'm glad she's turned away from me and doesn't catch my grimace. "He probably hasn't seen anyone in ages."

If only Mandy knew the truth.

***

After giving Mandy a short recollection of how I found the place—leaving out the six-foot-two guy with the hot body—she and I head straight for the porch light. My hands are aching from dragging her heavy suitcase behind, and damn—what the heck did she pack in there? A bookshelf?

"You could have left this in the car," I mumble for the umpteenth time.

"Ava, we've gone over that. Remember?" Mandy says slowly.

Yeah, apparently she can't leave her expensive Louis Vuitton travel bag in my old car 'out in the open for everyone to see.'

As if someone would steal a heavy bag in the middle of nowhere.

But apparently she can't wait for the rain to settle. In her words, "There's important stuff in there I can't possibly live a few hours without."

I fight the need to roll my eyes and drag the heavy thing up the stairs as she stomps behind, minding her steps so her new shoes won't be ruined.

It's my fault, really.

When she dragged the thing out into the mud, I should have let her do the heavy lifting herself rather than silently offer to help in the hope the physical labor would help me get rid of my racing thoughts.

Actually, one racing thought centered around one particular question: He's so frigging hot. Why the heck didn't I go out with him?

It would only have been one drink. One drink that most likely would have ended with me in his bed, eager to find out if he's as good in bed as he looks.

If given the chance again, would he want to settle things with me privately? Probably not, judging from the fact that he didn't look particularly happy to see me. In fact, it's safe to say he'd have preferred to leave me out in the cold if I didn't beg.

Ignoring the cold feeling of regret, I discard the thought quickly, not quite able to get rid of the 'what ifs' at the back of my mind.

The wind blows stronger now, each gust bruising my body. For a moment, the fear that he's changed his mind grabs a hold of me. But as I ascend the last step, I breathe out in relief.

The door to the house is now open, and a trail of light shimmers from inside. I can even smell the heady scent of wood burning in the fireplace. I imagine myself warming my hands on a hot cup of coffee while gazing dreamily at the glowing logs, the warmth slowly seeping into me after a long, tiring day.

"Should we knock?" Mandy peers at me before pushing the door open.

"Why do you bother asking?" I mutter, following her in.

What awaits me inside is Hot Guy's scowl as he glimpses Mandy's suitcase.

My eyes drink him in from head to toe, slowly brushing over his jeans and unbuttoned shirt to his rolled-up sleeves showing beautiful bronze skin and dark hair. In the porch light, he didn't look bad standing there with half of him bathed in darkness. In the dim light falling in from the kitchen, however, he's stunningly gorgeous. He's all so intimately familiar—as though I've known him all my life instead of only a few minutes.

I squint and think back to the place where we first met without giving the impression that I'm staring.

His face has been a part of my daydreams for so long that I feel as though I've known him forever. Maybe not so much the face as the chest and bulging biceps. Everything about him feels way more familiar than it should be. The fact that in my mind I've had sex with him more times than I remember is both hot and embarrassing—and now it comes back to bite me in the ass because I can barely look at him without the telltale heat of a major blush rushing to my face.

"Can I have a word in private?" he asks no one in

particular.

I assume he's talking to me, so I drop Mandy's suitcase and kick off my shoes, then shrug off the soaked jacket, hanging it up on a hook near the door. I turn to Mandy. "Wait here. I'll be right back."

My heart pounding in my chest, I follow him into the dimly lit kitchen, unsure what to say.

Will he kick us out?

It's quite possible, isn't it?

His expression is stony. His arms are crossed over his chest as he leans against the doorframe. Even though half of his face is obscured by the weak light, he's so gorgeous for a moment I forget what I'm here for as I peer up at the six-foot-two angry statue of the guy.

"I said no suitcase," he says quietly.

"It's not mine."

He glances over my shoulder to Mandy in the hallway. "If it's not yours, then that's fine."

This is so *personal.*

My jaw drops. It takes every ounce of my willpower to bite back a snarky remark.

He must really hate me, or more likely, he's trying to punish me. His arrogance is monumental. You can probably see it from outer space. And it irritates the hell out of me.

"Thank you for letting us stay," I say loud enough for Mandy to hear. "You're very generous."

Not.

He opens his mouth, then closes it, as though he wants to utter something, but then decides otherwise.

Eventually, he nods. "Follow me."

He gestures for us to follow him from the hallway into the living room.

I try not to gawk.

Compared to his flashy car, the room is rather simple and looks in dire need of renovation. There's a worn sofa on the east side, a whole library on the west side. A huge, old-fashioned fireplace adorns most of the north wall.

He disappears for a few seconds and returns with two towels, pressing them into our hands. Mandy peels off her soaked jacket and then joins me on the generously sized rug overlooking the ginormous fireplace. The warmth seeps into my skin, relaxing me.

"I'll get you some drinks," Mr. Hot Guy mumbles and takes Mandy's coat.

"Thanks. That'd be great," Mandy calls after him in what I've learned to recognize as her flirty voice— a mixture of low and sultry intermingled with just a hint of a smile.

I nudge her in the ribs and whisper, "Do you think that's a good idea? We don't even know him."

"What?" She shrugs, faking that she has no idea what I'm talking about.

As soon as he's gone, she turns to me. "What the hell!" she mouths in case he's eavesdropping. "Why didn't you say he was hot?"

I shrug my shoulders. "He's okayish."

"Okayish?" Mandy asks, aghast. "He's hot, hot, hot with a capital H!" She glances over her shoulder to the hallway then back to me. "Please don't tell me you wouldn't do him."

The admonishment is palpable in her voice.

I grimace as heat creeps up my face. If only she knew how often I've actually done him in my head, she'd be both appalled and proud of me.

"I've seen better guys out there," I mutter.

"Then I'm calling dibs."

"You don't get to call dibs. I saw him first." My head snaps to her. To my dismay, I realize she's smiling. Oh, crap. Who says things like that? We're not sixteen anymore. I've just managed to sound completely ridiculous.

I begin to dab at my hair with the towel, as I consider how to rectify my words. "What I was trying to say is that he isn't even your type," I add quickly, but it's too late.

She eyes me, amused. I can see her brain cells working. "You like him," she states, smiling like she knows something that I don't.

"No, I don't like him." I force myself to stare her down, even though my skin's getting hotter by the second. "Trust me, no woman in her right mind could possibly like him. I don't even know him but from what I've seen he's insufferable. Excruciatingly unbearable. Plain obnoxious."

"And so your type." She winks.

"Obnoxious is most certainly not my type," I protest. "In fact, you can have him. He's more your type anyway. He's arrogant, vain, and...and..." My mind struggles to come up with more adjectives to describe him. But he's in too close proximity, and faced with just how hot the guy is, words elude me.

He'd be perfect—if it weren't for his shitty character.

"I don't believe you," Mandy says.

"You should. I really don't like him. In fact, I can't stand him," I say. "And now drop it. Talking about a guy is getting boring."

Mandy keeps regarding me with a mixture of puzzlement and amusement. "You can't judge a book by its cover."

"You should have heard him when I arrived," I utter too low for her to understand.

"What?"

"If you think he's so great, you should date him," I say instead.

"So you wouldn't mind if I flirted with him?" she asks, cocking her head to the side.

I force a careful shrug. "Why would I?"

"Interesting. In that case, maybe I will," she whispers back and inches away from me, crossing her long legs in the process.

I shake my head and let out an annoyed sigh.

We barely arrived a minute ago, and she's already on the prowl, ready to conquer the next male specimen we've come across. Maybe she'll flirt with him to get me to ask him out on a date. Or maybe she'll do it because she thinks I'm not interested in him. With Mandy, you never know. Unless you specify loud and clear that the guy is yours, everything is a game to her.

It sure helps that he's handsome and not exactly the epitome of hospitality because she likes a challenge.

He probably won't be much of a challenge for her.

And then my gaze settles on the only picture frame in the room.

It sits on top of the fireplace, mirroring the slow dance of the flames.

I can't help that I'm drawn to it like a magnet. With a peek behind me to make sure he's not watching us from the doorway, I head over and lift it up.

My body freezes and my eyes narrow.

Seriously, what did I expect?

CHAPTER FOUR

I INSPECT THE radiant smiles of a loved-up couple: he's all dark hair and brooding eyes, arms wrapped around a blonde with sun-kissed skin and blue eyes that seem to come alive through the picture.

I don't know why, but disappointment courses through me. Jealousy rears its ugly head. The blonde is without a doubt beautiful. Her skin is glowing, her eyes shimmering. She looks young, carefree, happy. They both do.

I turn around to Mandy and hold up the frame, trying to keep my voice steady. "He's off-limits," I say. "He has a girlfriend. Maybe even a fiancée or a wife."

"So what?" Mandy retorts. "You don't know everything about men and relationships, Ava. Nothing's ever off-limits. Besides, we're not planning on marrying him, right? And last I checked, I saw no ring on his finger," she whispers and turns around, signaling that the conversation's over.

I shake my head. I know exactly what she's planning on doing: adding another notch to her bedpost or forcing me to add one to mine. She's had so many, it's both impressive and time-consuming. Or tiresome. Whichever way one might want to see it. I'm not a wallflower either, but my conquests pale in comparison to hers.

"See, cheating's where I draw the line."

"What?" Mandy says again after catching my glare. "You can't change a cheater, just like a leopard can't change its spots. That's nature." Her tone sounds resolute, as if she's made up her mind already.

For some reason, I'm not comfortable with Mandy chasing him, but I keep my reservations to myself. That's another beauty of our friendship: we allow the other to make mistakes, which we call life lessons.

It's all pretty deep and spiritual.

It's a thing between us no one else understands.

But the more I think about her kissing him, or anyone's lips on him for that matter, the more the thought makes me sick. Why's that? I don't own him. And I sure as hell shouldn't feel disappointment at the prospect that he might be seeing someone.

But I do.

"It's still cheating." I put the picture frame back on the mantelpiece and join Mandy, right before Mr. Hot Guy returns with three cups of steaming liquid that smells of black tea, cane sugar, and—

"I didn't know what you wanted, so I added a bit of rum to it," Mr. Hot Guy says, pushing a hot mug of tea into my hands. My gaze sweeps over his fingers. No ring. No shadow. Not even the presence of a faint tan line. For some reason, relief floods through me.

As I grab the mug out of his hand, I cringe at the surge of pain shooting through my fingers, but I don't complain, in case he changes his mind and decides to throw our unwelcome asses out after all.

"Thanks," I mumble and follow his invitation to take a seat on the large leather sofa overlooking the fireplace.

I sink into the luxurious cushions and let my gaze slide over everything and anything but Mr. Hot Guy, who's taken his seat opposite from me and seems to regard me with a frown lodged between his brows.

"You look familiar," he says after taking a gulp of his beverage.

My breath hitches, and I almost choke on my drink. With a nervous glance at Mandy, I turn my eyes back to him. "Excuse me?"

"I'm sure I've seen you before." His gaze locks with mine in a strange battle. "I just can't remember where. Care to refresh my memory?"

What the hell!

Is he suffering from short-term memory loss? Because I'm pretty sure he recognized me on the porch, so why the question? Taking a deep breath, I catch the glint in his eyes.

He must be playing with me.

The sudden knowledge angers me. Mr. Hot Guy is off-limits, and Mandy isn't exactly the kind of person you can tell everything without her wanting to meddle in one's private affairs. And then there's his girlfriend. I've no idea what he's trying to achieve, but I don't do cheaters. Ever.

Two can play this game.

Planting a fake smile on my lips, I stare him down. "I'm sure we haven't. You must be confusing me with someone else."

"No." He shakes his head. "I have a feeling we've met before. Ford, right?"

"The car?" I shrug. "It's a popular brand."

"I'm sure it is." His eyes lock with mine, forcing me to keep his heated gaze until I feel myself melting under his scrutiny. "But my feeling's never wrong."

"It is this time."

"You sure?" he asks.

"You're mistaking me for someone else."

"Ava's driving a white Ford," Mandy butts in, not really helping. "Where do you think you met her?"

I lift a hand to stop him before he gets a chance to reply. "It's none of your business, so butt out."

"Whatever." Mandy shrugs.

"Maybe I am confusing you with someone else," Mr. Hot Guy says.

"You are." I groan inwardly. Not because he's trying to expose me so openly in front of my best friend, but because I'm forced to look at him...and don't like what I see.

In the indirect light of the fireplace and several table lamps, he looks magnificent...and oh so intimidating.

He's beautiful, no doubt about that. His features are something you usually see on movie posters, and his clothes barely hide the Adonis body underneath them. But what makes him dangerous material to any woman's heart—and panties—are his magnetic eyes.

The kind that whisper sweet promises of nights filled with endless lust and clutching at the sheets in ecstasy.

The kind that draw you in with no guarantees of a tomorrow. Or even post-sex breakfast in bed. Come morning, he'll be gone, carrying your damp panties in one hand and your heart in the other. His eyes narrow on me, taking me all in, from head to toe.

"Hmm." He leans forward, and his knee almost brushes mine. The gesture is so intimate, I can almost feel his touch on my skin.

Why won't he just drop it?

Maybe he really has no idea where we've met.

Irritated, I turn away, sipping on my cup of tea and burning my tongue in the process because I don't know what else to do with myself.

"I don't think *we* have met," Mandy says. "I never

forget a face, and most certainly not someone like you. I'm Mandy, and this is Ava. We're from New York, by the way." She points her hand at me and leans forward, her ample bust on full display.

"Kellan Boyd," Mr. Hot Guy says, ignoring her attempt at flirting.

Kellan?

I fight the sudden urge to say his name out loud, just to hear what it sounds like on my tongue.

I lean back and deliberately turn away from him as I watch Mandy's reaction.

Her whole posture's changed. She looks kind of agitated. Is that shock etched in her features?

But why?

"Did you just say Boyd?" she asks slowly. "Like the Boyd brothers?"

Licking her lips, she crosses one leg over the other and brushes a strand of blond hair out of her face. The gesture is so innocent and yet provocative I almost cringe. She peers at me meaningfully, like I'm supposed to understand something major. I shrug my shoulders at her.

Does she know him?

Am *I* supposed to know who he is? Because I sure as hell have no clue.

Do you know who I am?

I remember his question. I didn't know the answer then, and I sure as fuck don't know it now, so I shoot Mandy a questioning look.

"The Boyd brothers own a string of nightclubs," Mandy explains to me in an excited whisper.

"That would be my brother, Cash. I'm just an investor," Kellan says coolly and raises his eyebrows. "What's someone from NYC doing around here?"

He's an investor.

I barely have time to digest the news before Mandy opens her mouth. "We're going to—"

"A road trip." I shoot her a venomous look that instantly shuts her up. As much as I love Mandy, I will *not* give off the impression that I'm in Montana to visit a stupid gig. And most certainly not that I'm a fan, and most certainly not a groupie, no matter how many chicks out there think Mile High's great.

Mandy replies with a shrug, as though it's something we do all the time, "Montana's always been at the top of my places to see before I die."

Which is a blatant lie, but out of her mouth, it comes so smoothly even I almost believe her.

"Really?" Mr. Hot Guy—Kellan—doesn't sound too convinced. "Judging from your shoes, I would have thought Club 69 was more your ambience."

His statement sounds more accusatory than

nonchalant. If I were Mandy, I'd feel insulted by the fact that he thinks he can judge me by the shoes I'm wearing. She might be more the urban type, and Club 69 *is* her ambience, but she has a huge heart for animals and the environment. She's definitely not some airhead. It's not something a nice guy would imply, but to my astonishment, Mandy just laughs and lets his comment slide.

Wait a sec!

What the fuck did he just say?

It takes a second or two for the penny to drop. I spin my head so quickly, a surge of pain shoots through my neck. I narrow my eyes to regard him, ignoring the fact that he's staring at me with the same irritating frown on his face.

Club 69.

Mandy said the Boyd brothers own a string of nightclubs. His name is Kellan Boyd and he's an investor. I might be jumping to conclusions, but that sounds like he's an investor in his brother's club.

Which would explain why he was driving away from the club on a Friday evening rather than arriving to party the night away.

I bite my lip hard, unsure how to respond.

Kellan keeps staring at me, one brow raised, as though he's waiting for my confirmation that I know who he is. But it's obvious from the knowing look in his magnetic eyes that he doesn't need it. Maybe it's a test to see whether I realize that he's half-famous or something. His oversized ego probably demands that every woman on this planet know his name and pant it in her sleep. I may not know him, but the two encounters we've had so far have led me to draw my own conclusions of the kind of person he is.

Bedroom perfection.

Arrogant prick.

Every woman has *that* one guy she'd like to fuck.

Well, he's mine. In my fantasies, that is.

However, I can't deal with someone like him. He's too confident. Too sexy. Too experienced. And he'll see right through the fact that I'm deeply, truly, madly attracted to him, even though he's absolutely not the kind of man I'd ever go for.

Ever.

I don't want him to know that I couldn't stop thinking about him.

"Do you like your drink?" he asks. His eyes are on me. It's clear the question is directed at me.

"It's good," I say.

The sudden change in topic has made me wary. My tone doesn't escape Mandy. Her gaze shifts from Kellan to me and then back to him, the big proverbial question mark etched on her forehead. It'll only be a matter of time before she sees the connection, and when she realizes he's the guy I told her about, she won't be able to keep her mouth shut.

"I'm a huge fan of Club 69, by the way," Mandy says. "I visited the new opening three months ago."

"You did. Was she there, too?" Kellan asks with a glint of amusement in his eyes.

"No!" I exclaim.

"Yes," Mandy says in that same moment, adding, "she drove me."

"Makes sense. That's why I remember her." Kellan's smile turns into a grin. "She looks just like someone whose car bumped into mine."

I choke on my drink.

He can't be serious!

"Really?" Mandy chimes in, giving me her you-didn't-tell-me glare. Slowly, she leans forward in mock interest. "She didn't mention—"

That he's so hot.

I can almost see the thought written across her forehead.

"She didn't mention my new Lamborghini?" Kellan cuts her off. His tone carries the annoying hint of fake surprise.

Mandy's jaw drops. "You drive a Lamborghini?"

"Mandy, you're not helping," I mutter.

"I do." Kellan nods, his eyes not leaving mine. "It cost me a few bucks to repair the chip she caused."

"A few hundred?" Mandy's gaze is going back and forth between Kellan and me.

"A few thousand," Kellan says coolly. "But it's okay. It was worth it because I got to meet her."

For a moment, I'm stunned and actually believe his words...until his gaze oh so innocently brushes my chest and settles there for way too long.

I wish I could slap his stupid grin right off his face, but instead, I find myself strangely breathless.

"Oh, my God," Mandy suddenly exclaims. "That's why you mentioned Club 69. You're—" Her voice breaks off mid-sentence as her gaze sweeps from me to Kellan and then back to me.

I shake my head, a warning look in my eyes.

"No way." She laughs. "This is *him*? The guy who hit your car? The one you said—"

"Shut up." I roll my eyes. "I've no idea what you're talking about. The rain must have messed with your brain."

She laughs again. "Club 69. You were there. He's the hot guy who *propositioned* you, and I'm quoting you there." She points at Kellan like he isn't sitting across from us, listening intently. "It's him. I can see it written across your face."

Kellan's eyebrows shoot up, and a glint of amusement appears in his eyes. "Hot guy, huh?"

He throws back his head and laughs—a raucous, hearty laughter that makes his perfect chest vibrate.

Suddenly, the generously spaced room is too small and I can't breathe. My vision blurs.

"Excuse me," I say and jump to my feet, snubbing Mandy's quizzical look as I grab her arm and yank hard. "I need to talk to you."

Somewhere, at the periphery of my perception, I hear Kellan mumble something about staying the night, but I can't be sure because all I can think is that this trip was one big mistake I shouldn't have made.

CHAPTER FIVE

"WHAT ARE YOU doing?" I ask as soon as we're outside. My voice is shaking. Not from anger, but from something indefinable. The temperature has dropped considerably, and the dark clouds are a lighter shade of gray, the wind softer.

The storm's calming down already.

"No, what are *you* doing?" Mandy sounds annoyed as hell. "You didn't fuck a Boyd?"

"Obviously, not everyone's life goal is to hook up with semi-famous guys," I mutter. "Besides, is someone else occupying your brain? The guy has a girlfriend."

"Which you didn't know when you first met him." Mandy's expression changes from anger to suspicion. "Why didn't you tell me you knew him?"

"I didn't recognize him," I lie.

I don't want to lie, but I need to. Mandy needs to drop the whole thing before I die from embarrassment.

"Let me guess. You forgot to mention he drove a Lamborghini?" She throws up her hands in mock surrender. "Oh my god, Ava."

Why's everyone obsessed with a stupid car? Particularly one that's not even worth its price tag, if you ask me. I mean, most human beings couldn't possibly afford the insurance rate, let alone the payment plan. And you can't park the thing anywhere without people gawking and at least a few thinking about stealing it.

It's insane.

"Again, I had no idea," I mutter.

"Yeah, right. Even someone like you must recognize it," Mandy says dryly. "There's nothing forgettable about the car, or the guy driving it, for that matter."

She's right.

There isn't.

But I can't admit that to her.

"You could have fucked him," she mumbles. "You know, get back in the game."

"Oh, my god. Will you just shut up about him?" I shoot her a venomous look and turn away.

"Fine. Whatever. I was just trying to help."

"How so? By pointing out the one wrong decision I can't change? Or that my love life sucks?"

She scoffs but remains quiet.

Of course, I regretted not taking him up on his offer three months ago. But what I regretted more was driving home and telling Mandy about it that night because the moment I did, she started calling all her friends to ask whether anyone might know him. Which they didn't, obviously. Next came the Internet searches. The Friday nightclub stakeouts. And eventually, the reproach that I didn't do what any woman with her panties in the right place would have done.

"You know..." Mandy starts. Oh, I know where she's heading, and I'm not having it. "You could always—"

"Don't say it," I interrupt.

She holds up her hands. "Fine." And then she walks back inside, leaving me alone.

The early evening air's crisp and cools my head. After spending a few minutes on the porch, I decide that seeing Kellan again is of no importance because tomorrow I'll be gone and his memory will be soon erased from my mind.

When I return to the living room, Mandy's nowhere to be seen. Kellan's hard body is sprawled across the sofa, his long legs stretched out, his arm draped across the cushions.

Fuck! I'm alone with him.

My heart speeds up. The entire situation feels way too intimate. My tongue flicks over my dry lips as my gaze sweeps over the room in a desperate search for Mandy.

Where the hell is she?

"She's upstairs," Kellan says coolly. "I offered to let you both stay."

"We agreed on three hours. We're leaving tonight." Gosh, why does my voice sound so clipped and hoarse?

"She told me your car broke down."

Damn my car.

We're stuck here. The realization makes me freeze in sudden panic. The fact that he's looking at me with a strange glint in his eyes doesn't ease the unnerving tension I feel in his presence.

"I'll be happy to send for a mechanic, but he won't be here before tomorrow. You're free to stay the night."

"Why the change?" I can't help asking.

Slowly, he lifts off the sofa, stretching up to his imposing height. "What do you mean?" He steps closer. I want to run, but instead, I find myself strangely enthralled by his green gaze, his stunning eyes keeping me captured on the spot.

"You wanted us gone," I say. "Why the sudden change?"

"I'm still torn about this." He shrugs. "But I know *you'll* change my mind."

The abrupt shift in his tone doesn't escape me. He's gone from broody and serious to mischievous in the blink of an eye. I can't figure him out. I can't keep up with him.

"I won't do anything to change your mind," I say.

"Why's that?" His fingers curl around mine and press them against his chest, right where his heart is. His pulse thuds rhythmically against my fingertips. "I've never disappointed."

His tone is so hoarse and erotic, I feel the urge to jump a step back.

The double meaning in his words is subtle, but there's no mistaking it.

A few seconds alone and we're drifting back onto dangerous territory. My heartbeat speeds up, and excitement courses through me.

I don't know the guy, but he has this knack of getting under my skin in a hundred possible ways, when all I want to be is the epitome of Zen.

"So you say," I mumble under my breath.

"Try me."

I blink in succession. No one's ever propositioned me like this.

It's so damn hot, I almost say yes.

But only almost.

A one-night stand is not my style. Not because I don't enjoy casual sex. I just like all the other things that come with a steady relationship, like falling asleep in each other's arms and waking up to a hot session of morning sex.

For some reason, Mr. Sex On Legs doesn't strike me as the guy who'd sleep over, and most certainly not someone who'd let you fall asleep cradled in his arms.

"I wouldn't *try* you if you were the last man on earth," I hiss, but for some reason, my low voice doesn't convey the disgust for cheaters and arrogant jerks I'm trying to go for.

"You're so ready for me, I could have you panting

my name in seconds. I bet you're soaked down there."

Who says things like that to a stranger?

I yank my hand from his fingers and push him away, without much success. "I bet you think being obnoxious is part of your charm."

"So I've been told."

"There's *nothing* charming about you."

"Obviously you haven't seen me naked yet," he says.

He's so arrogant I can't bear his ego anymore.

He inches just a little bit closer, until I can catch the tantalizing scent of his aftershave. He smells so good I want to wrap my arms around him, close my eyes and inhale his scent until it's all that fills my mind...and anything else that needs to be filled.

"Your bedroom's upstairs. It's the one with the animal print bedspread." He leans forward, and for a moment I fear he'll kiss me. My gaze is glued to his enticing mouth, and my lips part involuntarily, ready to grant him all the access he might want. His lips brush my cheek as they trail their way to my earlobe, his hot breath making my skin tingle. "It's also conveniently situated next to mine. Tonight, when you switch off the lights, I want you to know that I'm going to be jerking off to your picture in my mind. It won't be the first time."

F.U.C.K!

My air supply is cut off as I stare at him like an idiot. He's done it before? When? How?

I wish I had the confidence to ask him to let me watch. Instead, I find myself muttering, "You're such a creep."

"Don't pretend like you didn't do it after our brief meeting at Club 69." He laughs at my horrified expression. "Come on, Ava. Stop the double standards."

My face catches fire. I can't deny his statement. I'm too bad of a liar, and he's too full of himself to believe me.

Without waiting for a reply, Kellan turns and leaves, calling over his shoulder from the door, "If you need someone to help with your bags, you'll find me upstairs. In my bedroom."

The invitation's there. Unspoken but obvious.

"Thanks, but no thanks," I mutter, and then I head outside to grab my bags, my body hot against the chilly wind. At least, the rain has stopped.

CHAPTER SIX

DON'T EVER LET your guard down with a guy like him, unless you don't mind him dirty-talking his way into your panties.

I toss my pen on the bed, pondering if I should mention the jerk in my diary.

Because that's exactly what he's been so far, and he's proved it on numerous occasions.

As I heaved my suitcase up the stairs, Kellan just stood there, watching me from the door with a smug grin. Even though he kept quiet for a change, I knew he was checking me out, his eyes as dark and hooded as the night we first met. I walked past holding my head high, making sure not to touch him, even though I could feel him with every inch of my body.

My skin is still prickling from his gaze.

God, I can't get his name out of my head: Kellan, Kellan, Kellan—

He's in every thought. He's officially occupied my entire brain space, and I don't even know him.

A knock sounds at my door. I sit up straight and push the diary under my pillow just before the door opens and Mandy's head pops in.

"Can I come in?" she asks.

"Yeah." I tuck my legs under me as I watch her close the door and then settle on my bed.

The quizzical look from before is still etched on her face. "You okay?"

"I'm tired," I say, fighting the urge to ask where Kellan's gone. This is the right time to talk about him, but for some reason, I can't bring myself to. Maybe tomorrow. Maybe in the light of day he won't look so damn hot and this stupid attraction will be gone.

"We should get some rest. It's been a long day. Kellan's invited us to stay the night," Mandy says, wriggling her brows meaningfully.

I doubt 'invited' is the right word. He probably felt he couldn't possibly throw us out, in case we wouldn't make it through the night and he'd have to live with his conscience forever. Or maybe his big ego can't take rejection and he's still harboring the strange notion that I *will* bed him if he's being obnoxious about it hard enough. But instead of sharing my thoughts with her, I just nod. "Where are you sleeping?" I ask, ready to change the subject.

Mandy motions for me to follow her and leads us down the hall to a closed door. "The bathroom's in here," she says, as though she's the host and I'm her visitor. "I'm next door." She points to the adjacent door and opens it. Inside, I can see that her suitcase is already waiting to be unpacked.

He must have shown her to her room and helped her with the luggage.

The thought stings even though there's no surprise there. She's hot; she's confident and a hell of a lot of fun. The word 'rejection' doesn't feature in Mandy's dictionary, and I doubt Kellan's going to be the exception to the rule. He'll see that he's been going for the wrong friend in no time.

Which makes my blatant physical attraction to him all the more annoying.

"He's making us dinner," Mandy says casually as

she unzips her bag.

"Swell," I mutter. "Can he also make us wine?" Preferably a whole keg so I can drink myself to sleep and don't have to think about him anymore.

"I don't think grapes grow in Montana. The weather's not ideal."

I shoot Mandy a sideways glance.

"Oh," she says. "You weren't serious." She nudges me with her elbow. "Come on, the hot guy's obviously into you. What's up with the angry face?"

"The hot guy also has a girlfriend," I retort and turn to take in Mandy's room.

Just like mine, the décor is rustic yet simple with a low-roofed ceiling, fitted only with a rugged bed, night table, and a large, solid wooden cupboard. A few scarce pictures of birds adorn the otherwise empty walls.

"Honestly, I don't know why we're staying here," I say. "We could just ask him to drive us to a hotel."

"Because." Mandy waves her hand.

"Because what?"

She shrugs. "It's cozy here."

And free, which she doesn't add, and neither do I. We left home early and would arrive at the luxury hotel early, meaning we'd have to pay for the extra days.

"It is," I agree as my gaze sweeps over the room one more time. Simple and cozy—such a strong contrast to the red Lamborghini and the expensive clothes. I sigh and turn around to regard her. "But we're imposing. Give me another reason why we shouldn't leave."

"Because he's a Boyd," Mandy says. "I still can't believe you kept that fact from me for more than three months."

Oh, here we go again.

"I didn't know. Besides, what does it matter who he is when he's obnoxious as fuck?" I groan and head for the door. "You know what? I'll see you later. And if I hear his stupid name one more time, I'm leaving with or without you."

"Well, you can't. We're stuck, remember? The car's broken down, and we're not heading back home before we've seen Mile High. You might want to start to loosen up a bit and have some fun."

How could I forget the stupid tickets? They're the reason why we're here and I can't escape the one guy I want to escape.

"Whatever."

Mandy's laughter rings as I close the door behind me.

CHAPTER SEVEN

THE STORM PICKS up again. The night's one drawn-out opus of splattering rain and howling wind. I barely manage to get a few hours of sleep before a noise wakes me.

I sit up straight, familiarizing myself with my surroundings, my ears straining to place the sounds.

I'm still at Kellan's place. So, that part's not a dream.

The sky is still dark and starless, with nothing but the moon lighting up the room. I'm surrounded by the sound of the wind, the swaying of branches, the soft spattering of rain.

Pure, complete nature.

It must be what woke me.

Having lived in NYC all my life, I'm used to noise: the constant rumble of traffic, the honking, the hollow thudding of the music in nearby bars and shops, the shouting of the drunk on a Saturday night. I'm so used to my life in the city and the fumes that the complete absence of noise unnerves me.

It's supposed to be calming, and yet I find it peculiarly strange.

I feel as if I've been sucked into a black hole and spat out on another planet.

As if I've become the air itself, trapped somewhere between the earth and sky, and I don't know which way I want to go.

Somewhere in the distance, I hear the agitated chirping of birds, celebrating that soon a new dawn will break. Slowly, I sink back into the pillows and pull the covers up to my chin.

As soon as I close my eyes, I hear it again.

It's the same sound that woke me.

I cannot ignore it.

It sounds like...

I jump up, eyes wide open, my heart stopping, as I become aware of one fact.

It's coming from the adjacent room.

That's where Kellan's sleeping.

It's unmistakably moaning, interrupted by heavy breathing. And then soft voices.

Kellan has a woman in there.

I reach out for my phone on the table. The clock says it's four a.m. I left Mandy and Kellan barely two hours ago. My heart sinks as I recall the last few hours.

During dinner, which consisted of medium rare steak and bread, Kellan was friendly, respectful, and formal. I expected more sexual advances, but to my surprise, none came. There were no double meanings. No lingering looks. No more mentions of Club 69. Not even an intimate encounter that would put my willpower to the test. No mention of his girlfriend either.

The entire dinner focused mostly on our trip to Montana, Kellan's house—it's been in his family for generations—and a very long and heated conversation on the New York Yankees, Mandy's team, and Boston Red Sox, Kellan's favorite baseball team. Even Mandy, with her intense character and her big mouth, kept any snarky remarks to herself, for which I was very grateful. Except for a few glances Kellan and I exchanged, nothing happened—which both relieved and frustrated the hell out of me. At around two a.m., tiredness crept over me, and I excused myself, leaving Mandy and Kellan alone in the living room.

Which, maybe I shouldn't have, because now I have no idea what went down.

What is *still* going down.

I might have been so focused on avoiding him that the thought of him hitting on Mandy never occurred to me when it was a likely possibility. Their heated discussion could have easily turned into a heated situation with them ending up in his bed.

Upon our arrival, when Mandy hinted not so subtly that she'd go after him I didn't take her seriously. How could I have been so wrong? A pang of pain, raw and sharp, hits me in the chest. I can't help but feel betrayed.

I rise to my feet and tiptoe to the door, my heart beating in a frenzy. Fear chokes my throat as I head for Kellan's room and linger in front of the door.

It's cracked open. Caught in the throes of passion, they probably forgot to close it.

My heart lurches. I feel faint.

Every part of my brain tells me that Kellan can

fuck whomever he wants.

But every fiber of my being screams that Mandy knows I'm into him. That even though I told her she could fuck him, I didn't mean it.

Maybe she wants him for herself.

I have to know what's happening in there, if only to know where I'm standing.

I close my eyes, sickness washing over me as I picture the worst-case scenario.

I promise myself not to be angry at Mandy, but I know that's not a promise I can keep.

By fucking him, she's betraying every friendship code.

Should I make my presence known? Should I confront them? I have no plan. I just need to know.

Opening my eyes, I take a deep breath to prepare myself for what I'm about to see. As I crack the door a little bit wider so I can scan the room through the gap, nothing could have prepared me for what I see.

The truth hits me like thunder.

The bed is on the east side, facing the wall to my room. Kellan's alone, naked on the bed, his eyes shut. He's propped up against the pillows; the sheets are gathered around his ankles. A radio station is running in the background, voices chatting, but the volume's too low to make out the words.

There is no woman, no girl, no Mandy in sight.

He is all alone with his cock. His enormous, hard cock, which he now holds in his hand.

Holy shit.

I stare at his erection, the blood rising to my face. I know I should head back to my room, but I can't. I'm too mesmerized by what I see.

The picture in front of me is hot. Too hot. It's so much better than anything I've ever seen. And so intimate. I hold my breath as I take him in.

All of him.

He looks like a god engaged in his favorite activity, his beautiful face drawn in concentration.

One hand is wrapped around his cock, moving up and down in hard, determined strokes, the other pressed down on his balls, forcing back the orgasm he's chasing. His lips are slightly parted as another sexy moan ripples through his chest.

I stare at the engorged head glistening with wet arousal, and something twitches between my legs.

He's so caught up in his own pleasure that he doesn't hear me, even though I'm pretty sure my own heartbeat's so loud that even Mandy can hear it from her bedroom on the far side of the hall.

This is too personal. I shouldn't be watching him, particularly when I don't even have a good excuse or the right to be in his room. But there's something about him, about the way he seems so caught up in his arousal, that makes me want to stay, to break the rules.

Maybe it's the fact that it's night and I can be someone I'm not.

Shit.

I'm probably turning into a peeping Tom. I'm a voyeur.

I'll probably burn in Hell.

But I can't move. The movements of his hand speed up. His chest rises and falls. I can tell from the sound of him pleasuring himself—pumping up and down—that he's getting closer to orgasm.

I want to share that orgasm with him.

My own arousal grows with every move, every shaking breath he takes, every swipe of his tongue across his lips, and the deep groans of pleasure escaping his chest.

I bite hard on my lip until I can taste blood.

I want to touch him, taste him, feel him inside me.

I ache to replace his hand with mine as he strokes over the rim of his head. Suck his tongue into my mouth as he wets his lower lip.

I want to kiss him. To cup his heavy balls. To take

him into my mouth, if only to release the throbbing inside me.

I feel lightheaded.

He has captured my breath.

The air I'm holding—I have to let it out of my chest, but I can't out of fear that he could hear me.

I know he would.

But I have to breathe—fast.

Without blinking, I turn away, not bothering to close his door, and quickly walk back to my room. As soon as I've locked myself inside, the air comes out of me with a swishing sound.

I sink onto the bed, my heart beating against my ribcage, my head swirling, painful regret and trembling desire sloshing through me. My whole body is shaking, on fire.

I need him.

Why didn't I take him up on his offer?

Holy shit.

I had no idea he looks so hot in bed.

Watching him taking care of his needs is going to haunt my dreams. Even though we share everything, there's no way in hell I'll tell Mandy about it, or else she'll make fun of me for the rest of my life.

This is going to be a secret I'll take with me to my grave.

Holy. Shit.

Through the thin walls—God, is this house made of cards?—I can hear his heavy breathing and deep groans of pleasure. He's getting close to pleasure heaven. I'm frozen in time and space. All I can do is picture his face, his huge erection in his hand.

Walls may be separating us, but I know in my heart he's going to be my undoing.

Sure, I had imagined him, us, countless times in the past few weeks.

But I never thought I'd see him again. And surely not like *this*.

I close my eyes, my mind focusing on the picture of him on his bed.

But now he's no longer alone.

It's me who's doing all the naughty things to him. He's groaning while I'm pleasuring him. I like the thought that he's aroused because of me.

My hand slips into my panties. Between my legs, I'm dripping wet—for him. The muscles inside me clench, the heat unbearable. I slide two fingers inside me, imaging it's his fingers that glide between my wet folds.

To the sounds coming from next door, I begin to touch myself. When he comes, my own orgasm ripples through me.

CHAPTER EIGHT

A RAP AT THE door jolts me out of a dream involving the most beautiful yet infuriating green eyes I have ever seen. I don't bother to cover up my half-naked body as I shout, "Come in."

The door opens, but instead of Mandy's head popping in, it's Kellan who's standing in the doorway. I sit up straight, surprised to see him, all traces of sleep gone.

The image of his erection enters my mind, and I remember last night's events.

I remember what I did.

Oh, the mortification.

My face catches fire as I cross my legs to hide the after-orgasm effects.

"Slept well?" He sports the usual irritating, smug expression.

My heart skips a couple of beats.

Yes, I slept well.

Too well. All thanks to him.

In broad daylight, he still looks like the jerk I remember from our first meeting. A sexy grin tugs at one corner of his mouth, sending my insides into a jumbled frenzy of stirred emotions. The hair is definitely longer than it was back in NYC, and the crisp businessman look is gone. The slightest hint of dark stubble throws shadows on his cheeks and chin, and he looks surprisingly sexy in yet another pair of faded denims and a snug shirt that leaves little to the imagination. Without a doubt, he's the most stunning man I have ever seen. And I have absolutely no idea what to do with myself in his presence. I'm the most reasonable and composed person I've ever known. Nothing ever fazes me, and yet, for some reason, I can't be my usual cool self around him. Particularly not now, with all those vivid memories occupying my mind.

Does he know I watched him jerk off?

Impossible. His eyes were closed the whole time, and I'm sure I stood there no longer than two minutes. I mean, surely no one can hold their breath for longer than that.

But did he hear my moans through the thin walls?

I tried to be quiet, but how quiet can you be when you're lost in sexual nirvana?

That was the question that bothered me immediately after I came. Even if he heard me, why shouldn't I consider it only fair that he be embarrassed too? After all, fair is fair.

Why am I even pondering over what can't be changed now?

Because he can't possibly know.

I need to push this memory to the back of my mind—deny it, bury it deep inside my subconscious, so that not even a Freud follower could extract it. I'm going to lie to myself until the lie becomes the truth. How hard can that be?

Until then, it's going to be my secret.

My terrible, hot...hot...hot secret.

Oh, God.

No one has a cock like Kellan: big, engorged, perfect in its size and thickness.

No one redefines jerking off the way he does. He's the reinvention of holy hotness.

I'm such a lost cause. If Sigmund Freud were still alive, I know what he'd tell me, and it wouldn't be pretty.

"Everything okay? You look a little flustered," Kellan remarks.

"Yeah. I just had a—"

Bad dream, I wanted to say, but I can't, because then I would have to lie and claim the dream was most certainly not about him, nor about his gift of a manhood to the female population.

"You had what?" Kellan prompts.

"I just couldn't—"

Sleep.

What the hell!

I can't say that either because he might think that I heard him. If he so much as catches a whiff of the idea that I sneaked around last night, I'm so going down. Big and fast—like the way he pumped into his palm.

Shit.

The words *big* and *fast* are making me horny.

"Mmmh." Kellan nods as though he totally gets me, which I'm sure he doesn't. "So, you slept well? The fresh country air must have knocked you out."

"Yeah," I mutter. "I slept like a stone. No, make that a boulder." What the fuck am I saying? That doesn't make any sense. I let out a nervous laugh. Heat rolls over my body in thick, fast waves, and the tender spot between my legs begins to pulsate again. I need to get this guy out of my bedroom. "Thanks for letting us stay the night."

"No problem." He leans against the doorframe and regards me, amused. "It's nice to have company. Your friend told me a bit about you after you left."

Judging from Kellan's grin, Mandy's revealed all the crappy details of my failed love life and all the embarrassing, cringe-worthy incidents that came with it.

I'm all for honesty, just not to a hot guy.

Glaring at Kellan, I pray to God she's kept her mouth shut for a change.

If she didn't, I know I'll have to kill her and dump her body, and I'm not sure I have the guts for it.

The only reason I'm not taking the bait and asking what exactly she said is because I really need him to leave.

"I'm making breakfast," Kellan says casually. His gaze slides over me, from my tousled hair down to my breasts almost spilling out of my bra and the not exactly matching but comfortable panties I thought were fine for a road trip. My heavier bag is still in my car, as finding my way around this place at two a.m. didn't seem like such a good idea. Besides, I didn't feel like dragging the thing through the mud all by myself again, so I had no other option but to sleep in yesterday's underwear. To my mortification, Kellan's gaze remains glued to the way the silk panties seem to stick to my hips and ass. "How do you like your eggs?"

The question is harmless enough.

If it weren't for the sparkle in his eyes...

Dammit.

I thought we were past that.

For some reason, the picture of eggs runs through my mind. And then it disappears and makes room for something else. I imagine myself running my fingers through his hair and pulling him on top of me, my legs wrapped around his narrow hips, his weight pinning me down as his huge cock enters me.

Our gazes meet, and something flickers in his eyes.

Awareness.

Knowledge.

Something else.

Something so deep, it travels through my abdomen and settles in a deep pull between my legs.

As if sensing my sexual response to him, he starts to smile—the same, irritating grin he tossed at me during our first encounter. I don't have to ask him what he's thinking. He knows I'm attracted to him. I mean, what woman in her right mind with her panties in the right place wouldn't be? And judging from his smug expression, he didn't expect anything else from me. In fact, the way he stares at my chest suggests he isn't averse to a bit of touching either.

His ego certainly fits the chick magnet of a car and the attitude that came with it the night we first met. The kind of attitude that comes with experience. Years of dating jerks have taught me to spot it from a mile away.

Thank God I'm immune to whatever Kellan Boyd's charm is. Maybe he's used to being the center of attention, but he's most certainly not going to flicker anywhere on my radar.

"I like my eggs like you take them," I say coolly.

He doesn't even blink. "Can I convince you to try the bacon, too? Because you strike me as a meat person."

And here it is again: the slightest hint of sexual innuendo accompanied by another lingering look at my chest. A tremor rides my core as I shrug, forcing myself to remain as unfazed as humanly possible.

"Sure. I'd love some bacon. Make it extra greasy."

His brow shoots up, and his face brightens just a little bit more. "I love a woman who loves to eat," he states with what I assume is admiration, his eyes roaming over my body again. "You have a nice body. Lots to grab and hold on to."

Wow.

Talk about direct.

I'm not even sure any woman would take 'lots to grab' as a compliment.

I pull the sheets up to my chin to cover up. I even throw him a venomous look for not even trying to pretend to look away, but I don't quite succeed. "Is there anything else?"

"As a matter of fact, there is," he says and pauses. Before I can open my mouth and ask him what the hell he wants, he continues, "Yeah, before I forget. Your friend left."

"She left?" I ask, surprised.

"Yeah." He nods. "About twenty minutes ago."

I regard him, stunned, my heart beating frantically against my chest. Mandy just left me here—with him? "Are you joking?"

"Feel free to check her room."

A wave of something hot sprouts somewhere inside me—not the emotional kind, but the sexy kind, the kind that crawls right under my skin and makes it tingle. "Maybe I'll do that." I stare at him, ready to challenge him, but Kellan just laughs.

"Okay. While you do that, make sure to be on time."

"For what?"

"Breakfast. What else?" He winks at me. "It'll be ready in fifteen. Feel free to put on some clothes...or not. I'd rather you didn't anyway." The irritating grin doesn't leave his face as he turns around, calling over his shoulder, "By the way, I prefer my eggs hard, just like everything else about me."

He closes the door behind him.

I swallow hard and stare at the empty space he left behind.

Eventually, I shake my head and pull the covers over my face, groaning loudly.

Mandy left without telling me? And what the fuck did Kellan mean by putting on some clothes...or not? I thought I had made myself clear back in NYC that I wasn't interested in him.

My impression of him seems to shift from one end of the spectrum to the next, just like my emotions shift from guilty awe to the desperate need to hate him. He looks like a decent but sexy kind of guy when he just smiles. But once he opens his mouth, every single thing that comes out of it seems to irk me.

It's like sex is the only thing he ever thinks about.

How the fuck can someone like him focus on work long enough to make a living and drive the half a million car he does?

Okay, I'll admit I Googled the price tag of his Lamborghini.

Judging from what I've seen so far, he's filthy rich with a filthy mouth and even filthier morals.

I've never been around a guy like him.

Even though breakfast sounds like something I'm very much in need of, the idea of being alone with him doesn't seem too appealing. But if I avoid him, he'll think I'm doing it because he's so sexy I can't take it.

Which is kind of the truth.

I can't take just how much he gets under my skin.

Obviously, this nonsense has to stop.

Mandy has to come back now.

Full stop.

Grabbing the phone from my night table, I dial her number, but the instant beep confirms I have no signal.

Crap!

I toss the phone onto the bed and jump up.

Maybe Kellan will let me use his landline to call her, which means I'll have to join him downstairs.

Clutching at my toothbrush and my makeup bag, I head for the bathroom down the hall. On my way there, I peer inside Mandy's room. Her bag's still here; the contents of her suitcase are neatly stashed inside the wardrobe. I can't believe she's taken the time to unpack, as though she's not planning on leaving today, as per our agreement.

It still doesn't make sense why she'd just leave without asking me to tag along.

Unless....

I freeze as the sudden realization hits me.

She left so I'd get to spend time alone with Kellan...and get rid of the cobwebs between my legs.

I know that because that's exactly what someone like Mandy would do.

Obviously, I'll have to tell my idiot best friend her attempt was in vain.

I won't sleep with him. Full stop. I'm a woman who has morals, or at least someone who attempts to have morals.

As soon as I step in front of the mirror, I cringe.

My hair is a mess, and my eyes are swollen, framed by dark circles.

I look like a ragdoll.

Kellan didn't seem to mind much though.

He seems to want me, just as much as I want him. I just don't have the faintest idea why.

Why am I even asking myself this question?

Whatever the answer is, I have to run from him without letting him know that I'm doing so. While I wouldn't mind a bit of fun, my heart beats a bit too fast around him, which is never a good sign.

I throw on yesterday's jeans and top, run a hand through my hair, then apply some mascara and a sheer shade of red lipstick. Finally, I head out the door, confident that I can do this.

CHAPTER NINE

I CAN'T DO THIS.

Breathing in and out, I let my gaze brush over the kitchen, which is a manly thing decorated in lots of dark wood and expensive stainless steel.

The kitchen is huge and probably the only modern part of the house, with its east side entirely made of glass. Outside, the woods stretch out for miles. In the distance, a lake shimmers in the bright light. Without a doubt, the place is quite the sight.

But compared to Kellan, it's nothing.

He busies himself with pouring two mugs of steaming coffee and shoveling several layers of what I assume is toast onto a plate next to boiled eggs, cheese, bacon, and waffles. Next, he resumes making an omelet as well. He takes his sweet time, which gives me plenty of opportunity to stare at the dark tips of his hair brushing the collar of his shirt. From his broad shoulders to his low-hanging jeans and cowboy boots—everything screams rural life.

And holy hotness!

If I didn't know any better, I'd doubt he's the same person from NYC who was dressed in a tailored suit and exiting the most expensive car I've ever seen.

So, what's he doing here?

Buried deep in my thoughts, I don't realize that he's turned around and is now regarding me.

"If you like the view, I'll be happy to provide a more in-depth one," Kellan says. The frown lodged between his stunning eyes contradicts the humor in his voice. "In fact, I'm not averse to touching either. I give and take in equal measures."

I can't believe he caught me staring.

And what's with this guy and the sexual innuendoes?

Heat spreads to my face. I turn around hastily,

but I know he glimpsed the telltale onset of a major blush.

"There's nothing to like," I mumble.

"Sure. So you keep saying, but I bet your panties would tell a different story."

My breath hitches but only for a moment, until I remember Kellan's only flirting. He cannot have any idea how much his statement is true.

I cross my legs and watch him as he places two plates and coffee mugs on the table, then plops down in the chair to my right. As he does so, his leg brushes mine. I become so aware of the sudden physical contact that my breath dies in my throat and I almost jump up, my skin seared.

"You told your friend about me," he says.

His statement is so sudden I look up in surprise. "What makes you say that?"

"It's a fact."

"Yes." I take a sip of my coffee and burn my tongue in the process. "Obviously I did in case you were a creep or stalker or whatever."

Damn Mandy!

Why can't she ever keep her big mouth shut?

Kellan gestures at my plate. It's still in front of me, untouched. "Do you like your omelet?"

Trying to play nice, I grab the fork and taste it. "I

do."

"I'll take that as a compliment."

I incline my head. "You should. You're a good cook."

"And you're a good guest."

"Thanks, I guess," I mumble. "You said you got your car repaired?"

Thankfully, he pulls back, and I find myself able to breathe again.

"You can't repair a Lamborghini, Ava." He's looking at me like I'm completely mad for even suggesting such an outrageous thing. "I tried and then I traded it in for a new one."

"Ah. That makes sense," I say dryly. "Now that you got rid of the dent, will you buy a new one if you need a tire change, too?"

"Probably," he says, not even picking up on my sarcasm. "And how's your car?"

I shrug. "Same old. Same old."

"Why didn't you take the money? You could have easily had it repaired." His gaze pierces me with such intensity, I almost flinch.

"What?"

"I wrote you a check," he says slowly. "Why did you throw it back at me?"

I flick my tongue over my lips, lost for words. His

gaze is glued to my mouth, and for a moment, his eyes glaze over, as though he's a million miles away, overtaken by the thoughts in his head.

What can I say?

That I would have felt cheap taking money from him? Which obviously makes no sense whatsoever.

"It was too much," I mutter. "You weren't realistic. Besides, I didn't know you."

He nods and looks away. The air is heavy with something I can't define. I don't know what to do with myself, so I just take another sip of my coffee.

"Are you always so—"

"Sensible? Rational?" I suggest the two words Mandy has been throwing at me for years.

He shakes his head. "No. I was thinking more along the lines of sincere and brutally honest."

The way he sums up those personality traits makes them sound distinctly negative.

Maybe I should have shut my mouth about the tire changing part.

"So, where's Mandy again?" I ask, eager to change the subject before we insult each other some more.

"She's headed into town."

"I can't believe she would just leave without telling me. Did she say why?"

He shakes his head. "No, only that it's urgent and

that she needs something from the shops."

I glance out of the window. It's still windy, but the clouds are gone. When Mandy says something's urgent, it usually isn't. A sliver of hope colors my voice. If Mandy decided to walk, then the streets are clear and we'll be gone by midday. She'll be back soon, and I'll no longer have to be alone with him.

"She should have told me," I say, even though I know I sound like a little girl who's afraid of being alone with her first crush.

"You were sleeping," Kellan says, grinning.

I regard him intently. "How do you know? Did you peek into my room?" Realizing my blunder, I add quickly, "Obviously not *my* room but your guestroom."

"Maybe I did." He winks.

I narrow my eyes as I try to read his expression. His face is relaxed; his lips are twitching. "I don't believe you'd do that," I say after a pause.

"You're right." His smile slowly disappears. "Except..." He trails off and leans back, crossing his arms over his chest.

"Except when?" I prompt.

"Except when I'm welcome, Ava. With you, it's only a matter of time."

My breath catches in my throat. Our eyes

connect, and something happens between us. It's like a current, and I know in that one moment that if I let go, there's no coming back. The waters in there, between us, are deep and dark and stormy, much like the sky in Montana. They leave no room for hesitation. No uncertainty. I know in that instant that he's waiting for me to invite him to my room.

I wish I'd just do it.

The thought is both intimate and frightening.

"How far away is the next town?" My voice trembles as I force my gaze down.

"Why?" he asks. "Are you getting bored of me already?"

"No, I was just wondering."

"Don't get your hopes up. The next big town with shopping facilities is almost two hours away. I told her she wouldn't make it far, but she wouldn't listen. Said something about shopping and hiking being her thing and all." His eyes flicker with amusement, a sign that he saw right through Mandy's lie.

I'm not surprised. Who in their right mind mentions shopping and hiking in the same line?

"How did she leave?" I ask because I don't believe for a second that Mandy's gone hiking.

"She borrowed my truck." Kellan cocks his head, misinterpreting my gloomy expression. "What? You think I have your friend tied up in my basement?"

"Well, do you?" I raise my brows.

"I'm into tying up, but not your friend...she isn't exactly my type." His words are deep and dark, full of unspoken promises. His gaze brushes my lips and lingers there. "I prefer the curvy kind I can tie to my bedpost."

"Did you just suggest I might be curvy *and* bedpost material? That's so—"

Sexy?

Wrong on so many levels?

I shake my head and laugh...until I remember he has a girlfriend.

Before I can stop myself, I blurt out, "Yeah, you like the blond kind, too, don't you?"

It was meant as a joke, but the words that come out carry the slightest hint of bitterness and jealously.

That's so not what I was going for.

Kellan regards me, amused. "Not so much the blond but the quirky kind. The kind that hits my car."

I can't figure him out for the life of me. I know I shouldn't ask, but my curiosity gets the better of me.

Mandy mentioned the Boyd brothers own the famous Club 69 venues, and Kellan definitely owns the arrogance of Mr. Universe, which is often a sign that he's successful. That and the fact that he drives such an expensive car. Yesterday at dinner, he kept evading my questions. To be honest, I've no idea what the big deal is. It's not like being a nightclub owner is something worth hiding, although I guess everyone needs a break from reality.

"What exactly are you doing, Kellan?" I ask. "Jobwise, I mean."

"I like to entertain my guests."

"As in clubs?"

"Not in that kind of way. You have the wrong Boyd. I invest in my brother's clubs." Another evasion and so clearly a lie. He points to my plate, his tone a bit sharper than before. "Tuck in."

The accent comes through so pronounced it vibrates its way through all my hidden spots, and I almost topple off my chair. If he notices my growing discomfort at being alone with him, he doesn't mention it.

Obviously I can't force him to tell me more about his life.

I take a few hesitant bites of egg omelet and force myself to chew and swallow slowly. The rich taste of full-fat registers somewhere at the back of my mind, but all I can focus on is the scent of aftershave wafting from him and the fact it's doing strange things to my body.

Like impairing my breathing.

And making it very, very difficult to focus on anything but him.

"Caught a cold last night?" Kellan stops eating and turns to me. His piercing gaze reminds me of dark green meadows and the mystery that comes with them.

"Why?" Narrowing my eyes at him, I put down my fork and take my coffee again to warm my hands. I might be hungry, but there's no way I can eat around him. Not when we're alone in his way-too-masculine house and he's looking at me with a combination of disdain and intensity that makes me too aware of my body's reactions to him.

"You sound breathless. And I haven't even made you come yet." His brow shoots up, and a lazy smile tugs at the corner of his lips.

He's such a jerk!

"FYI, it was cold outside. I froze my ass off out there and probably caught a cold."

"Or you're into me."

"I can assure you I'm not." I raise my chin and stare him down with as much frostiness as I can muster. "I'll grab some aspirin from town." I emphasize the last part so he won't get the impression I want to stick around.

"No need. I have some." He gets up. His back is turned to me as he begins to rummage through the drawers. Eventually, he pushes an emergency kit toward me and sits back down. "Feel free to take whatever you need."

"Thanks, but I won't be around for much longer," I say.

In fact, sticking around is the last thing I'd do, but I keep that to myself.

His frown returns, and for a moment, his eyes remind me of emeralds—cold and hard. But the impression disappears quickly and makes room for the nonchalant, almost contemptuous expression that he seems to sport whenever he looks at me. It's either contempt or lust, like he can't decide which way to feel about me.

I bet the words 'jerk' and 'arrogant prick', which pretty much sum up our first encounter back in NYC, have etched their way into his ego, and now he's scarred for life at the idea some skirt doesn't think he's God's gift to the female population.

He can't take rejection.

It's no longer a question. It's a fact.

"You know," he starts with a smug grin, "the

streets out of town are flooded. There's no hotel so, as things stand, you'll have to tolerate me for a little longer. You can keep busy by helping out with the livestock."

A kind of challenge flickers to life in his gaze, like he thinks I'd never dirty my hands.

The condescending prick!

I add that to my mental dictionary of words that perfectly describe Kellan.

"When's the mechanic coming?" I ask.

He shrugs. "I don't know."

"What do you mean you don't know? Did you call him or not?"

"The lines are still down. The storm must have hit a phone pole."

I take a sharp breath and let it out slowly. "So you haven't called him, like you said."

"I never said I did. I only said I would." His eyes catch mine, the glint in them naughty and devilish. "But no worries, you're not imposing, if that's what you're worried about. The guestrooms have been vacant for so long, I'll be happy to entertain you. I'm very good at it, as you've probably noticed."

"I'm sure you are." I cock my head to the side, my voice dripping with sarcasm. "Do you have enough food for the three of us?"

I can't quite picture Kellan being the kind who stocks up before a hurricane hits.

"This house was built to last," he says, amused. "My family owns thousands of acres of land. There's plenty to live on. You wouldn't be starving. So, what do you say? Are you going to help me with the farm?"

I don't know why, but he kind of looks smug. And then I remember.

He doesn't think I have what it takes for physical labor.

"Sounds like a date." I take a huge gulp of my coffee, emptying half the mug, and jump up with a triumphant smile on my face.

He downs his coffee and stands, a smile creeping up his face. It's only then that I realize what I've just said.

Holy shit!

What the fuck's wrong with me?

"Obviously not a date but—" I wave my hand in the air as more heat rushes to my face.

His smile widens, revealing two rows of perfect, white teeth. Teeth I can't help but imagine nibbling on my body and tugging gently at my sensitive skin.

The thought instantly makes me horny.

Oh, God.

I'm a lost cause.

"Not a 'date' date," I say through clenched teeth.

"Obviously. Let's call it earning your bacon while you're lying in my hay."

He can't possibly expect payment. But, in spite of his smile, his expression is so honest, I'm not sure he's not serious.

I clamp my mouth shut to keep back a snarky remark because, let's face it, I'm flat-out broke and might just have to work to earn my keep. Judging by the way his gaze seems to brush the front of my top, I'm not sure what that work might entail.

"If you think I'd ever fuck you in exchange for staying here, you're wrong. I'd rather sleep outside, in the dirt."

He leans into me, his breath brushing my lips. I can smell the faint scent of coffee and bacon, the heady mix of aftershave and *him*. An instant throb forms between my legs.

"It was a joke, Ava. I'd never expect you to pay for anything. Be my guest for as long as you want. The fucking part is voluntary, though I'm pretty sure there'll be lots of that."

He pulls back and I stare at him, open-mouthed and struck speechless.

Nope, I still don't get him.

CHAPTER TEN

I'VE NEVER CONSIDERED myself ugly, but I'm no blond model material either. My figure is not bad, with a bit of extra padding here and there. Guys always seem to like my generous chest size, but that's not impressive either.

No one like *him*—rich and instant-panty-drop sexy—has ever hit on me.

You rejected him, and now he thinks you're a challenge.

That must be my answer.

Combine spectacular looks with a bruised ego in a guy, and he's major trouble. It's like he turns into a bloodhound, sniffing you out, pursuing you relentlessly. Once the job's done, he'll lose interest and be gone before you even realized what just happened.

"I know I keep asking the same stuff, but I can't figure you out." I take a deep breath and let it out slowly. "How does the dirty talking usually fare for you?"

"What dirty talking? I haven't even started yet."

I sigh at his infuriatingly sweet tone. "Okay, let's try again. So, what is it that you do? Irritate the hell out of a woman so she gives in just to get rid of you?"

A smile flashes across his lips. "I don't usually need to. Women usually throw themselves at me. But—"

"But?" I raise my brows at him, silently coercing him to enlighten me.

"But I might not have any other choice with you."

"Ah." I nod knowingly, mocking him. "Maybe not everyone is into you, you know? Does that make sense?"

Before I know it, he grips my chin between his fingers and leans forward. Our breaths intermingled, I'm forced to meet his green gaze, and I don't like what I see there.

Longing.

My own longing for him to kiss me is reflected in his eyes.

And then there is something else.

Determination.

Raw, hard, primitive determination.

The kind I don't possess.

He's used to getting what he wants. I knew that from the first moment I saw him. What I didn't expect was that, for some reason, he might be wanting *me*.

"I'm everyone's type, Ava," he says, his voice low. "You just have to realize it."

He lets go, his fingers leaving a tingling sensation on my skin.

I shake my head, more out of need to convince myself that no man could have such an effect on me than disagreement. "Be that as it may, you're not everyone's type to handle, and I can assure you I'm not interested in getting involved with a guy like you."

"And what kind of guy do you think I am?"

"Mmh, let me think." I bite my lip in mock contemplation. "The kind of guy who thinks you're on every woman's bucket list of things to do before they die."

"Wow. You have me down to a T." He eyes me, amused. "So, why don't you join the crowd?"

I let out a laugh. "Seriously? Is that even a question?"

"It is." He nods. "Women usually throw themselves at me. Except you. You seem to be the exception, which poses the important question: why do you keep rejecting me?" His question sounds genuine, like he's given it a lot of thought and can't for the life of him figure out the answer.

"You're too much," I admit.

"Too much of what? Sexiness?"

"No, dude." I shake my head in disbelief. "You're too much to handle. Too much obnoxiousness."

"I never thought I'd hear a woman say something like that to me. It's usually the other way around, you know?" His smile breaks into a grin. "Are you sure you're even a woman?"

I scowl. "Trust me, I'm as much of a woman as you're a man."

"Prove it."

He's playing me.

I cock my head, annoyed that he'd think I'm so easy to trick. "If you think I'm going to flash you my breasts while you get to show me your private parts, you're wrong."

Yeah, no need to show them to me when I've already seen them.

And they're *huge*.

There's a strange look in his eyes. I still don't know if he saw me watching him last night, but I sure as hell won't be asking.

"I'm messing with you. But you've got to admit it would have been nice."

I smirk. "Yeah, if we were five-year-olds."

"If I were a five-year-old, I would have said, I'll show you mine if you show me yours. But like I said, I never have to ask. It's always the other way around." He leans forward. His stubble grazes my skin, and for a moment, I think he's about to kiss me. His hot breath brushes my lips as he says, "I'm perfectly well-endowed and will be happy to show you if you ask...nicely."

He leans back, his green eyes challenging me with so much fire it takes my breath away.

I'm stunned. Lost for words. I don't know what to say. But I know how I feel. I'm turned on by the memory in my head.

His hand wrapped around his hard cock is all I can think about. It drives me crazy. It takes all my willpower not to look down at his crotch.

"Not going to happen," I mumble, more to myself than to him.

"Now it's my turn," Kellan says coolly. "You told me your opinion of me, so it's only fair that I tell you what I think your problem is."

My breath catches in my throat.

I so don't like where this is going.

"I'm not interested in what you think my problem is because I don't have one."

"You see, Ava," Kellan says slowly, "you're a good girl, which is why I irritate you. I'm the kind of guy you've avoided all your life. The kind of guy you're too scared to fuck because you're too scared to let go of your inhibitions."

"That's not true." I open my mouth to protest some more. He presses the tip of his index finger against my lips, instantly silencing me.

"Don't misunderstand me. You enjoy sex, and you look like you're not half bad at it. But I'll take you beyond the boring, predictable kind you're used to. In fact, I can teach you a few things you'll really enjoy. Things that will make your last orgasm seem like a waste of time. Then you'll see why bad boys who are 'too much for you' always get the girls."

Coming out of this jerk's mouth, it all sounds like an insult.

He's so right about me, I feel a strong need to vehemently deny it. But I can't because he'd know. Sure, I have experience, but none of my previous partners had a body like his.

They all had been nice guys.

None of them had been arrogant and rich.

Or so fucking self-assured that I might just want to find out if his words carry any truth to them.

I'm about to tell him to fuck off in not so nice words when Kellan releases me, leaving me both breathless and strangely elated at the thought that he wants me.

He hasn't answered a single one of my questions.

However, he doesn't need to. It's not like I'm interested in his life story or in his job. He's looking for fun. That part's pretty obvious. And as much as I'm trying to deny it, the truth is I'm into a bit of fun, too.

We might just have something in common.

Except I'm single and he is not. That's never a good basis for anything.

To get involved with someone like him, someone to whom I feel an intense attraction, even if on a purely physical level, could mean that I might get attached along the way.

While people fuck, they also fall in love.

My world never splits its color into white and black. I always get trapped somewhere in between.

I can easily imagine myself falling in love with him.

And then what?

I'm not sure I want to take the risk of having to face that question.

In the silence of the room, Kellan busies himself around the kitchen. His sexy back is turned on me as he grabs the coffee pot and a tray with waffles, and then returns to the table, placing them in the middle together with a bottle of syrup.

When he sits down again, I can't bear it any longer.

I need to know.

"How can you flirt with me so openly?" I ask. "You're in a relationship."

"I am?" He looks up, surprised. "Wow. I had no idea."

My eyes narrow on him. "Well, are you?"

"It depends." He tops up our coffee mugs, taking his sweet time, which annoys me to no end. "If you plan on marrying me, then yes, I'm already in a relationship for life. But if you're just down for fucking, no, I'm not. Don't get me wrong. I love relationships, as long as they don't involve me, or kids. Or to put it another way, the only relationship I have is with my cock. I nurture it. I take good care of it. I teach women like you to have fun."

Wow.

He sounds like a player, which was pretty much my first impression of him.

It shouldn't come as a surprise, and yet it does.

The news that he's single is a relief, but it also leaves a burning question in its wake.

"What about the woman in the pic?"

"Which one?" He tilts his head, thinking.

"The one in the living room." I frown. "Why? Do you have more than one?"

"Guilty as charged. I have keepsakes of all of my trophies," he says smoothly, one brow raised. "But if we're talking about the one in the living room, that's my sister. I'm on the market today, happy to oblige."

"Today?" I let out a laugh.

Who says that?

"And tomorrow," he adds. "Obviously I want you to know what you're getting into, considering that your friend and I talked about you after you went to bed last night."

A whooshing sound bursts into my head, making it spin.

"Yeah, you keep mentioning that." A long

moment passes during which I consider my next words. "So, what exactly did Mandy say?"

"That you talked about me."

I swallow hard to get rid of the hot rush surging up my neck. "Yeah, in case you were a creep, which I think I've mentioned already."

He inclines his head in mock agreement. "Or I got under your skin and you wanted her to hear all about it. It's a preconception that women don't talk about their sexscapades. In fact, they do it just as much as men."

Of course he'd think that.

I smile sweetly. "Well, I won't argue with you on that one because you seem to be the expert. But I can assure you in my case, it's not true."

"You don't talk about your sexscapades?" His brows shoot up in amusement.

I sigh patiently.

What is it with this guy and his tendency to mangle my words?

"That's not what I was trying to say."

"So you do," he says.

"No, I was referring to you getting under my—" I break off as I realize he's messing with me and shake my head.

"You regretted not having slept with me."

I roll my eyes, even though I know the gesture is so immature a guy like him will see right through it. "No. And no." And before I can stop myself, I add, "No!"

"Strange, because she says you regret it," Kellan says softly.

I stare at him.

Oh, my god.

I'm going to kill Mandy.

"She did?" I jump to my feet. "Where's the phone?"

"In the living room. Not working." He stands but doesn't move from the spot. "Relax. It was a lie. She didn't actually say that."

I cross my arms over my chest as I regard him coldly. "Why would you lie?"

"I wanted to see your reaction."

"Right." I'm not a fan of confrontation. The entire situation has my mind racing. The last thing I need is for him to think I harbor regrets about not having spent the night with him.

"Please sit down, Ava," Kellan says and walks around the table. Even though I don't take shit from men, I find myself following his order. I can feel his presence behind me a moment before he leans over me, so close his breath brushes my earlobe and sends a shiver down my spine. "But you have to admit it's something she could have said because it's the truth."

"You know nothing about me." My voice comes out slightly choked.

Dammit.

His proximity does strange things to my body, and the fact that I've seen him naked doesn't exactly help.

"On the contrary. You're quite the open book." With that, he returns to his seat and pours what looks like half a syrup bottle over his waffles.

"Wow." I stare at him mesmerized as he starts eating. For the life of me, I can't understand how anyone can shovel down that much sugar. "Do you always eat so much for breakfast?"

"Always." He looks up, amused. "What can I say? I'm generally a hungry person who likes to eat out."

He's not talking about dining at restaurants. I can tell that from the naughty glint in his eyes.

My skin prickles at the implication and my heart races.

Kellan dips his finger into the puddle of syrup on his plate and holds it up to my mouth. "What about you?"

His gaze pierces mine, waiting.

The challenge is there.

I gingerly wrap my lips around his fingertip and let my tongue glide over it, then pull back.

Kellan's eyes remain glued to my lips as my tongue flicks over them to lick off the sticky syrup.

"As far as I see it, we're adults," he says, his voice slightly hoarse. "Consenting, sexually active adults who should have a bit of fun."

Wicked fun sounds about what I'd like to have with him. If it just weren't for the fact that I'm way too into him, and I get easily involved. Too easily, which makes for a dangerous combination.

He laughs at my gloomy expression. "I was talking about having a bit of fun outside. The livestock? Remember?"

Oh.

"Of course."

He points to my shoes. "You cannot wear those."

I look down at my boots. "Why not?" Okay, so they have heels, but they're not stilettos.

"Tell me, Ava, have you ever been on a farm or climbed a mountain?"

"No," I admit. "But they're way more comfortable than you think, and I'm willing to learn."

And I didn't have time to pack sneakers.

His gaze is quizzical as he regards me and points

to the food on the table. "Dig in. You'll need the energy."

"Why? A horse isn't exactly hard work."

He cocks his head, and slowly, a grin breaks across his face. "Who said anything about horses?"

CHAPTER ELEVEN

LAST NIGHT'S RAIN has stopped, but a strong gale is still blowing. Mud cakes my boots and sticks to my jeans as I trudge after Kellan for what feels like miles. The ground is one giant bucket of sludge that seems to slow down my pace and make my usual walks around Central Park seem like an afternoon stroll through the backyard to water the plants.

My legs have never hurt so much in my life. In fact, my thighs are burning, and I consistently feel like I won't be able to take another step. But somehow my groans and huffs keep me going.

Or is it my ego that just doesn't want to admit defeat?

Or is it the fact that he warned me my boots weren't suitable for hiking, yet I wanted to prove him wrong?

Sure as hell, Kellan doesn't seem to break a sweat. It's frigging cold outside, but he's adamant he doesn't need a jacket. From behind, his shoulders look magnificent—broad and strong, the muscles barely contained by his shirt. His thighs are built like tree trunks, and for a careless moment, I imagine myself sitting on his lap, my legs wrapped around his narrow waist, his green gaze piercing mine as he cradles me against him.

But the sexiest thing about him is his tight ass. I wonder if it's as hard as his biceps. It sure looks like it's been carved out of stone.

"Ava?" His voice pulls me back to reality. I clear my throat, thankful that his back's still turned on me and he can't see the telltale heat of a major blush creeping up my face.

"Yeah? What did you say?" I manage to croak.

"I asked whether you're from NYC, too, or just your friend." He seems to be having a great time, all cheerful and buoyant as he strikes up a conversation.

"Yep." My voice sounds so strangled, I might just be on the verge of having an asthma attack.

"What really brings you to this part of the world?" He says it like Montana's the Antarctic.

"A road trip," I say because that's about all I can squeeze out through my taxed lungs.

Kellan shoots me an amused look over his shoulder. "Just finished college?"

As if.

I've worked my ass off since I turned sixteen.

I roll my eyes. "No, I finished college two years ago. Like I said, just a road trip."

His laughter rings through the air, taking me by surprise. It's so deep and rich and full, I trip over my feet and barely manage to avoid taking a tumble facedown into the mud—which I'm sure he'd very much enjoy.

"Okay, if you *must* know, we're here to see Mile High." He stops and turns around, waiting until I catch up to him.

"Really?" he asks, resuming his walk.

"Yeah, really," I say in the most bored tone I can muster.

"You don't sound excited."

"Sorry, I can't help myself. I'm not really a fan." I shrug, feeling the need to apologize. "I just don't get all the hype about this band." I peer at him sideways, surprised to find that he's listening intently, holding my breath as I try to catch his expression. There's nothing on his face.

"So I gather the trip wasn't your idea."

I shake my head, more out of irritation with Mandy for coming up with her grand plan than out of need to confirm Kellan's statement. "I'm just doing my best friend a favor. If it were up to me, I would have sold the tickets and enjoyed this road trip, but Mandy is a big fan. She's like a sister to me. And then there's my job." He glances at me, and I feel the need to clarify. "I've been offered an investigative position with a business magazine. That's been my dream for ages. But it's demanding work. There won't be much time left for friends and family. Mandy had it all sorted out, you know, see a bit of the world before we get stuck behind a desk for the rest of our lives, so I went along with her plan."

"Sounds like an optimistic outlook. What happened?"

I grimace. "She took a shortcut."

"In the middle of a storm? In your old car?" He sounds incredulous, which is an understandable reaction, given that he doesn't know Mandy, or how durable my car was...before we entered Montana and the engine failed.

"In her defense, I'll have to stress that it wasn't raining when she decided to cut through God knows where. But she definitely knew that a storm was on the way." I cannot help but feel a bit defensive of her.

"Now you're stuck here." Kellan stops and turns to regard me. To my surprise, I find that his smile is genuine, maybe even kind, as though he understands that the trip hasn't been a pleasant experience so far.

It's been scary and dangerous and pretty unpredictable.

Just like him.

Kellan reaches out and brushes a strand of hair from my face. The gesture is slow and innocent, but because he's standing so close, it almost feels intimate.

"I'm glad we met again," he says.

"Yeah?" I frown. My voice is low and slightly hoarse, probably from the cold wind that's left a cotton ball sensation in my mouth.

"You don't sound convinced."

"I'm just surprised. After all, you didn't seem

particularly happy to see me."

"I might have overreacted a bit."

"Well, I put a dent in your precious Lamborghini."

He lets out a laugh. "Yeah, you did, but it's just a car. I guess I'll survive the shock." Another gust of wind. It's so strong, it almost knocks me over. Kellan wraps his hands around my waist to steady me.

The gesture is too intimate.

I take a step back to put some distance between us. "What are you doing here, Kellan?"

He frowns. "I grew up here. I enjoy the countryside. Don't you?"

"It's not so bad."

"No?" The skin around his beautiful green eyes crinkles, and his expression softens even more. "So you're not such a big city girl after all."

Which is kind of not true.

I am a city girl. I love shops. For the life of me, I cannot imagine living far away from civilization.

However, my mouth clamps shut.

It's the nicest thing he's ever said to me. His words please me, probably because he's been a jerk so far.

He's warming up to me. For the first time, I'm enjoying our conversation. He sounds like a decent guy when he's not trying to rip off my clothes with his spectacular eyes or verbally bring me to orgasm.

Or so I think...until he turns around and starts walking, calling over his shoulder, "Well, let's see how much you can handle. It'll be interesting to see if you still think the same once the farm work begins. Now, let's hurry, woman, before the next storm catches us and we have to spend the night in the barn, naked and huddled together for warmth."

"You didn't just say that." I lunge forward to smack his shoulder, but he's faster, almost two steps ahead of me. "Speaking of farm work, where are we going?"

He throws me a glance over his shoulder. "Why are you asking? Are your feet hurting? Do you already need me to carry you?"

My chin juts out defiantly. "No. I can perfectly carry myself. Thank you."

That's so not true.

"It's not too far. We're almost there." He grins and then we walk some more.

He remains silent as we ascend the hill. Once we stop, I see what he's so excited about.

At the foot of the hill is a huge barn with open fields to either side. A tall fence stretches around it. The red-painted wood panels build a beautiful contrast to the gray-blue sky and the dark woods behind it.

Woods the color of a storm intermingled with magic.

Just like Kellan's eyes.

A tingle shoots through my abdomen, settling in a delicious pull between my legs. Suddenly I'm reminded that I haven't been laid in way too long, and all I want is for him to touch me.

Oh, fuck, what is it with this guy and my sexual attraction to him?

It's not like I haven't been attracted to others before. It must be the setting—cut off from the world with what looks like a guy who knows how to survive out here. It's all so primeval, it probably talks to me on a primitive level.

I roll my eyes at the strange direction my imagination's taking and recall the chick-magnet sports car he drove back in NYC.

Primeval, my ass.

Kellan is a player who's probably had more dips in the dating pool than there are fish in the sea.

That's what attracts me to him. He's standoffish, bordering on rude.

Taming the bad boy is probably every woman's secret fantasy, and I'm most certainly no exception.

But my head's screwed on pretty tightly. He's more Mandy's caliber anyway.

Whatever happens, I'm not going to let him sink his hook into me—even though I know I might have trouble stopping myself from thinking about it whenever he's around—particularly after two months of obsessing over him and seeing him taking care of himself.

"Still want to help?" Kellan asks as we reach the barn.

I stare at the bright, red-painted building with white trim. Up on the hill, the barn looked big, but standing in front of it, it looks huge—much larger than his house, almost as large as an airplane hangar. I definitely know now what he meant when he said I'd need extra energy.

The hike has already drained me, and we haven't even started work yet—whatever that may entail.

God, a waffle would be delicious.

In spite of the mud caking my boots and my aching muscles, I set my jaw and peer all the way up into his striking green eyes. "What do you think?"

A soft smile tugs at his lips, and his brows shoot up with what I *know* is the slightest hint of admiration. The knowledge makes me smile, proud of myself. Kellan's still looking at me, and for a moment, he opens his mouth, as though to say something, but swiftly changes his mind.

"We'll have to inspect the damage first," he says casually, turning away from me. "Storms around here aren't particularly kind."

I nod, even though this is news to me.

He continues, "Do you really want to help?" I nod my head, and his gorgeous smile widens a little. "Okay. Then stay close to me and don't do anything rash."

I frown because I've no idea what the hell he's talking about. What could I possibly do rashly?

But there's no time for asking because Kellan takes off. I follow behind, watching him as he opens the main door to the barn, the muscles straining his shirt. The tendons in his forearms flex and stretch while a sexy groan swooshes past his lips.

At last, the door opens with a groan, and he motions me inside.

The interior is divided into huge stalls with top and bottom opening doors and halls to the left and right. To my left, there are cows. On the right, there are stalls with horses. At the far end, there's the storage area where he keeps the feed and the hay. Dust is flying as we walk.

"The barn's over one hundred years old," Kellan

says. "The land has belonged to my family for generations."

"Wow," I say, impressed, and peer up, spinning in a slow circle.

The morning light is spilling in through the high windows, and the pungent scent of hay, dust, and manure hits my nostrils. It doesn't smell bad, just earthy—different from the city.

I keep close to him as he opens the stalls and inspects one horse after another, then guides them outside with a smack on their haunches.

I don't know much about horses, but these ones are huge and well groomed. Even I can tell that Kellan takes great care of them.

"Are you afraid of them?" Kellan asks.

"What? No."

It's not the entire truth. I'm not afraid of horses, per se.

But these look like something out of a gladiator arena—the kind that could trample you to death.

"Good. Maybe I'll teach you to ride them, if you're up for it."

"What makes you think I cannot ride?" I ask in a bold moment.

He cocks his head, his eyes running over my body. "I can tell."

I don't bother with a reply. There's no point in telling him that he's wrong because he isn't.

But damn, coming out of his mouth, I never know whether to feel insulted or not.

For what feels like an eternity, he works in silence, swiftly moving from stall to stall, inspecting the wood panels and the large windows, opening more doors, refilling food. An hour later, he's done, seemingly pleased, and we head back outside.

"This is it?" I ask. It wasn't so bad.

"No, we still have to take a look at the bulls. Their barn's about a mile away."

A mile?

I'm not sure my legs can carry me that far, and yet I force a smile to my lips. "Sure." I point at the barn. "Shouldn't we do a bit of cleaning first?"

"I don't usually have my guests cleaning out the stalls, unless they ask me to." He winks, and my breath hitches in my throat.

In the sunlight he's so gorgeous, it's unreal. His green eyes seem to catch and reflect the golden light. The wind ruffles his hair, blowing a strand into his eyes. I want to brush it aside, but refrain from doing so.

He beats me to it anyway and rakes a hand through his hair, the motion slow and sexy. I look away and wrap my arms around my waist, not because I'm cold but because I need to put something between us, even if the wall is imaginary.

"Can I stroke the horses?" I ask. My glance travels to them. They're feasting on the grass, their muscular bodies strong and majestic.

"No, but you can ride one, if you want," Kellan says. "Come on, I'll introduce you to them."

Without waiting for my reply, he grabs my hands and guides me while telling me their names and recalling how he got each one of them.

I try to listen, but all I can think about is his fingers on my skin, the heat of his body, the strength emanating from him.

"This is Brenna," Kellan says. "She's the quietest, most patient quarter horse I've ever had."

"She's beautiful." I stroke her muzzle, almost expecting Brenna to bite or otherwise express her displeasure. To my surprise, she seems to like it.

"You should ride."

"I can't," I say.

"Can't or won't?" Kellan asks.

"I can't ride," I say dryly. "You, being the expert, have already figured that out."

"You'll pick it up in no time." He looks up at the sky and frowns. Dark clouds are gathering in the distance, but it doesn't look like it'll rain soon. "Wait here while I get a saddle."

I wait until he's out of hearing distance before I turn to Brenna. "You seem to know him well. You won't tell me too that I should sleep with him, will you?" She gives a snorting sound, and I laugh. "Exactly my opinion. He's hot, but just because someone's hot, that's not enough of a reason to bed him." I reach over the fence to stroke her neck when I notice something moving.

The barking carries over too late.

I turn around the moment Kellan yells from a distance, "Sniper, no!"

But it's too late. All I see is the blur of a rich black and tan mutt before paws settle on my shoulders and I tumble backward, landing on my backside. The impact is softened by the blanket of mud reaching up to my calves and now covering half of me. But I don't have time to digest the fact that I've just landed on my backside in front of the hottest guy in history – oh, the mortification.

"Sniper, no," Kellan commands. "Get off her now."

I stare into the softest brown eyes. Sharp, exposed teeth are barely inches away from my face, but there's also a pink tongue that hangs out.

"Ava, don't move," Kellan whispers, the undercurrents of his voice filled with worry and—

Fear.

From the corner of my eyes, I watch him inch closer very slowly, palms slightly raised, his voice whispering soothing words to the German Shepherd.

Oh, he can't be serious.

I roll my eyes and struggle to sit up as I push the large dog aside. "Good boy," I praise and pat his oversized head.

"No, don't touch him," Kellan says.

Seriously, he really sounds panicky.

"Why not? He's such a sweetie."

And he is.

The dog licks my wrist and leans into me, almost throwing me back into the mud. His enthusiasm and excitement are contagious, and I find myself laughing.

It takes me a while to rise to my feet and look up all the way into Kellan's eyes. His gaze is strange, filled with a heat so scorching hot it burns my skin.

No one's ever looked at me like that.

"He likes you," Kellan says, taken aback. His voice carries a mix of admiration and respect, but his face shows something else. "Do you have a dog?"

"No, my parents never let me have one." I look at

Sniper, who's jumping up and down, begging me to rub him in his dog language. "Why?"

He shrugs. "I was just wondering. This dog doesn't like anyone but me."

"And me." I run my hands through Sniper's coat, then begin to rub his ears.

"It took me half a year to get him to let me touch him," Kellan remarks, watching me with a strange expression. "He's a military dog with PTSD. I adopted him. So no, it's not normal."

"Everyone likes me," I mumble.

His brow shoots up, his usual arrogance returning. "Not everyone."

His statement hits me like a slap in the face. My head snaps to him. "What the fuck's that supposed to mean?"

He shrugs and moves closer. His fingers curl around my upper arm, and before I know it, I'm back up on my feet again, Sniper instantly forgotten.

Kellan's standing close, looking down at me, his hot breath warming my lips.

"I don't like you," he whispers, his expression dark, his eyes hooded.

What. The. Fuck?

As I stare at him, I realize he's probably jealous.

Jealous that his dog likes me.

"Are you always this blunt?" I shake my head and yank my arm out of his grip. "Wait, don't answer that. I think I know the answer."

"Trust me, you don't."

The air around us seems to have cooled down a few degrees.

What's with this guy, blowing all hot and cold? Why can't he just be like a normal human being and at least pretend to be charming until he's deceived his way into my panties?

"I don't like you either," I say and turn around to leave. His grip on my arm holds me back.

"Ava?"

"What?" I snap at him for no reason. It's such an immature reaction, but I can't help feeling hurt. Hurt that he doesn't like me. Hurt that he's jealous when it's not even my fault. Hurt that he can't be happy that his dog likes me.

"I don't like you," he says again.

"You made that part perfectly clear."

"No, you don't understand." He takes a deep breath and lets it out slowly. "You're not unlikeable. I don't like you because I want you. You should take that as a compliment. The women I didn't like were always the best lays."

My mouth opens and closes.

"You're such an asshole, you know that?" I say through gritted teeth.

"Why? Because I just told you that I want you?"

"No, because you're implying that I could be just another one of your conquests. That's all I am for you, right?" My eyes are ablaze as I step forward and poke a finger into his hard chest. "Did you ever ask those women whether they liked you?"

He steps back and smiles at me, the kind of smile I wish I could smack right off his face. "No need to. Their screams always said it all."

With that, he heads back to the horses, whistling for Sniper to follow after him. The dog doesn't. Panting, he sits on his haunches and looks up at me, waiting.

"Now, that's a good boy," I say, smiling, and pat his head. "I don't like him. And I bet you don't like him either."

CHAPTER TWELVE

THERE'S A DIFFERENCE between longing and living out a fantasy. There's also a difference between desiring intimacy with someone who's your dream guy and wanting something that you know is bad for you. Dream guy or not, I know it can and won't end well with Kellan.

I stand rooted to the spot for a good five minutes before I decide that whoever Kellan is, he's definitely not someone you want to let too close to you or your heart.

For one, he's too good-looking. Beautiful people always get away with anything.

And second, while I've met my fair share of bad boys, and, as such, am rather familiar with their game, Kellan takes it to a whole new level.

He's too arrogant for his own sake.

He behaves like every woman is fair game and the world is his playground. If he thinks he only has to ask and I'll jump on his bandwagon, he's mistaken. The fact that he wants me and makes no secret out of us never being more than just a fling makes him a whole different kind of dangerous.

It's all too tempting.

I don't know how to deal with someone like him.

Keeping away from him is no longer just an option. It's become a priority because there's no way I'll ever turn into one of the women he's used and left behind.

"I'm heading back inside," I call out and begin my ascent before he can stop me.

"What about work?" he shouts.

"You can do it yourself. I have no intention of staying."

"Fine. Suit yourself. Let's see how far you get without me."

Wow.

The guy really assumes I'll need him just because I'm a woman.

Talk about being sexist.

"Condescending jerk," I say and head in the direction from where we came.

"I heard you," Kellan yells after me.

"I hope so." I turn back to him, my gaze boiling. "Because that's my honest opinion of you." I continue walking with Sniper glued to my ankle, glancing over my shoulder a few times to see whether Kellan's coming after me. He makes no attempt to follow.

That's fine by me.

Sniper is a much better companion anyway.

The house is a long way up the hill. From where I'm standing, I can't even see it, but I'm confident it'll barely take me ten minutes to reach it, fifteen minutes tops. I huff and groan as I trudge through the mud, and realize climbing up a hill is way worse than climbing down. I've barely managed to walk a few yards when a gust of wind whips against my face. I lose my equilibrium for a moment and tumble backward.

I fall on my backside, and a scream escapes my throat.

The pain shooting through my ankle is

excruciating. My vision blurs. I bite my lip hard to stifle the yelp lodged deep in my throat. Sniper barks once, then twice, and then he runs off, probably frightened by my scream.

"Fuck. Fuck," I mutter as I try to scramble to my feet but find that I can't.

My hands go to my throbbing ankle. It burns when I touch it.

"Are you okay?"

Kellan's voice reaches me a moment before he does. I nod and look up at him through the curtain of unwanted tears clouding my vision. Sniper barks again. He's standing next to Kellan, eyeing us both.

"Good boy," Kellan says to the dog. "He came to get me."

"I'm fine," I squeeze through gritted teeth, even though I'm anything but. The throbbing pain in my ankle shoots up to my knee in long pangs. In spite of the wind, my back is slick with sweat. I broke my arm when I was five and had my tonsils removed at nine, so I know what physical pain feels like. However, this hurts so much, I might just pass out.

My ankle feels like it's been run over by a truck.

"I'm fine, " I say again. Pushing up on my arm, I try to stand—to no avail.

"Let me see." Before I can protest, Kellan's pulled

off my boot and his fingers are on my bare skin, inspecting, prodding.

His touch is torture.

"It hurts," I choke out.

"I hope it's not broken," he mutters.

I rise up on my elbows to get a better look and instantly wish I hadn't. A large, purple bruise is forming where the bone is located, and my foot looks like it's about to swell.

Kellan presses his fingertips against it, and I whimper. He holds my ankle in place, then presses some more, moving his fingers around.

"Not broken," he declares eventually. "I think it's just a minor sprain, but it could be worse. I'll take you back to the house and get it bandaged up for you."

"No, thank you," I mutter. "I'll be fine."

"Ava, you're not fine. You can't walk. You need help."

I do, but I'm still angry with him.

"I don't want your help," I hiss. "I don't need help from someone who doesn't like me but wants to use me for a good fuck."

He lets out a breath. "What I said was out of line. I didn't mean it."

I scoff. "Yeah, right. What part? The one about

wanting me or not liking me?"

Sighing, he sits down next to me. "About not liking you. Obviously, there are parts of you that I like."

I stare at him in disgust.

Is he talking about my body?

He makes it sound like that's a good thing.

"Forget it." I make a move to get up, but he holds me down.

"I don't know you, obviously. I can only judge from what I've seen so far. You're likeable in general. I do enjoy your company, otherwise I would have sent you away."

He likes my company—the thought makes me smile just a little bit. "You're just saying that because you want to help me."

Kellan shakes his head slowly. "No, I'm saying that I sort of care for you. That's all. I find that difficult to deal with."

His words strike me speechless.

Our gazes lock, and something passes between us. A moment later, another jolt of pain shoots up my ankle, and I wince.

"That's it. I'm not taking no for an answer," Kellan says, our strange moment broken.

I nod and hold my breath as he lifts me up in his

arms like I weigh nothing and cradles my head against his shoulder as he carries me back to the barn.

The shooting pain becomes a dull, consistent throb, and I bite my lip to hold back a swear word.

We reach the barn, and he saddles a horse, then helps me up, both of my legs dangling on one side. He places himself behind me, one hand holding the rein, the other wrapped around my waist to keep me secured in place as he guides the horse.

Even though it's the last thing I want, I press my palm against his thigh to hold on for support. His muscles are hard and defined. Broad from riding and God knows what else. His chest feels like steel against my face.

"Hold on to me." His voice is gentle. I nod and do as he requested. "Ready?" he asks.

I nod, and the horse jolts into action.

Up close, he smells amazing. I inhale the blend of heat and shower gel, of nature and something so heady it makes me want to press my lips against his skin just to see what happens.

Good thing he's sitting behind me, oblivious to the nature of my thoughts and the irregular beat of my heart.

Get a grip.

He's just a guy, albeit the hot and forbidden kind.

Like my mother used to say, all women go through the phase of liking a bad boy…they fuck one, cry over one, and then they marry the boring and safe accountant next door.

I've tried my hand at the dating part plenty of times. Most of the guys I went for were boring, and just plain jerks, who thought sex follows shortly after the drink tab and is a mandatory part of any first date. However, none of them were like Kellan.

My fingers travel up just a little bit—obviously in need of something to hold on to. Something hard is prodding my hip—I can't tell if it's the saddle or if the situation is getting Kellan excited.

The thought gets me so hot and bothered, I suck in a gulp of air. My lungs feel devoid of oxygen, and my breath is coming in odd little bursts. The picture of him naked and sprawled out on a bed instantly enters my mind. Certain parts of him are blurred, like even my fantasy knows that nothing I've ever seen before could measure up to him. I want to look, if only to see whether that part of him is as delicious as the rest. But I refuse to give in to my perverted brain's command.

CHAPTER THIRTEEN

AFTER WHAT FEELS like an eternity, we reach the front porch. Kellan finally unmounts and secures the bridle to the veranda, then lifts me in his arms again.

He pushes the door open and carries me into the kitchen, setting me down at the table. He leaves for a few minutes and returns with a first aid kit, a towel, and a bowl. I expect him to return to his chores. But instead, he settles besides me, his proximity too close for comfort as he starts to inspect my ankle again.

His hand feels rough against my skin.

As if he's worked on a farm all his life.

For the life of me, I cannot imagine him to be a nightclub owner, the kind that parties all night, and yet his expensive car suggests he does. At the same time, it's strange to think that a rich guy like him enjoys pure physical labor. It makes me wonder about his past, who he is, what he does.

"This wouldn't have happened if you didn't try to run from me. I told you to stay close," Kellan remarks, his hoarse whisper sending an instant jolt through my body.

Of course he would think that.

"I wasn't running and most certainly not from you."

"Yeah. Ava—" He hesitates. Words linger unspoken.

The way he says my name—it's too hoarse. Too intimate. It rolls off his tongue like it belongs there.

Like he owns it.

My body instantly tenses, and I curse my bad luck for not only propelling me to Montana and into the arms of this man, but also for bestowing him with an arrogance that makes him way too observant.

"Whatever it is you want to say, don't," I mumble.

"I can't deal with your kind at this point in my life. Not when everything's finally going according to plan."

"My kind. Really?" He finally stands and then kneels at my feet. His fingers begin to busy themselves with my swollen calf, applying a wet towel. I wince when he touches the sore spot again. "Here we go. May I ask what that is again?"

"Thank you for asking. I'll be more than happy to enlighten you. You're the arrogant prick kind that seems to think a woman's legs are there to be pried open. And if you stomp on some hearts in the process, then so be it. I bet it comes with the job description."

"You have me all figured out, huh?" He stops and looks at me, his eyes flickering with amusement.

I raise my chin defiantly. "You bet your ass I have."

His eyes flicker again.

Big mistake to challenge him like that.

Why can't I ever keep my mouth shut when it matters?

I want to take my words back.

Only, how?

"You still haven't answered that one thing I want to know," Kellan says. His gaze is dark, hooded. I've no idea what the fuck he's thinking, and not knowing drives me crazy.

"I didn't realize you had asked a question," I remark.

"I never said I had. I keep wondering about something."

"Yeah? What's that?"

His huge palms go around the sides of my face, holding my head in place. His lips come close until his breath feels like soft butterflies against my mouth. He's towering over me, his proximity unnerving, but what makes me hold my breath in anticipation of his next move is the way he looks at me through those burning green eyes.

As if he wants to kiss me.

I want him to.

I want him to so bad, I feel myself leaning into him—just for a second—but it's enough to bring a wicked smile to his lips.

"That's what I thought," Kellan says.

"You thought what?"

He's going to say something stupid that'll piss me off big time. I just know it. And yet, I still want him to answer the question I shouldn't have asked.

"That you want me." His tone is confident and nonchalant, like there's no way in hell he could have drawn the wrong conclusion.

Up until this moment, I could have denied it.

But the faux pas I've just made isn't one I can take back.

Yes, I want him.

But we don't always want what we need. What I need is someone who's reliable, someone with whom I can build a future if I fall in love, someone who takes relationships seriously. Kellan's the opposite of commitment and stability. He's the opposite of everything I've ever known.

I could easily fall in love with him, but rather than my happy ending, he'd be my downfall.

He's a beautiful distraction from reality with the prospect of having one's heart broken.

I raise my chin and stare him down with what I hope are daggers of ice in my gaze.

He stays silent.

"All right," I say. "Maybe I want you a little bit. You're not exactly hard on the eye, and I've had a bit of a dry spot." I pause, regarding him to catch his expression—a blink, a smirk, shock, anything to give away that he might be affected by what I'm saying. "But just because I find you attractive doesn't mean I'm going to jump into bed with you. That's all."

I pause again, waiting for his reply. The glint of

amusement never leaves his eyes as he just shrugs, seemingly uninterested to find out the answer.

"Your point being?" Kellan prompts.

"I'm not interested," I say coolly.

"See, that's why we have a problem. I don't believe you." I frown and he adds, "You're in denial. I know you feel about me the way I feel about you." His fingers settle beneath my chin, forcing me to meet his gaze. "I'm attracted to you, and yes, it's all fun for me, but at least I'm being honest. What irks me is that you're not. The way I see it, you're single, I'm single. We're both not looking for commitment." He shrugs again. "No harm done."

Whoa.

He just won't stop assuming.

I blink several times as his words keep circling in my mind. "Who said I was single?"

"Your friend. Mandy."

"I know her name," I mumble, still staring at him. "You asked her?"

"Didn't need to," Kellan says. "The moment she found out we sort of met in front of Club 69, she basically blurted out your entire résumé, in particular emphasizing the last three months of your life."

He jiggles his brows at me meaningfully. I'm

supposed to catch his drift, which I do...unfortunately.

After I went to bed, they talked...a lot.

Mandy's such a traitor! From now on, I'm going to consciously unfriend her.

"What exactly did she say?" I ask warily.

Kellan laughs, the sound grating on my nerves, and I have no idea why.

It's not like there's anything annoying about it. In fact, it's the most beautiful laugh I've ever heard. Too bad such a sexy voice and amazing outer packaging comes with the shittiest character I've ever met.

"I could tell you, but what's in it for me?"

"Nothing." I stare at him. "I could ask her, you know. She's my best friend."

"I don't see her around. Do you?" He glances at me. "Haven't you been wondering why she's gone AWOL?"

I narrow my eyes in suspicion. "I knew it," I say slowly. "She told you something before she left."

"My lips are sealed." He zips up his lips, the gesture so funny I let out a laugh.

"Her attempt's in vain. I'm not going to sleep with you."

"You sure?" he asks. "I like it when you squirm."

He's so full of himself.

Struggling to keep calm, I draw a deep breath and let it out slowly. "I don't squirm."

"Back there, on that horse, you did."

"I'm not going to argue with you," I say, shaking my head.

"Because you don't have a case."

I choke back a laugh. He's challenging me. I can see it in the way his mouth pulls up into a grin that's so sexy I fear it'll set me on fire. I can sure feel it between my legs.

What could I possibly respond with when he's right and he knows it?

I *did* squirm against him, and to be honest, I'm pretty sure, given the chance, my traitorous body would do it again.

In the silence of the room, I watch him apply a lotion that reeks of the usual hospital scent. "So, you're a physician or trained in the medical field?" I point at my ankle, eager to find out more about him.

"Nothing of the sort." He wraps a bandage around my ankle. "I'm just good with horses. They're not so different from women."

"Ah." I nod in mock agreement. "You're really charming. Anyone ever tell you that?"

He laughs that raucous laughter of his. In spite of

the insult he's just thrown at me, I find that I'm not insulted at all. I don't know why, but I wouldn't have expected anything else from him.

"Horses are loyal as long as you take care of them," Kellan explains, ignoring my statement. "But their emotions tend to get the better of them, and they'll always put themselves first. They won't hesitate to stomp over you and desert you."

His words catch me off guard.

His smile is still in place, but the dark glint hasn't left his eyes.

Something about his tone makes me think he was in a bad relationship.

Maybe that's why he is the way he is.

"I'm sorry that you think that way. But I can assure you, not all women are the same." I brush my hair back out of my face, wondering what the heck happened to him in the past that he'd generalize the entire female population.

Everyone has their closet full of emotional baggage. It comes with the people we let into our hearts and lives. Obviously, I'm not here to prove Kellan wrong, which is why I clear my throat and think hard on a change in topic.

Through the kitchen window, I watch Sniper outside. He's sprawled out on the lawn, his head between his paws. From his relaxed posture, I can tell he's in doggy slumberland.

"He's a good dog," I say out of need to keep the conversation rolling.

"He is."

I turn back to regard Kellan. "You say you adopted him?"

"It's a long story."

"I have nothing but time, as you must have gathered." I point at my ankle.

He lets out a laugh. "With a sprained ankle, you have indeed."

He puts the first aid kit aside and takes a seat beside me. Together we turn to watch Sniper.

"He's a military working dog who was supposed to be put down," Kellan says.

"Really? But why? He's so sweet." I cannot help but be disgusted. "Besides, as a military working dog, he's probably very useful."

"He was." Kellan pauses, hesitating. "Sniper was one of the best in the service. He was trained to find booby traps, bombs and mines, track enemy troops and missing persons. All you had to do was let him familiarize himself with a scent and he'd run off and find the person. He was relentless." He shakes his head in admiration, his eyes lost in reminiscence.

"He saved so many soldiers. But then..."

I hold my breath. "But what?"

"His owner died in a bomb blast, and he stopped listening to anyone."

"He was supposed to be euthanized for not following?" I ask incredulously.

"It was more than that. He started to attack people that got too close. Every loud sound was traumatic for him. It got so bad, he wouldn't eat. He wouldn't let anyone touch him. He wouldn't work." Kellan glances to me. "He was deemed dangerous, uncontrollable, useless."

"Until you saved him."

He nods again. "I did because I felt that I had to." His voice is so low it sends a shiver down my spine.

"What do you mean?" I ask breathlessly.

He looks away, taking his time with a reply. His eyes are glazed over as he stares into the distance, his mind a million miles away.

"Sniper's owner was my best friend," Kellan whispers at last. "When she died, I felt like I owed it to her to take him in."

I stare back at the dog, thousands of questions running through my mind.

His best friend was female and she was a soldier. I can't imagine someone like Kellan being friends with a woman, and most certainly not with one who fought for her country.

Heck, I can't even imagine him living on a farm.

And yet, it seems to be the case.

It's as if Kellan's a completely different kind of person than the one I imagined him to be. The flirtatious side of him is just the beginning. I feel like I'll have to peel back layers over layers, remove piece by piece of him, to get to know him.

Maybe he isn't as bad as I thought.

Maybe underneath the player he's portraying, he's a real person with emotions, someone who is capable of forming meaningful attachments.

"I'm glad you adopted him," I say softly. "And I'm so sorry about your loss."

He nods, and then the awful silence resumes.

CHAPTER FOURTEEN

"YOU'RE COLD," Kellan says, misinterpreting the brief tremor rocking my body. Or maybe he's just as eager to drop the subject.

I nod, suddenly seeing my chance to escape this situation.

Our conversation.

Him.

"I'll take you to the living room," he says.

"No, Kellan."

Ignoring my half-hearted protest, he lifts me off

the chair and carries me inside, only stopping when we reach the couch. Slowly, he sets me down, arranges a few cushions behind my back, and then wraps a blanket around me—the motion is so intimate, it makes me uncomfortable.

I don't like a guy taking care of me because I fear that one moment in the future when I involuntarily let my guard down, and his guard is still up. Like any other human being, rejection doesn't agree with me.

Kellan's impossibly good looks aren't the actual danger to my inner equilibrium. It's all the small things he seems to do and not make a big deal out of. Like riding home with me and making sure I'm not freezing my ass off.

Been there. Done that. Never again.

Just like him, I have my own emotional baggage. Just like him, I'm not willing to try again.

"I'll bring you something to drink," Kellan says and heads out of the living room, finally leaving me enough space to breathe.

In his absence, I relax against the cushions. The sun is streaming in through the open curtains, bathing the mahogany wood in an orange glow.

There's something strange about this room. It's too manly, too rough. But there's also a tenderness about it. It's the décor, I decide. The odd female touch in the form of a delicate picture frame and an empty glass vase.

He used to live with someone. This someone is gone now.

My gaze is involuntarily drawn to the picture frame Mandy inspected last night, and the blond woman in it.

He said she was his sister. Was he telling the truth? I'm thinking of his best friend, a soldier. What were the odds that he was in a relationship with her before her death?

He didn't say it, but I could feel the sadness radiating from him, the way was hard for him to talk. As soon as I said sorry, he closed up.

His sudden change of topic only confirmed it.

"Sorry it took so long." Kellan places a glass on the couch table.

I didn't hear him coming in, and so he catches me off guard. My thoughts can't possibly be written across my forehead, and yet I feel like he can look right through me and see that I'm trying to figure him out.

"Thanks." I grab the warm glass, eyeing the yellow liquid.

"It's Riesling Hot Toddy," he answers my unspoken question. "Warm white wine with honey, lemon, and cardamom. It'll warm you." He points to my ankle. "Is it still hurting?"

I shake my head and find that at some point the throbbing must have stopped. "No."

"Good. You should be able to walk again in a few hours."

"I hope so. I mean, I don't want to impose. We've already overstayed our welcome."

"Don't worry about it," Kellan says and sits down next to me. "Like I said, I enjoy your company. It's a nice change."

I bury my face in my drink, forcing myself to take slow, measured sips. It tastes delicious, sweet, and refreshing.

"Do you live here alone?" I avoid his gaze as I ask the question, afraid to give the impression that I care.

"I do." A slight pause. "Do you live alone back in NYC?"

Just like before, he's avoiding talking about himself. Either he's the monosyllabic type, or he doesn't want me to know too much about him. Either way, I find his evasive nature rude.

"I don't." I stare at him, unwilling to say more. If he wants to remain shrouded in mystery, then so do I.

The corners of his lips twitch. "I know. Mandy said you've been living together since your first day of college."

I grimace.

What else escaped her big mouth?

"She also said that you're starting a new position next week and that you have no time for relationships," Kellan continues, seemingly enjoying his advantage over me.

"I never said I didn't have *time* for relationships. I just don't want one."

He nods, like he knows exactly how I feel. "Relationship gone bad in the past?"

I take a deep breath and let it out slowly. Finally, I shake my head. "Nope. Not really."

It's a lie.

Someone hurt me—bad—but I can't tell him that. He wouldn't understand, not when I'm sure he's probably broken thousands of hearts.

His brows shoot up in obvious interest. "Not eager to share?"

I shake my head again.

There's no way in hell I'll disclose my romantic past to someone like him. If I want to unburden myself, then I'll listen to Taylor Swift songs to feel better about all the things that have gone wrong in my life.

"I'm a good listener." Kellan leans forward, elbows propped on his knees, as though his physical proximity could prove his point.

I frown at his sudden interest. "Why do you even want to know?"

"Because I like to know about my competition."

A simple statement. Just like that, he seems to think about competition.

I laugh. "I doubt Kellan Boyd knows what competition is."

"You're right. I don't usually have competition." He hesitates, which gives me the opportunity to regard him intently, trying hard to read the sudden shadow crossing his features. His green gaze seems a shade darker. Troubled. And determined.

I clear my throat and look away when his fingers clasp my chin, forcing my eyes back to him. "I'm not afraid of competition, Ava."

"I never believed you were."

"Good. I won't make a secret out of the fact that I always get the woman I want. You won't be the exception, Ava."

His monumental ego is back.

I open my mouth, then close it at the way his mouth seems to draw closer to me.

My breath is caged in my chest, waiting, expecting, fearing *that* one moment when his lips will crash down on mine.

The world around us seems to stand still while my head becomes a big void of nothingness, my senses straining to tune into him. He's so close. I can smell him. I can see the way the light reflects in his irises, splitting it into different shades of green—all beautiful, all breathtaking.

"You're different," he whispers.

"How so?"

"I don't know. Just different."

"Is that a good or a bad thing?"

"I don't know, either. Is not wanting me a bad thing?"

"You tell me." I cock my head, a smile tugging at my lips. "After all, you're the one with the long list of conquests."

"None of them matter," Kellan says. "None of them get my attention like you do." He glances at me. "There's something about you that drives me crazy."

"I believe it's called rejection." His eyebrows rise, so I feel the need to clarify. "I rejected you, and now you think you have to conquer me."

He shakes his head. "No, it's more than that. I

want you. I want you like I've never wanted anyone before. I just can't explain it...I can't explain you."

My breath hitches, stolen by his words. When did things take this turn? One moment he's flirting with me, the next he's saying something like this. I'm not sure that I like the change.

"What are you saying?" I whisper, my voice shaking.

"I'm saying..." He hesitates. "I want to know more about you. I want to know what makes you tick. And—" he pauses again, his eyes glued to my lips "—I want to kiss you. To know if your lips are as soft as they seem."

All air swishes out of my lungs, as though it's just been knocked out of me. He's waiting for my permission, I realize. "Is that a good idea?"

"Only one way to find out."

His hand moves to the back of my nape, pulling me softly to him, and then his mouth meets mine in a slow, delicious kiss. Even though his lips barely brush mine, the electric jolt running through me is all-consuming. My nerve endings are on fire. My whole body is.

He holds me like no other. His kiss is balm for my soul.

The tip of his tongue slips between my lips, and I

moan against his mouth, the sound lost between us. He tastes manly and minty, his hot breath burning me from the inside. The picture of those lips on my nipples appears before my eyes—those lips traveling down my abdomen, kissing me. My fingers are trembling as they brush the front of his shirt, the open palm of my hand settling on his lower ribcage. His warmth is seeping through the thin material, searing me.

I want to push my hand underneath his clothes to feel skin against skin. To taste him the way I want him to taste me. But I don't do any of those things.

Because this one kiss is already my undoing.

His lips are doing unthinkable things to me, creating feelings I have never had before. They remind me of a summer breeze, soft and warm; of a winter tale that mesmerizes and entrances; of the wings of a thousand butterflies, light and soundless, as they flutter around.

I wish I could stop this one moment, capture it, because I know it won't last.

Because a guy like him doesn't stay in a woman's life. He breezes through and leaves only havoc behind.

I press my lips against him, over and over again, letting his tongue meet mine in a slow dance. And then I can feel his hand traveling up my inner thigh.

A delicious jolt travels through my clitoris and moisture pools between my legs, readying me for what he has to offer. Only, I'm not sure if I'm ready.

I squeeze my legs shut, but the friction only manages to intensify the want inside me.

Too soon, Kellan pries his lips away from mine, his hand withdrawing from my body.

I open my eyes and find him staring at me. He's just as breathless as I am. His eyes are dark, full of desire. His gaze is penetrating every layer of me, reaching my core. "I'm not a patient man, Ava. But I can wait if something's worth waiting for."

"Don't do this." My voice is shaking as I push him away and stand, disgusted at just how desperate this man makes me. I have to get away, but where could I possibly head without appearing like I'm running from him?

His fingers brush the back of my arm, and my breath catches in my throat.

"You sound upset. I'm sorry," he whispers. "I shouldn't have kissed you."

Coming from someone like him, his apology takes me by surprise. I want to tell him that there's no need to apologize. That I enjoyed kissing him. But I can't. I've been hurt so often that opening up is not an option. I brush my fingertips over my lips. They're still tingling, reminding me of how good it felt to have his mouth against mine. They remind me that his presence does something to me. My resolve is crumbling. I fear he'll pull me to him and I'll give in, just because I miss the intimacy of having another body against mine, inside me.

It's been too long.

The attraction I feel for him reminds me of that.

I can feel the shift inside my head.

It's not like I haven't hooked up with guys before.

It's not like I want him to put a ring on that finger.

I'm available. He's available. Except, is he? Who's the blond woman in the picture on the fireplace? Why don't I believe that she's his sister?

Because he won't elaborate.

Because the one man I loved in the past lied to me. Told me the same bullshit story.

"Ava?" Kellan's voice is a deliciously hoarse rumble.

What's the harm indeed?

I'm not a cheater—that's the harm. I won't do to others what others have done to me.

"I was in love with someone," I whisper at last.

The words are out before I can stop them.

My reply has his instant attention. His shoulders tense; his whole body does.

"He cheated," I continue as I glance up at him. "He was my first love. My first in everything. I gave him my whole heart, and he broke it." I take in Kellan's face, expecting nonchalance, but there's nothing nonchalant about his expression. "Now you know why I reject you. It's because I won't go through something like that again," I say. "I'm sorry. It's not personal. It's not you. It's me. I'm so sick of guys who play with your emotions. I won't ever get hurt again."

"I had no idea."

I shrug and turn my back to him. "It's okay."

"Do you want me to beat him up? I'm good at it."

His question takes me by surprise. "You would do that?"

"Give me his address and I'll get it done." He smirks. "Actually, I don't even need his address. His name will do."

I let out a laugh. "You can't be serious."

He returns my smile. "You might want to say it one more time and see what happens."

I sigh and touch his hand, squeezing it gently. It feels so good, rough, as if life has shaped him, too. "No, thank you. But I do appreciate the offer."

"You sure?" He cocks one eyebrow. "You're not saying that because you have pity on him?"

"It's over. Definitely. I've moved past him. To be honest, I'm not even sure what I saw in that guy. It's definitely a good thing we're over."

Kellan's hand moves up to my face and I hold my breath, excited at the prospect that he'll kiss me again. But he doesn't. "I don't know who he is, but he's damn stupid for letting a beautiful woman like you go. It's his loss."

And then he withdraws his hand and gets up, his focus turning to the window. "It's about to start raining again. I have to get the horses in."

"I'm sorry I can't help you with the farm work. Is there something else I can help you with?" I ask.

He runs his fingers through his hair and then shakes his head. His expression is casual, his eyes two dark pools of emotions I cannot read.

He's unperturbed.

Whatever our kiss did to me, I'm not sure it had the same effect on him. Or maybe he's so good at hiding it because he does it so often.

The thought stings, but I didn't expect anything else from him. He's made it pretty clear that he doesn't date. He only ever fucks.

At least he's honest—unlike my ex.

"You need to rest now. You'll be okay to walk in a few hours," Kellan remarks. "I'll be back this evening."

He glances at me one more time before heading out. For a moment, I stare at the empty space he just occupied, wondering how I could possibly learn to read a guy who's a closed book.

CHAPTER FIFTEEN

KELLAN'S RIGHT. THE pain in my ankle lessens over the course of a few hours.

After our kiss, it seems that he can't get away from me fast enough. Or maybe he really is busy.

From the open window in the kitchen, I watch him take Brenna, saddle and mount her, then kick her into a trot. His eyes meet mine. I give him a short wave before he disappears with Sniper by his side. I stare into the open space for a long time, alone with my thoughts, confused.

One moment, he tells me he doesn't like me, the next he's expressing his readiness to beat up my ex.

He's a man shrouded in mystery and contradiction.

Eventually, I sigh and hobble to my feet, giving up trying to make sense of him.

I've no idea what to do with myself in this strange house as I head through the hall to familiarize myself with all the rooms.

The space is huge. All the rooms are tastefully furnished in a rustic style, but carry a male touch. The ensuite bathrooms are clean but empty. Devoid of life. Like Kellan hasn't had any visitors in a long time.

I inspect the contents of the fridge and decide to make us ham sandwiches and salad for dinner, then head to my room to take a short nap.

It's early afternoon when the sound of chopping wood and hammering carries over through the open window. The dog barks a few times, and Kellan laughs—the sound causing a strange jolt in my chest.

Even though I shouldn't even be thinking about making an effort, I apply a bit of lipstick and straighten my clothes before I head back into the kitchen.

Kellan seems surprised when he sees me standing

in the doorway, juggling two plates and two glasses of lemonade.

"You didn't have to."

I shrug. "I wanted to. You're kind enough for letting us stay."

He mumbles a "thanks" and we eat on the front porch in silence.

"The mechanic is going to pick up your car later today," he says.

I swallow the last bite of my sandwich before I reply. "I thought the landline wasn't working."

"It isn't." He gives me an amused glance. "But the one in the barn is."

"You have a working phone in the barn and didn't tell me?"

"I never got the chance because you just took off."

"You were rude."

"I was." He turns his head to me and playfully bumps his shoulder against mine. "I need to apologize."

"I wasn't nice either, so don't."

"I knew the hill was slippery. It's my fault you fell. How about I make it up to you?" He takes another sandwich, bites into it, and chews slowly.

"How?"

"I want you to stay for a few more days," Kellan

says.

"I'm not sure I can."

"Because you know I'll keep making passes at you?"

I shake my head. "No, that's not it. I know you will. Strange as it may sound, I think I've gotten used to you being annoying."

A smile lights up his face. "Then stay. I want to see how far I can go with you."

"You don't give up, do you?" I roll my eyes in mock exasperation.

"Never." He grins. "Wait here." He gets up and rounds the house, then returns with a pair of brown hiking boots. "These are for you."

I take them out of his hands and turn them around to inspect them. "How did you know my size?"

"I removed your shoes from you, remember?"

The sound of tires hitting gravel carries over, followed by Sniper barking.

"Here, boy." Kellan grabs his collar and guides him to the garage, locking him inside.

A moment later, Mandy calls out, "Are you guys decent?"

I roll my eyes at her and shoot Kellan an exasperated look. I find him gazing at me, but his expression isn't quite as irritated as mine.

Because he doesn't want to be decent with me. He's made that part pretty clear. And because he's not a guy who beats around the bush; he seems to like to keep all women informed about his intentions.

"I can't believe you just said that," I say to Mandy as we head back inside.

She shrugs and squeezes out of her jacket, tossing it at the foot of the couch the same way she does back home. Kellan glares at the jacket like it's the poor fabric's fault, but doesn't comment.

So, he's the tidy kind. I add that to my mental drawer of information I've gathered about him.

"Did you find the town?" Kellan retrieves the jacket and drapes it over the back of a chair.

Mandy freezes as she hears insistent barking, ignoring Kellan's question. "Wow. Is there a dog in there?"

"It's Sniper," I say.

Mandy watches us with a knowing smirk on her face. "Look at you, guys. You already look like an old married couple."

"Not a fan of marriage?" Kellan remarks, brows raised.

"Actually, quite the contrary," I say, amused. "She

finds old, married people cute." I grimace at him. "Don't get her started, unless you want a rendition of The Notebook with all its literary merits and its relevance to today's society."

A blank question mark flickers on his face, and I smile.

He has no idea what The Notebook is.

If he continues to be a big jerk, I'll let Mandy unpack her all-time favorite movie, which I'm sure is safely stashed in her suitcase because she never travels without it, and dare him to watch it from the beginning until the very sappy ending.

"Did you know there's a freaking western movie out there?" Mandy ask and plops down on the sofa.

"She's probably talking about the landscape," I say and look at Kellan, barely able to hide my smile. Something—is that amusement?—flickers in his eyes.

He's looking at me intently as he asks Mandy, "How far did you get?"

Holy shit.

Is there something growing on my nose, or why the fuck won't he look away? If he continues to be so weird, Mandy will get all suspicious and then will start drilling me for details, her dirty imagination making up things that will never happen.

"I got as far as the next town," Mandy says slowly.

"You drove all the way?" I ask incredulously.

"Why wouldn't I?" Mandy retorts, slightly annoyed. "I wish I hadn't bothered though. All I found was a string of taverns glued together. And get this. There are no shops. Not even a Starbucks. I don't know how those people survive. It was literally impossible to find a working phone. Or an Internet café. Even the post office and the police station were closed." She raises her brows the way she always does when something strikes her as unbelievable.

"That's probably the storm's fault," Kellan says patiently. "Phone lines are often down during and shortly after bad weather. The main roads are also blocked by uprooted trees. It takes a while to clean it all up, which takes all the manpower the sheriff can get."

"Yes." Mandy draws out the word. "But that usually only happens in movies. I need to get a manicure and make a very important phone call. Not to mention the fact that I *really* need to check my emails. Maybe you could point me to the nearest hotel, preferably one that has a spa and deluxe rooms. And I wouldn't mind a well-stocked mini bar. Anything to help me sleep through the days I'm stuck in the middle of nowhere."

"Of course." Kellan winks at me. "The hotel's down that way." He points out the window, in the direction of the barn, and I can barely stifle a snort.

Now that Mandy thinks I'm interested in Kellan, she no longer sees the need to pretend, so she's basically returned to her true NYC persona. Gone is the pretend off-the-grid nature fan she was about to morph into last night when she thought Kellan and she might turn into an item...if only for a night.

"I didn't see it," Mandy says.

"That's because there's nothing there," I say.

Her eyes narrow on Kellan and me. I can see her little head working. "Did you guys have fun?"

"She sprained her ankle." Kellan points to my bandaged leg, ignoring her question.

"Oh." Mandy looks at me, disappointed. "In that case, we can't leave just yet."

"I can walk around, though it still hurts a little," I say. "But my ankle's not the reason why we need to stay. It's the car. The mechanic's not been here yet, so I don't know how long it'll take to get it repaired."

"Damn. And there's no way we can borrow his?" She gestures at Kellan like he's not standing there listening.

"Mandy!" I give her my usual 'don't you dare' glare. "We're already imposing."

"What?" She shrugs. "We need to check into our hotel. We'll be losing a day."

I shoot Kellan an apologetic look. "Even if we could leave, the streets are still blocked."

"What are your plans for tonight?" Kellan asks, his gaze cemented on me.

He doesn't want me to leave.

The realization hits me like a wall.

I shrug and look at Mandy, her attention jumping back and forth between Kellan and me, like a ping pong ball, as she's analyzing our every move and word.

"What are your suggestions?" Mandy says. "Ava likes to go out just as much as she enjoys an evening in." Now she sounds like she's in a TV reality show and trying to get the guy to choose me instead of the two other desperate floozies.

"I was planning on getting to bed early. You know, catch some sleep," I say.

Mandy shoots me a dirty look.

"What?" I mouth and frown.

"You're a lost cause. I'm going to take a shower because I'm most certainly not staying in tonight," she mutters and walks out. She calls over her shoulder, "And you're not staying in either. There's got to be something remotely exciting to do in this town. And I'll find it, dammit."

"I think she wants you to go out with me," Kellan remarks, amused, as soon as a door slams down the corridor and we're alone again.

"Yeah, she's not very subtle at expressing her wishes." I brush my hair out of my face and look all the way up to meet his impossibly green gaze.

That was a big mistake.

"Is there a bar somewhere around here?" I ask.

"Sure, there is. And it serves the best beer in the state." Kellan's arms are crossed over his chest as he regards me with that challenging flicker in his eyes.

Does *he* want me to go out with him?

I can't imagine a guy like him needing someone like me to keep him company. And yet, his expression says it all.

He wants me around.

I heave an exaggerated sigh as I consider my options. I'm not afraid of being on my own, but the idea of being stuck in my room with no one to talk to isn't exactly appealing.

Wherever Kellan's going, there are bound to be people.

I won't even have to sit at the same table.

Or talk to him.

I won't even have to look at him.

Heck, I bet I can shut him out completely until I won't even know that he's around.

"Let's hit it."

His brows shoot up.

"I mean the town." I gesture with my hand. "You know the saying."

He shakes his head.

"Everybody knows the saying 'let's hit the town'," I say. A thought occurs to me—I don't even know how old he is. "How old are you?"

"Twenty-eight. I thought you would have Googled me by now," Kellan remarks. I stare at him, unsure whether he's joking or being serious.

Did Mandy say something? Because I swear to God his stunning green eyes are twinkling with knowledge that yes, I tried to Google him after our first encounter, even though I didn't know his name.

"Not everyone's obsessed with you," I say through cringed teeth, already regretting my decision to go out with him. But I can't go back on my word now, lest he think his words might carry a morsel of truth to them.

"Hmmm."

That look again, like he knows more than he should and is annoyingly smug about it.

I swear to God, I'm on the verge of saying

something I might come to regret to wipe that grin right off his face.

"I've never been obsessed with a guy, ever."

"That is, until you met me, right?"

"No." My tone comes out defensive, my voice conveying my annoyance because he's so damn right. "Honestly, you could own all the nightclubs in the world, and I wouldn't be interested."

He shakes his head. "Like I said, you got the wrong Boyd, baby. I'm just an investor in my brother's business."

I look up at him to see if he's lying. Yeah, that's what my cheating, lying ex did to me.

Kellan keeps denying it, and his expression is honest, so it must be true.

"I'll leave you to get dressed," he says and heads down the corridor to his bedroom, I assume.

"What's wrong with my jeans?" I mutter and grimace at the air.

Of course guys like Kellan like a woman all made up and probably wearing barely more than a piece of fabric to cover their modesty.

It's what they're used to.

If he expects me to turn into Mandy, then he'll be thoroughly disappointed. Not in the least because I don't own Mandy's wardrobe...or long legs to show off. So I refrain from squeezing into clothes that will only accentuate my shortcomings.

I sigh and head for my room, where I change into a dark blue pencil skirt that reaches down to my knees and a white button-up blouse—my usual work attire. I top it all off with ankle boots and a thin jacket.

It's all very demure.

It's all rather suited to an office environment.

I stand back, disappointed.

I look like a secretary or a librarian.

Regarding myself in the mirror as I apply a thin layer of red lipstick, I've no idea why I packed the kind of clothes I did. But it's too late to ask Mandy for help because a knock raps at the door. Before I can answer, Kellan's voice bellows, "I'm leaving in two minutes. Don't be late, woman."

Without a doubt, he's piling on the caveman charm.

I swiftly roll my hair into a bun, then, deciding that it might be too much, I let my hair cascade down my back in a waterfall of brown, messy waves.

"I thought I might have to drag you out of there," Kellan remarks as soon as I join him in the hall. There's an easy smile on his lips as his gaze brushes over me, his eyes narrowed, expression veiled.

My hands turn damp and my skin begins to tingle just a little bit.

Damn!

I have no idea what he's thinking, and it makes me nervous.

Even though I shouldn't give a fuck, I want him to find me sexy.

Kellan inches closer and places his big hands on my hips, keeping me at arm's length as his gaze drinks me all in.

"Is that what you're wearing?"

There's a twinkle of amusement in his eyes.

He's laughing at me.

I can't believe the audacity.

"You said you wanted me to change. Well—" I push his hands away from my body and take a step back. "—here I am. Take it or leave it. I'm a grown-up woman, not one of your usual floozies who dress to impress you. If you want a hooker, I can call one for you. This is all you'll be getting from me."

His head shoots back, and a roar of laughter erupts from his chest, the sound vibrating all the way down to my core.

In spite of this man's arrogance and the fact that I know that's something you *don't* want in a guy, I can't help but want him.

I want him with all my body.

I crave his hands all over me.

Crave feeling his fingers slip beneath my clothes and enter all those places I didn't know could come to life from a man's mere voice.

"What's so funny?" I narrow my eyes as I take in the shirt stretched over his broad shoulders. The top button is undone, revealing taut, tanned skin. His jeans hang low on his hips, and there's that clearly defined bulge that keeps drawing my attention to it.

The picture of him stroking his cock flashes before my eyes.

For a moment, I lose focus. It's all a bit too detailed—especially the part of his face drawn in pleasure. The telltale heat of a major blush rushes to my face.

Damn, he looks so good I want a piece of him.

"Can you handle it?" Kellan asks.

"What?" I frown at his irritating grin.

Holy shit!

He just caught me staring at his crotch. I can only hope my face isn't on fire. Though, judging from my burning skin and his smug expression, I'm most certainly wrong.

"I've handled way more than this," I mumble.

"I was talking about your ankle and a night out in

those shoes, but..." He winks and lets his gaze brush over my lips. It's all so lascivious, I can almost feel him on my skin, and it sends a shiver through me. "...I'm glad to hear you'll be able to handle certain parts of me."

I smirk. "You're such a—" I shake my head, lost for words. Whatever I say couldn't possibly deflect from the fact that I *was* thinking about handling certain parts of him.

Either he has mind-reading abilities, or he's so full of himself, he assumes that his dick's every woman's fantasy.

"Jerk?" Kellan prompts. "I think we've already established that."

"Oh, God, Ava," comes Mandy's voice from the door. "You didn't!"

She's dressed in a short denim skirt and cowboy boots with fringes, the ruffled low-cut top putting her cleavage on display. Her outfit suits Kellan's blue jeans and snug shirt to a T. It's like they coordinated in advance, which annoys me to no end.

Mandy and Kellan seem to have so much more in common than Kellan and I do, starting with the looks and attitude, to the dressing style.

I don't need to ask what Mandy's thinking because, as usual, she's quick to share.

"You look like a secretary."

"I like secretaries," Kellan leans in to whisper in my ear, his hot breath brushing my earlobe. "In fact, they're my favorite kind. You sure know how to stoke a fire in a man's pants. I wouldn't mind pinning you to that couch, pushing your panties aside, and licking your hot pussy until you're ready and I can take you hard from behind."

My pulse thuds in my ears, drowning out all the dirty things he'd like to do to me. But I don't need his account to help me get the picture.

The image of my face buried in his sofa while Kellan's hands hold my hips in place, entering me from behind, makes me jump in my skin. I almost choke on my breath as I jump a few steps back, freeing my heated body from his sweltering breath.

"Let's go." I swoosh past him, walk down the stairs, and yank the door wide open in the hope the darkness will hide my burning face.

Kellan laughs, and I know I am what amuses him.

I thought my outfit would put him off.

That he's the kind who likes double Ds spilling out of push-up bras and short skirts riding up oiled legs. That he might not be into that never even occurred to me.

He likes a challenge. I should have known it. And

of course his caveman ego would make him think I dressed like this to get a reaction from him.

I got a reaction big time. I can see it in the swelling of his pants.

Now I'm screwed.

I know it.

It's the memory of our kiss that's making me lose it, and there's nothing I can do about it.

I can't help myself. I want more.

CHAPTER SIXTEEN

ACCORDING TO KELLAN, it's a thirty-minute drive to the bar. However, in his SUV, in spite of the mud caking the tires, we make it in fifteen. He drives like a maniac, which is most certainly the reason why he bumped into my car.

I sit in the passenger seat, grasping at the armrest for support. When the SUV finally comes to a screeching halt, we're in front of what looks like another oversized barn with a big flashing neon light showing a rodeo rider sitting on a bull.

As soon as we step through the open door, I can see it's full. A live band is playing, and people are dancing.

Kellan and Mandy will fit right in. I can see that the moment we enter and join the crowd of patronage. There are people of all ages, all singing and chatting and having a good time.

As we head straight for the bar area on the left side, I peer around me at the vastness of the space. The wooden décor screams Western chic. The hayforks hanging on the walls would be a major security breach back in NYC, but not here.

Here, they actually give the place an authentic atmosphere.

As we approach the bar, countless eyes turn to take us in. Back in NYC, we'd be barely more than shadows. But here, off the grid, where everyone seems to know everyone, I bet we'll be the talk of the town by tomorrow morning.

My work attire doesn't seem to help either. Everyone's staring at me like I've just stepped off a different planet. I wouldn't be surprised if people assumed if I was Kellan's accountant or attorney.

Mandy disappears after coming up with a bullshit excuse that she has to visit the restroom when I know for a fact she's going to check out the live band.

Kellan waves over a bartender to place an order while I turn away to take in the scene.

"I think I'll have to punch in a few faces tonight," Kellan whispers in my ear, his hot breath brushing the nape of my neck as he leans into me. His palm is flush against the small of my back, riding so low his fingers are almost caressing my ass.

"Why? Because every woman in the room hates me?" I ask, ignoring the evil glances addressed at me.

"Forget the women. I'm talking about the men."

"Got it. Wearing an office outfit isn't something people around here do," I mutter. "You could have told me."

"Women wear business outfits, just not in this establishment, which is why you'll be every guy's wet dream tonight," Kellan whispers again. His hot breath is on my earlobe now, doing incredibly sexy things to my body. My nipples stab the fabric of my shirt, begging to be sucked into his hot mouth. His fingers travel a little lower, brushing the contours of my hip bone, then moving to my ass. "Damn, woman, you're so hot you'll be *my* wet dream."

My head snaps back to him and our lips almost meet before I jolt back, seared by the want in his green eyes.

Where the hell did that come from?

And what the fuck was I thinking not following my first instinct and staying away from him?

We're at the bar, his hand on my ass, and people are still staring. No one knows me, but they know Kellan. Even though I shouldn't care because I'll be gone in a few days, I don't want to be the talk of the town. I don't want people to think that I'm his squeeze or fuck or whatever Kellan calls his conquests. He's pretty much made it clear that he doesn't do relationships, and I'm not stupid enough to think I could possibly be the exception.

The bartender approaches us with our beer bottles, exchanges a few words with Kellan, and then leaves again.

"You could have told me to wear something more inconspicuous." I throw him an icy glare, which earns me a laugh in return.

"Ava, you wouldn't be inconspicuous wearing a paper bag over your head. It's the ass."

"What about it?"

"It's hot." As though the word doesn't convey the right meaning, his gaze lowers to my backside appreciatively and he licks his lips. My clothes seem to evaporate before my eyes. "I'd know a thing or two about what to do with it. You'd like it. I'm incredible at that."

No doubt about that.

Slightly breathless, I scowl at him.

His eyes gleam a shade darker than usual. "Think about it. The invitation's standing."

"There's not going to be any ass play, today or ever," I say in the kind of raspy voice that betrays just how much I'd like him to touch me and show me what I'm missing.

His brow shoots up in amusement. "Why? Because you'd like it too much?"

"No."

"Ava," he whispers.

"What?"

"I know you'll enjoy it." He raises his bottle. "Here's to us meeting again. To new beginnings."

I eye him cautiously as we clink our bottles, and then we chug down a few gulps. I feel the effect instantly. My head is lighter, my limbs like jelly.

"Wow. You're right. This is the best beer I've ever had," I say.

He leans forward. I expect my body to go rigid, but instead I find myself strangely relaxed.

"You'll be panting my name as I take you on the ride of your life."

Emphasis on the ride.

It takes me a moment to realize he's resuming our conversation from before.

He's talking about my ass.

Oh, my gosh.

That monumental ego of his is back.

I roll my eyes so hard it almost hurts. "No." I draw out the word again. "Because I don't do that."

"You've never tried? Or you tried but didn't like it?"

Whoa!

When did a harmless dress code conversation take such a dirty turn?

"I'm so not going to answer that, Kellan." I cross my arms over my chest and manage to draw his attention to my hard nipples.

"Because you've never tried," he says, as usual convinced that he knows everything.

Arguing with a guy who thinks he's the living and breathing equivalent of Adonis is a waste of time. Arguing with one who thinks he's all that *and* all-knowing is like banging your head against a wall. I like my head the way it is, so I'm not even going there.

I swat his hand off my ass and put a few inches of space between us. "No. Because it's none of your business."

"Fine." He throws his hands up in mock surrender. "But just some food for thought. The uptight ones are always the ones that enjoy it the most. Give me a night, and by morning you'll be screaming for more." He guzzles down half of his beer as I stare at him.

Wait, did he just call me uptight?

I should be offended, but I'm not in the slightest.

He hasn't hit a nerve. I haven't tried all the things he's tried. Maybe because I've never met someone who really rocked my boat and made me want to abandon all my inhibitions.

So what?

I'm not ashamed of it.

"Yeah, right." I laugh. "I'll be screaming all right...for you to get the hell out of my room before I throw something at you."

"Hmmm."

I laugh again. "Hmmm? That's all you have to say? Did I just manage to shut up your insufferable ego?"

His green gaze pierces into me, shimmering, flickering.

Oh, shit!

I did it again.

I've just managed to challenge him.

Why can't I ever keep my big mouth shut?

"No, baby. You haven't shut me up. On the contrary, there's so much more I can say and show. My promises are always accompanied by actions."

In spite of all the people staring, he closes the distance between us. His hard body is pressed into me, his hand at the small of my back, holding me glued in place. I throw my head back to look all the way up, and instantly regret it. His lips lower over mine, hovering less than an inch away. I can feel his breath on me. I can feel the heat of his body. I can feel something hard against my belly.

He's hard for me.

His tongue flicks over his lower lip. Before I realize what's happening, his mouth crashes down on mine, wild and hungry.

I'm so taken aback by his taste, I can't move. I stand rooted to the spot, caught up in him. The band's break is over and the music resumes.

Kellan's lips part from mine.

Slowly, he begins to move, his hard grip forcing me to shift with him, like we're dancing. The music in the background shifts to a country ballad, as though to suit our movements.

I lean into Kellan, not because I want to. I have

to.

It's what this hard body demands of me.

Even though we look like we're dancing, I know that's not what he's doing.

He wants me to feel his erection. He wants to know how I'll react to him wanting me.

Damn.

I should be pushing him away. Laugh it all off because it's something guys like him do. Push their boundaries. Check whether they can score.

And yet, all I do is let him take the lead.

Surrender control.

His breath mingles with mine. It's labored. Scorching. It's on my skin. Inside my head.

I want him.

All of him.

Now.

I feel someone's presence behind me and turn sharply.

It's Mandy, and she's smirking at me.

"Gee, get a room. Or use the restroom. Or whatever. I don't care." Her voice penetrates the layer of lust rendering my brain useless.

My palms spreading across his chest, I push Kellan back. His hands leave my body without protest.

"We were just dancing," I mutter to her.

"Of course you were." Mandy blinks her eyelashes at me. "And I was talking to the president of China. Look, he's sitting at the bar over there."

Stupidly, I follow her line of vision to the old man nursing a half-empty glass of what looks like scotch, his hooded eyes buried in his drink, his expression vacant.

She was being sarcastic, obviously. The fact that I didn't catch on immediately is a sign that Kellan's touch just caused my IQ to drop at least ten points.

"We were just dancing," I repeat stupidly. Then I mutter, "Need to use the restroom," and dash off before anyone can question my sanity…or morality.

Inside the bathroom, I stare at the reflection in the mirror, ignoring the redhead coating her glossy lips in another layer of sparkly pink. She eyes me curiously but doesn't say a word as I keep staring at my rosy cheeks and sparkling eyes.

Holy shit!

I almost made out with Kellan out there, in front of everyone.

I can't believe I just let him touch me like that. I let him kiss me in public.

Who is this person? Because I sure as hell don't recognize myself.

I'm not an exhibitionist. I don't even kiss in public so as not to offend anyone who might feel offended by a public display of affection.

Only, that wasn't exactly affection.

It was raw want.

And I enjoyed it way too much.

"Gum?" the redhead asks and pushes a packet of something fruity toward me.

I shake my head and toss a hesitant smile her way. "No, thanks."

"I'm Trish," she says in the same slow drawl like Kellan's.

"Ava."

"New in town?" Her perfect eyebrows rise in question, and her fingers lift to brush a strand of glossy hair out of her face.

"Just passing through."

"You staying with Kellan?" His name coming out of her mouth is like whiplash against my skin.

Her brows shoot up again, which I sense is an expression she does often when she wants an answer. But there's something in her gaze. Like it's more than just curiosity.

It's surprise.

The door opens, and a bunch of giggling girls I'm not sure are even old enough to drink enter.

"Excuse me," I say and head for a stall, barricading myself inside before Trish can continue her conversation. I'm not usually rude, but I've had enough of Kellan for one evening.

CHAPTER SEVENTEEN

I WAIT UNTIL I think the restroom's cleared before leaving the sanctuary that's my stall and returning to the bar area.

Kellan and Mandy are sitting at a table, engaged in small talk with a guy who's obviously very much interested in what Mandy has to say.

As soon as Mandy sees me, she waves at me. "She's back." She turns to the guy next to her. "This is Ava. Ava, this is Josh." Mandy leans into me and yells in my ear a little louder than is necessary, "He's a friend of Kellan's."

Of course he is. He even looks the part: all tall and muscular, with blue eyes the color of mountain rivers and sandy hair that, coupled with his tanned skin, gives him the same bad boy appearance Kellan has about him.

I can see they're related somehow before Josh speaks up to set things straight. "We're cousins, actually. Our dads were brothers."

Ah.

I nod and shoot him a hesitant smile, deliberately ignoring Kellan's heated stare. His fingers brush my leg beneath the table and I pull away, crossing my legs to make it harder for him to reach them.

The guy says, like we already know each other, "Let's get the lady a drink."

Mandy laughs, and like on cue, a woman in her early forties, wearing an infectious smile and the lowest cut top I've ever seen, approaches our table with a tray full of shots and slices of lime.

We don't do shots...ever. And for a very good reason. Last time we did, bad things happened.

Someone wants to get us drunk, or why else would you ply a woman with tequila? And I have a pretty good idea who's behind this grand plan.

I peer at Mandy, who just shrugs her shoulders at

me and takes a glass.

"No, thank you." I shake my head at the waitress and steal a glance at Kellan, who's downright staring at me.

"Wine? Beer?" the other guy asks. He's basically giving us options, so the shots weren't his doing.

"You need to loosen up a bit," Kellan says. "Live a little."

"Are you calling me uptight?" I laugh. "Oh, wait. You did already."

Given that I have so little self-control over myself even when sober, I shouldn't be drinking more than I've already had, but the peer pressure is too much. Besides, this is a bar. No one's having soda, unless it's to accompany the scotch.

"Can we have another round, please?" Mandy says to the waitress. I watch her snake her way through the crowded space.

The music in the background's getting louder.

"So you both grew up here," Mandy says, her voice way too chirpy, her tone way too flirty.

She's found her very own Kellan, and now she's ready to charm her way into his bed. Or he into hers. Judging from his hungry eyes and the way his gaze seems to keep brushing her cleavage, it won't take long before his hands will be all over her.

Just like Kellan's were on me a few seconds ago. Classy.

I turn away, angry with myself for not leaving at once, as the conversation continues without me.

"We grew up together. Always got ourselves into trouble over this and that," Josh says to Mandy. "It was usually his fault though. The guy always knew how to attract it."

"Like you were a saint," Kellan says.

"The way I remember it, I actually was...until you came along." Josh's tone is light, jokey. "You compromised me. You compromised all of us."

Kellan laughs, the sound sending jolts of pleasure through me. His voice is so deep and raw, so sexy, I can't help but steal another glance at him. As though he can feel it, his sinning eyes turn to me, and our gazes meet. My heart jumps into my throat, and a soft tingle erupts between my legs.

"I'm two years older," Josh goes on to explain to Mandy. "I remember a time when my days didn't consist of Mom or Aunt Becky yelling at me because of something Kellan did. From the moment he was born, I swear the guy didn't understand the meaning of no. And because I was the oldest, I was always to blame."

"No one forced you to trudge along." Kellan

shrugs, his tone still light-hearted. But there's affection in his eyes.

He cares about his family, I realize. He probably cares about them more than he wants to let on.

"Dude, you stole your dad's rifle to track down a cougar by candlelight in the middle of the night."

"He attacked two foals," Kellan says. "It was my job to protect the horses."

"If I wasn't there with you, you could have burned down the barn with all the horses in it."

"Oh, my God." Mandy giggles. "How old were you?"

"He was ten," Josh says.

"Nine," Kellan clarifies. "And in my defense, that cougar had been bothering my dad for weeks. I was just trying to help. Being a good son and all. The cougar cost us seven good horses, and that's not counting the foals."

"Yeah, you were helping all right," Josh says, laughing.

The picture of a nine-year-old boy with dark hair and beautiful green eyes pops into my head. I can picture him so well. His hair brushing the collar of his shirt. His pants covered in mud and dust and hay. His dad's rifle slung across his back as he tries to find the animal that's been giving his dad trouble.

His mom almost having a heart attack as she finds her little boy carrying a firearm and going for an animal that could attack him.

In spite of myself, I smile at the picture. It makes the grown-up Kellan so much more likeable. I don't want to like him, but somehow I can't help the tightness spreading across my chest.

It's clear Kellan loves his dad. It's also clear he likes being around horses and that he takes great care of them.

"I'm a cowboy at heart. It runs in my blood," he says.

"That's true," Josh agrees, then leans forward. "You should see him riding a bull. If he weren't already famous, he...fuck." He glares at Kellan. "Dude, don't kick my leg."

"I'll do more if you don't keep your trap shut."

The waitress arrives, placing a tray down. "If you gals are stupid enough to marry one of them Boyd boys, be warned. That story doesn't even begin to scratch the surface of truth about their blood. I should know, for I married one back then, when I didn't know any better."

I peer up at her, past her incredibly full cleavage on display, to the twinkling eyes encircled by deep laughter lines.

She smiles, the skin around her eyes crinkling even more as she winks at me.

"I'm Ava. This is Mandy." I reach out my hand.

"Sharon." Ignoring it, she gives my shoulder a brief squeeze, then pulls up a chair and plops down in spite of Kellan's murderous look.

"I know Mandy. We met this morning."

"I asked her for directions," Mandy explains. "Sharon was kind enough to show me the way to the police station."

"Which was empty, by the way," Sharon says, raising a bottle in the air. "That deputy of ours is never here when we need him. Cheers to that."

"Amen."

Josh snorts and raises his bottle, waiting until we all follow suit. I don't want to drink with them, but I don't know how to politely decline, so I obey everyone's silent urgency. The beer burns my throat so bad, for a moment I'm rendered blind.

"It's tequila beer. You need to follow it up with the lemon," Kellan whispers in my ear.

He's so close, his leg brushes against mine under the table. His hot breath on my earlobe is all I can think about.

I bite into the slice of lime he holds up to my mouth and realize the sour tang kind of washes away the burning sensation. But it does nothing to get rid of the throbbing between my legs. The fact that he brushes his thumb over my lips, as though to wipe away some residue, only makes it worse.

He's using any bullshit excuse to touch me, but for some reason, I don't stop him, which makes me even angrier with myself.

"See, he's compromising you already, and the evening hasn't even started yet," Josh says.

From the corner of my eye, I notice Josh's hand is on Mandy's naked arm the moment he finishes the sentence.

He's going for it. And all she's doing is leaning into him and laughing.

She's so natural at this. Watching her, I know I'm nothing like that. I want to run. I want to hide. And yet, something keeps me glued to my seat, my breathing not quite functioning every time Kellan seems to lean too close to talk to me or touch me oh so innocently.

"It's all in the Boyd blood," Sharon says, throwing me a look of pity. "Compromising women is their family legacy."

I stare at her, then at Josh. Both used the same word.

Compromise? As in one's reputation?

I've no idea but don't get a chance to ask.

"Hey, Sharon. Get your sweet ass over here or hang up the self help sign," a guy from the bar yells to her. "Some of us are thirsty."

"Hold your horses, Trent. I'm coming." She rolls her eyes at me and stands, leaning toward me until I catch a whiff of her perfume. "A word of advice, sweetheart. Don't let this one get into your panties until he's earned them. God knows he has enough of a collection already, and you look like a nice girl. You don't want your heart broken if you can't break his in return."

"Go away, Sharon. No one needs your advice tonight," Kellan mutters.

Sharon laughs and disappears in the crowd.

What was that all about?

I want to ask him who Sharon is when Kellan grabs another beer bottle and pushes it toward me. "Ignore her."

"I don't think that's a good idea." I shake my head, not sure whether I mean that it's a bad idea to ignore Sharon's advice or have another drink with him.

In fact, I think both of them rank pretty high on my things-not-to-do-in-Montana list.

"As you wish." He downs his drink.

I scan his face as he tunes back into Josh and Mandy's conversation. Is he mad that I declined him? He doesn't look like it. But then, I know nothing about this man, except for the few tidbits of information, that he's close to his family and collects panties—the dirty kind.

I like the family part. It makes him a nice guy. The panties part? Uh, not so much.

"You okay? You look a little flushed," Kellan says, genuine concern etched in his features.

"I'm fine. I'm just—"

Jealous?

Maybe a little bit, which I'd never admit to him.

I wave my hand, like it's nothing really.

Kellan regards me for a few moments. And then, to my surprise, he leans closer, though there's nothing sexual about the way his fingers brush my hand.

"How's your ankle? Still hurting?"

Staring at his hand on mine, I shake my head in response. "It's all good. Thanks to you."

"Good." Kellan intertwines his fingers with mine and pulls me to my feet. "Come on."

"Where are we going?" I ask, but don't put up a fight.

He only answers after we've reached the door. "I

haven't shown you around yet."

CHAPTER EIGHTEEN

SIGHTSEEING AFTER DUSK is another bad idea that's just made my bad-ideas-in-Montana list.

A balmy breeze whispers around us as Kellan leads me out of the bar and into the dark street. A group of teens squeeze past us, pushing me into him so hard I almost take a tumble. His hand reaches around my waist, steadying me until I've regained my equilibrium.

"Hey, guys, watch it," he calls after the teens, his voice conveying more anger than is necessary.

"It's okay." I touch his arm.

Kellan shakes his head. I can feel the waves of anger wafting from him. Suddenly, he seems a million miles away.

"Hey." I touch his arm again, this time to get his attention. "They're just kids having a good time."

His attention returns to me, and for a second I think I see something in his eyes.

A fierceness that isn't lust.

A spark that isn't want.

He's protective.

My body's still pressed up against him. His arm is still wrapped around my waist.

I use the proximity and rise on my toes to kiss the corner of his mouth, though only manage to reach up as far as his chin.

"What was that for?" Kellan asks, his tone just a little hoarser than it should be.

I shrug and ease out of his embrace. "You're not such a bad guy after all."

"Coming from you, I'll take that as a compliment." His lips twitch, the heaviness between us gone.

"I didn't say you were a good guy either."

His arm goes around my waist. "I know almost nothing about you."

The statement takes me by surprise. My eyes rise to meet his, and I flinch at what I see in them.

For a moment, it's like I'm looking at a different person...someone who's genuinely interested in me, not in peeling off any layers of my inhibitions.

Or maybe it's a ploy to do just that.

Either way, I sort of like the sudden gentleness about him.

"I'm a single child. Both of my parents are composers."

"Ah," he says. "That's why you hate music."

"No." I frown as I consider his statement. "Maybe. I'm not sure." I shrug. "Does it matter? They wanted me to follow in their footsteps, but I wasn't really interested. For the life of me, I just couldn't figure out the cello. Surely you can imagine how disappointed they were that I didn't inherit their talents. I wasn't a child prodigy. They were so enthusiastic and pushy, until one day they realized their plans of raising the female version of Beethoven or Mozart were nothing but a pipe dream."

"So, what did you do?"

I shrug. "I moved out, went to college to study journalism, and now I write articles."

"About what?"

I laugh. "Whatever pays the bills. I'm a journalist. I dig out all the crap I can find about companies and expose them."

"Sounds like you're no-nonsense."

I glance at him to take in his expression. He's seems honest, serious. "I am. I always try to uncover the truth. If you dig hard enough, you'll find that most companies have secrets, but some are shadier than others."

His brows shoot up in interest. "Yeah? Like what, for example?"

I shrug. "Like writing off charity donations when the charity's just some bogus company. Or a company cutting employees' pension funds while raising their board members' salaries." We resume walking. "Josh mentioned brothers," I start, ready to shift the focus on Kellan. "How many siblings do you have?"

Kellan hesitates, but only for a moment. "One sister. Two brothers."

"Must be nice to have a big family," I say. "I've always wanted siblings."

"You can always borrow mine."

I laugh. "Only if they're nice. So, what were you doing back in NYC when your life seems to be here?" I can feel him tense before I've even finished the question.

He doesn't pull his hand back, but his grip loosens, the soft butterfly strokes on my skin ceasing.

For a moment, he's perfectly still, his eyes hooded, his expression cagey.

"Business," he says matter-of-factly and clears his throat. "Montana's beautiful, but not the only beautiful place in the world."

A tactical change of subject. It's not even a subtle one.

The feeling he's hiding something is stronger than before.

As soon as I get back home, I know I'll be trying to find out as much as I can about Kellan Boyd.

That's a promise to myself.

I nod, sensing the usual 'one day I'll take you there' BS guys always dish out. But it never comes. I take off down the dimly lit road, unsure which direction to take.

"You said you wanted to show me around. This is your chance."

His laughter echoes behind me a moment before I feel his arms on my body again, guiding me into what looks like a deserted dark alley.

"And I was planning on using it. There's

definitely something I need to show you."

I peer around me, unsure what exactly we could possibly see in the dark. My confusion intensifies when he opens a gate leading into someone's back yard and pulls me inside, closing the gate behind us.

"We're trespassing," I hiss.

"Are you afraid of being caught?"

"No," I say slowly. "But someone's not going to be happy."

"Well, that someone isn't going to be me." Kellan laughs and pushes me against the gate, capturing my hands in one of his and raising them above my head.

Holy shit!

We're in someone's back yard, and Kellan has me pinned against the gate, his mouth inches from mine as his other hand begins to roam over my body.

"I've waited so long for this," he whispers, his hot breath sending an electric tingle down my spine. "Do you have any idea how much my hand hurts?"

The sudden memory of him jerking off pops into my head, and wow, it's hot.

"I know what you did last night," he whispers. "While you were taking care of yourself, I was imagining myself replacing your fingers with mine."

My breath halts. The shock is short, but sweet.

Heat pools between my legs.

If he were to touch me down there, he'd find me dripping wet and ready for him.

He lets go of my hands and unbuttons my top. The cool breeze brushes over my skin, beading my nipples, a moment before his hot mouth encloses one, sucking it into his mouth for a second, then moving on to the other one.

The moon is hidden behind rainclouds. Away from the street, the light of the lamp doesn't reach us. We're hidden from the street, but the house isn't too far away.

"Someone might hear us," I whisper and moan involuntarily as his fingers pull my top out of my skirt and move across my stomach back to my breasts.

The entire situation is completely inappropriate. We're probably breaking a few laws, too. And yet, all I can do is catch my lower lip between my teeth as a myriad of sensations awaken, all at the same time.

"You're right. Someone might hear us," Kellan mutters, not really helping. "Let's be quick, then."

His fingers are like fire on my skin, his touch on my breasts not as gentle as I imagined.

Rough has never been one of my preferences, but coming from him, his decisiveness does strange things to my body.

Tossing my head back, I moan in response, the mixture of pleasure and pain taking over.

"What are you doing?" I ask in a sudden moment of lucidity.

He doesn't reply. He just lets go of me and slides up, his body pressing me against the gate.

I can feel the entire length of his erection pulsating against my abdomen. He's hard as a rock, ready to take me to pleasure heaven, which I'm sure is the plan if I let him.

"Kellan." His name slips out of my mouth. It sounds like a question. I don't know what to do. I'm not Mandy, who can so easily live in the moment and think about consequences later.

It's just a hook up.

Enjoy it.

"Yes, baby. Just like that." Kellan groans, and I realize I've just pressed myself flush against him, closing the remaining space that might have been between us.

Our gazes meet. In the moonlight, I can sense the mixture of apprehension and lust more than I can see it.

He trails his hands down my hips and lifts up my skirt, then steps back to appraise me. My pale skin looks white and smooth in the darkness, all the faults I never liked about myself hidden.

His eyes drink me in. All of me. I'm holding my breath, waiting for his reaction.

"Damn, woman," is all he says. A moment later, his lips crush mine. His tongue is forcing its way into my mouth, probing, tasting, while his fingers brush the front of my panties.

My breath hitches as my clit pulsates to life against his insistent fingers, and I moan into his open mouth.

I can feel my wetness coating my panties, readying me for his hard cock. I want him inside me so bad, I whimper, almost considering begging if he won't speed things along.

So much for my resolution to stay the fuck away from him.

So much for my decision not to join his collection of conquests.

How many were there?

How many will there be after me?

I shake my head to get rid of the seed of jealousy settling at the back of my mind.

It doesn't matter. He'll be a sweet, delicious memory by the end of the week.

He'll be the one past indulgence I'll think about when I'm old and settled into my boring, middle-class life, chasing after two kids and the passion I once felt for a stranger.

"This means nothing," I whisper, more to convince myself than him.

"Hmm." Kellan stops to bite my lower lip, sucking it into his mouth. His fingers pry my legs apart and squeeze beneath my panties.

His groan reverberates from his chest. It's deep and sexy and all the answer I need to know what he's thinking about my wet pussy.

"You're ready for me." Kellan's voice is hoarse, dripping with want. "I could fuck you right now and you'd be milking me for all I've got."

"Then fuck me."

I don't know where that came from or who this woman is, because it's sure not me.

His fingers trail my folds. A gasp escapes my mouth as they find their way inside me, and I spread my legs a bit, rocking against his big hand.

His thumb finds my clit and presses gently while he plunges two fingers in and out of me.

It feels so good to have him inside me.

Desire rolls over me in sweet, long waves.

"Ava, look at me." His command enters the periphery of my mind.

Unwillingly, I open my eyes and meet his gaze.

Half of his face is veiled in darkness, reminding me of our first encounter in front of Club 69. This has been my dream for so long, I know it'll be my undoing.

"Yes, baby, look at me and tell me how much you like this." His tone is low, barely more than rasps of breathing.

"Kellan." His name is all I can say, over and over again. His eyes are fixed on me, feasting on my lust, as his fingers work their magic, taking me to the brink.

"I'm so close," I think I whisper, but I'm not sure because all I can hear is the thrumming of my blood flooding my veins.

The pulsing between my legs intensifies. I close my eyes, ready to succumb to my imminent orgasm.

"No." The word is sharp, forceful. An instant later, Kellan's magical fingers stop and his hand is at my chin, forcing my head up. His index finger traces the contour of my lower lip.

"What are you doing?" I practically whimper, and my eyes flutter open, my gaze imploring. The throbbing between my legs intensifies, but it's not the good kind.

I've never felt so unsatisfied. So...empty.

"I want you to come on my tongue. I want to taste

you." His tone is gentler, but there's a forceful undertone to it, like it's his way or none.

"You want to—" My voice breaks.

I'm too wet for what he wants. I'm so slick he could slide inside me, all of him, right to the hilt, and I'd probably moan his name in the process. And I don't even know why. It's never happened before, with none of my few boyfriends. As a result, I don't know how he'd react to it.

I don't know whether he'll like it.

"We could just fuck," I say. The word fuck is barely more than a wanton whisper.

"No." His groan is almost feral as he slides my panties down my hips. I lift my legs one by one, helping him remove them even though that's the last thing I should be doing.

I know that. I'm not stupid...just momentarily rendered brainless.

"I'll fuck you when I say so," Kellan says. "Until then, you take what I give you."

"You're such a jerk."

He was one before, and he'll continue to be one.

A jerk who needs to be in control.

I'm not surprised to find that a guy like him finds his thrill in power.

"A jerk who's going to make you come hard."

Maybe.

I'm so on edge, I'm definitely ready to see that happening.

"Tell me what you want me to do," Kellan demands. His thumb traces my lower lip again while his hard cock presses against my abdomen. I can taste myself on his skin. I can smell my scent on him.

I flick my tongue over his thumb hesitantly and hear him catch his breath. "Fuck me."

I've never begged a man to take me. That I'm doing it now is a sure sign that I'm losing my morals in Montana.

"No. That's not what I want to hear." His hands trail down the front of my shirt and gather on either side of my hips, pulling me to him.

Waiting.

Stalling.

Forcing me to ask him for the one thing I'm not comfortable doing.

This is the moment to shut down this little episode between us.

And yet, I find myself wondering what it'd be like to have his mouth between my legs.

He brings his lips close to my ear. "Say it, Ava. Tell me what you'd like me to do."

"Taste me," I whisper, instantly ashamed of myself as I repeat his words. "I want to come on your tongue."

Others have gone down on me. I've never come.

I'll let him try, if it makes him happy...so we can move on to the fucking part.

Kellan smiles, his smugness so obvious I'd slap it right off his glorious face if I weren't so damn horny.

"If you hold back or fake it, you'll regret it." The threat lingers in the air. It should make me afraid of him, eager to get the hell away. Instead, I can't help but wonder what kind of punishment he'd have in store for me.

A slow trail of heat begins to throb to life. My clit's on fire.

I like the idea of surrendering all control to him. And that's exactly what I'm going to do.

I push my chin out, my eyes challenging him. "If you want all of me, you'll have to earn it. I'm not easily pleased."

He chuckles, the self-satisfied sound speaking volumes. "Your pussy won't stand a chance against my tongue."

Oh, gosh.

I've never met anyone so delusional...or full of himself.

If he weren't so darn sexy, I'd—

In one swift motion, he's kneeled before me, his hands cupping my ass, bringing one leg around his shoulders. My balance is so off, I have no choice but to lean into him. To open myself up, leaving my most private spot at his mercy.

"Ready for the ride of your life?" Is that another chuckle before his mouth descends upon me?

"Ride?" I ask stupidly, cursing the fact that my head's just turned into a big, empty cloud, when his hot tongue dips into me. The movement comes so unexpected, I almost whimper and thread my fingers through his hair, unsure whether to pull his mouth closer or push him away.

My leg wraps tighter around his shoulder, bringing his mouth closer to my entrance. His tongue dips in again, then licks all the way back up to my clit, through my swollen folds, moving back up to my clit.

I suck in a gulp of air and close my eyes, my fingers still tangled in his hair as arrows of pleasure shoot through my core, my pussy tightening around nothing, begging to be filled.

"I've been thinking about your wet pussy," Kellan whispers appreciatively between another dip and lick, then another and another.

"You taste even better than I imagined." His voice is deep, hoarse, sexy as hell. "I'm going to make you crash so hard, you'll be spoiled for every other man after me."

"No false modesty," I more moan than whisper.

His tongue focuses on my clit for a moment. His mouth sucks the little mound between his lips, then he flicks his tongue across it.

I moan and arch my back.

It feels so damn good, but it won't be enough.

Laughter echoes somewhere to our right, reminding me that we're in someone's back yard. We could be discovered any minute with my skirt literally hitched up around my waist. A surge of adrenaline rushes through me, the excitement almost pushing me over me edge.

"Be quiet," Kellan whispers, but his tongue doesn't ease up on me. It slides through my slickness, leaving a hot and moist trail behind just long enough for the wind to cool me down, before he begins again.

He's such a professional at doing this.

Too calm. Too focused.

Of course, he's probably licked more pussy than he can count. I, on the other hand, feel like I could be dying on the spot. Both from desire and sheer mortification at what we're doing. And from being so ready to give him what he's been wanting all along.

Somewhere, a door closes. Then a click.

Footsteps thud in the distance.

Thump. Thump. Thump.

"I think someone's coming," I whisper needlessly and try to push his head away. He grabs my ass tightly, holding me in place as he adjusts his mouth.

"Kellan," I whisper, mortified.

His tongue is more unrelenting now. Barely giving me time to breathe between the hard flicks on my clit. My pussy tightens, squeezing the air, the delicious pull of an oncoming orgasm forming, but not quite there.

The footsteps stop, and a male voice begins to talk quietly...into a phone?

I can even make out a few words.

Oh, God.

We're going to be found out.

Talk about bad timing.

"Kellan." His name swooshes out of my mouth in another silent moan.

"Hush! He'll be here soon." The way he says it, it sounds like he knows the person. I want to follow up his remark with a question. I even open my mouth when he thrusts a finger into me, then another, stretching me, filling me.

I nearly cry out, the sound lodged deep in my throat.

It's getting harder to breathe.

Kellan's tongue flicks faster while he finger-fucks me hard, rubbing against that one special spot inside me I know will have me crying out his name.

Red-hot waves of lust threaten to crush me. My legs begin to tremble. I bite my lip hard so I can't cry out. The taste of blood registers somewhere inside my mind, but I don't care.

All I want is more.

More of him.

More of this.

I think the footsteps are heading for us now, but I can't move.

Whatever Kellan's doing to me is way too good to stop him.

"Oh, God." A moan erupts from my chest.

The familiar blackness of an orgasm is descending on me a moment before my body lights up, then crashes in flames. A tremor rocks my entire body over and over again.

Faintly, I think I feel Kellan set me down and place a hasty kiss on my lips.

He tastes of me.

It's so darn sexy, my core flares up again.

Yes, I definitely want more of him, until the lights in the back yard go on.

CHAPTER NINETEEN

"KELLAN, IS THAT you?" a male voice calls out.

Oh, my God.

I jump back and only manage to rattle the gate, drawing attention to us.

Kellan laughs and pulls down my skirt. "Hey, Ryder. How's it going?"

"You son of a bitch." A dark figure reaches us in a few long strides, and I groan inwardly, filled with humiliation.

This guy is definitely corrupting me.

I can't believe I just came barely a few steps away from one of his friends.

"I heard you were back, but I didn't realize—" The guy stops mid-sentence, and for the first time, he seems to see me.

Like, really see me.

There's something familiar about him. His eyes are dark in the night, but I don't fail to notice he's the same height as Kellan.

Even the same build, as far as I can tell.

I can see the resemblance.

"Ava, this is my brother. Ryder, Ava. She's from NYC," Kellan says coolly. His hand grabs my ass possessively, like he has a claim on me.

"Well, hello, Ava," Ryder says. "I'm glad you guys were enjoying my back yard. I like my guests to come more often."

My face flushes with mortification.

I don't know what the fuck he meant by that about, but I'm pretty sure he isn't talking about regular invitations to a barbecue party.

Kellan laughs. "The lady definitely will. I'll make sure of that. Thanks for not arresting us."

My head snaps in his direction?

Is that supposed to be a joke?

I take in his wink, and the penny drops.

Oh, my fricking God.

His brother has to be a cop.

"My dear brother's the deputy," Kellan explains.

The fricking deputy? The one everyone seems to be missing.

"What are brothers for?" Ryder laughs.

I swat at Kellan's hand on my ass, the slap so hard the sound reverberates in the night.

"I'm going home," I mutter and rattle at the gate.

"Let me—" Kellan starts.

"No. I'll find my way back. Thanks." I shake my head and shoot him a deadly look, even though he probably can't see it in the darkness. "It was nice meeting you..."

"Ryder." He stretches out his hand, and I take it.

"Sorry about the—" My voice chokes.

I rush past him, head held high, trying my hardest not to look back.

It's the walk of shame.

I might have lost any sense of decency, but I still have my dignity, right?

Right?

CHAPTER TWENTY

AFTER RETURNING TO the bar, I make up some bullshit excuse, and Kellan drives both Mandy and me home—the silence in the car deafening in its intensity. I barely mumble something about a headache before dashing for my bedroom and barricading myself inside for the rest of the night.

Holy shit!

I can't believe I let Kellan compromise me like that. Sure, I had the orgasm of my life, but...

What. The. Fuck?

In his brother's back yard?

With his brother barely a few steps away?

Knowing his brother's the deputy?

The bastard *knew* Ryder would be back any time. He *knew* Ryder could hear us.

Why the fuck would he take me there to have his wicked ways with me?

Because I'm another conquest for his panty collection. That's what I am. I can't even pretend that I don't know it. Like I can't pretend I didn't hear Sharon's warning.

And I even asked him for it.

That's probably the worst part.

Practically panted his name and begged him to take me...

In his brother's fucking yard.

He likes to brag about his conquests, or why else would everyone know about his damn business?

This episode is definitely a new low since meeting Kellan Boyd.

Stripping off my clothes, I leave them in a puddle at my feet and step into the shower, furiously washing away the memories of Kellan's mouth on me. I lather tons of shower gel into my skin and let the hot water burn my body in the hope that Kellan's image will disappear from my mind.

But he's all I can think about.

My body's aching for his touch. Even though I just had a release, I want more of it.

I want all of *him*.

I switch off the water and step out of the shower. Wrapping a fluffy towel around me, I head back to my bedroom.

My mind is made up.

Even though I can't leave until the car's been repaired, I *will* stay away from him, even if that involves living like a vampire, AKA sleeping through the day and only venturing out at night.

It shouldn't be too hard a task.

The rap at the door jerks me out of my thoughts. My heart stops—hoping, praying, then hating the thought—that it's Kellan.

It's probably Mandy anyway. I can't deal with her questions right now, not in the least because it's all her fault. She wanted me to go on this trip.

If it weren't for her and her stupid plan to see Mile High, I would never have Kellan seen again. I would never have been stuck here. I would never have been so embarrassed.

Another rap, this time a little louder.

Ignoring the urgency it seems to convey, I put on a T-shirt and pair of shorts, and slip beneath the covers, then turn off the lights.

He or she'll get the message.

I'll make sure of it.

But, damn, keeping my raging hormones in check has never been so hard.

CHAPTER TWENTY-ONE

IT WAS ALL a mistake. It was all a mistake. It was all a mistake.

The way the same sentence keeps circling inside my brain, I could swear it's some sort of mantra. Or one of those songs that, once you hear it on the radio, you simply can't get out of your head.

It was all a mistake.

It's like invisible strings keep me tied to that one memory, forcing me to watch it on replay over and over again.

Needless to say, I'm up all night, my sleep evading me as my brain keeps replaying the same events, like a broken record.

I'm up at dawn, staring out the window at the rising sun. Stripes of pink and purple streak the sky in the distance, the colors not matching my mood. I'm tired and yet restless from all the frustration building up inside me.

It's going to be a very sunny morning, yet I don't know how to face the day.

It depresses me to no end that I cannot be outside, taking a walk, enjoying the scenery, out of fear that I might meet Kellan.

I've never been so on edge, every part of me sensitive, my body begging for release. Obviously, I don't need a cocky, self-centered guy to do it for me.

I know which buttons to press to make myself come.

The trouble is that if I so much as touch myself, Kellan will be all I can think about. Consequently, I'd rather deny myself the pleasure than inflate his oversized ego even more—even though he'd most certainly never find out.

It's after six a.m. when I head for the kitchen. I need my morning cup of coffee, and no man can keep it from me. Secretly, I hope Kellan and Mandy are still sleeping at this ungodly hour.

But just to be on the safe side, I'll be quick about making the coffee, and then return to my bedroom.

The kitchen door's ajar, and the clinking sounds of a teaspoon stirring something inside a cup carries over. I'm about to turn around and walk back to my room when I hear the sound of a chair pulling.

"Good morning. You're not avoiding me, are you?" Kellan calls from inside.

I can't see his expression. But I can hear the amusement in his voice, and it irritates the hell out of me. Raising my head high, I step through the doorway into the kitchen and head straight for the coffee maker.

"Avoiding you?" I laugh, squeezing as much nonchalance into my voice as I can. Though I'm pretty crap at the nonchalance part. "You wish. I slept in. I hadn't slept in in ages, so I thought I'd use the opportunity."

"You call getting up at six a.m. sleeping in?"

"I usually get up at five." That part's a lie. I spend so many late nights at the office that I rarely make it home before midnight and often don't get up before ten a.m.

I help myself to a cup of coffee, deliberately avoiding Kellan's penetrating stare, which is burning a hole in my back.

"Judging from the way you look, I doubt you had an ounce of sleep. You were probably too busy thinking about my dick inside you."

I almost jump in my skin when I feel Kellan's breath on my earlobe.

Holy shit!

Does he *have* to stand so close? And does he *have* to be so crude?

The guy's obviously never heard the term personal space, or why else would he keep invading it?

"You should have asked me to help you out." His finger traces down the nape of my neck, scorching my skin. "I'm always happy to oblige."

I step aside too quickly and manage to spill half of my coffee over the counter and down the front of my shirt.

"Aaaah." A faint yelp escapes my lips. "It's hot."

"Let me help you," Kellan says, amused. Before I can realize what's happening, his fingers are busy undoing the buttons of my blouse and pushing it aside to reveal my bra.

"Seriously?" I ask. "That was so not necessary."

"Pouring coffee over yourself can easily result in first-degree burns."

He grabs a napkin and is patting the liquid off my chest. His green eyes are glued to my breasts, and he licks his lips lasciviously. The way he looks at me, I feel stripped bare of my clothes, completely exposed to his gaze and touch.

I should slap him, but instead I find myself strangely aroused.

No one's ever looked at me with so much want.

No one's made me instantly hot for him.

Is that his thing? Making a woman feel wanted so she'll gladly part her legs for him?

Even if it is...oh, fuck it!

My fingers wrap around his hand, but instead of pushing him away, I press it against my chest, holding him in place.

Our eyes connect, and my breath hitches.

Something passes between us.

I don't know what it is. I only know that it makes my head spin.

"I'm already burned," I whisper.

"So am I."

His lips come closer to mine, until his mouth is less than an inch away. I can feel his hot breath. I'm wondering what he tastes like.

In a bold moment, I lick across his upper lip, then pull back. A feral sound escapes his lips. His hands go roughly around my waist, pressing me against his body.

He's hard—just like last night.

"I want you," he mutters.

He seems surprised, as though feeling that way about a woman for longer than a few days isn't usually the case.

"Seems like you didn't have a good night either," I say, a little smug.

"I actually did. Twice." His hands cup my ass and press me against him. His erection feels amazing against my core. I moan unwillingly. "But that was just my warm-up."

"Ava?" Mandy's voice calling from the hall rattles me.

I push Kellan aside and walk past him, my face on fire, just in time before Mandy's head pops in.

"I'm in here," I say needlessly and peer up at her.

The suspicion is written all over Mandy's face. Heat shoots up my neck to my cheeks as I realize I'm only wearing my bra, holding my blouse in my hand.

I turn away, but I'm pretty sure you can see my blush from a mile.

"What were you two up to?" Mandy asks casually, like she hasn't seen us in ages and is trying to catch up.

I'm pretty sure she can see that I'm half naked.

"Breakfast," Kellan says.

Wow, he's the god of casual.

I dare to peek at him. He's leaning against a counter with his arms crossed across his chest, his biceps bulging. And there's something else that's bulging.

I swallow and peel my gaze off his jeans, albeit unwillingly.

He's big. I saw that firsthand when he took care of his needs. I noticed it again last night, but I hadn't realized just how huge he is until now.

And he's making no secret out of his erection. Apparently, he doesn't give a damn about the fact that everyone can see it.

"Eggs Benedict for me, please," Mandy says and takes a seat at the table, arm outstretched, as though she's waiting for someone to hand her a cup of coffee.

"Those are Lila's, my best hen." Kellan holds up a bowl with eggs. "I don't have a Benedict."

I snort and immediately press a hand against my mouth to stifle it. He has a sense of humor. I like that. Our gazes meet, and something passes between us again. Heat gathers between my legs, and the same slow throbbing sensation from last night returns with a vengeance.

Oh, God. What is it with this guy and my chemical reactions to him?

It's like I'm a walking pill of female Viagra.

"What about you, Ava?" Kellan asks softly.

The way he says my name, I swear the temperature has just risen a few degrees.

"I'll take whatever you have."

Our gazes remain locked.

He moistens his lower lip.

I can see the wet trail on it and wish we were alone so I could run my tongue over it and taste him the way I've wanted ever since meeting him.

His thoughts mirror mine. I can see it from the way his gaze brushes my bra and lingers there—way too long. He's not even subtle about it.

Under different circumstances, he'd probably say something way too inappropriate, but he won't with Mandy present. I'm not sure whether to be grateful to her or annoyed to the point of kicking her ass out of the kitchen.

"What happened last night? You two disappeared outside, and when you came back, you couldn't get away fast enough," Mandy says, drawing my attention back to her.

I could kill her for being so direct.

Instead of following my murderous urges, I sit down at the table and try to focus on someone other than Kellan for a change. "Nothing happened. I was tired."

Kellan shoots me a strange look. I grimace at him, lest he open that arrogant mouth of his and say all the wrong things, and take a sip of my coffee.

"I think it was all a bit too much for Ava," Kellan says. "She didn't expect everything to be so intense."

I almost choke on my coffee. In an attempt to hide it, I hold my breath to stifle the scratching sensation in my throat until my eyes begin to water.

I can't believe the audacity.

"You don't have to talk about me in the third person, Kellan," I say. "I'm right here."

Of course, he'd think his tongue is God's gift to the female clitoris.

"So, what did you do out there?" Mandy asks, her usual prying self.

I peer at Kellan, who's looking at me, brows still raised in amusement.

Dammit!

He's letting me do all the hard work.

"Talking," I say.

Kellan lets out a most irritating snort, and I shoot him a murderous look.

Now Mandy will never believe me.

"Hmm. I bet," she says and stares right at me.

I shrug and remain silent as Kellan fills our cups.

"Anyway, guys, I have an announcement to make," Mandy says and takes a sip of her coffee. "I'm leaving today."

I stare at her. "What are you talking about?"

"Well, I wanted to talk to you last night, but you wouldn't open the door. I wanted to tell you that Josh, his cousin—" She points to Kellan. "—is taking a trip to Helena. I want to go with him."

I shake my head, confused. "But that's not where the gig takes place."

"I know," Mandy says. "I'll be back in time to see Mile High."

"What about...our plan?"

And me? I want to yell.

Mandy shrugs. "You wanted a vacation. That's exactly what you're getting. Kellan will take good care of you. Won't you?" She slaps his shoulder to get his attention.

"I'll make sure to feed her," Kellan says and winks at me.

"See?" Mandy says. "Problem taken care of."

I stare at both of them, lost for words.

Is it just my impression, or did he already know

that Mandy was leaving, because he sure doesn't look particularly surprised?

"Can I talk to you?" My fingers clutch around Mandy's upper arm, and I yank hard.

"Sure."

She leads me to the privacy of her bedroom. I realize all her things are packed.

"What's up?" she asks as soon as the door's closed.

"We've barely been here for a day, and now you want to leave again? What happened? Why the sudden change of heart? What happened to our vacation in a five-star hotel?"

"You said you weren't keen on it," Mandy says.

"Yes, but that was back home. I never said I wanted to stay here either."

Mandy stares at me. "Look, this is your one opportunity to bury the past. You can't stay single forever just because one guy let you down."

I let out a snort. "Kellan and I don't have a relationship. He's not even into relationships."

"Yet," she says slowly.

"It's not going to happen. Ever."

"You can't know that."

"Trust me, I know."

She sets her jaw. I can almost see the sappy

scenes from The Notebook playing before her eyes. She wants a happy ending so desperately, it's ridiculous. "That's not what Josh said."

"What *did* he say?" I ask warily.

"I think you should hear it from Kellan. I'm sorry, Ava, but I have to do this. I promise I'll be back soon."

She hugs me tight and quickly lets go, dragging her suitcase behind her as she leaves. I dash for my room to grab a clean shirt before I sprint after her.

CHAPTER TWENTY-TWO

THROUGH THE WINDOW in the hallway, I watch Mandy get into Josh's pickup truck and leave. I could head after her, beg, force her into staying, and yet I'm doing none of those things.

As soon as she's gone, I return to the kitchen.

"You knew she was planning on leaving, didn't you?"

"She talked to me yesterday. You never gave her a chance to tell you." Kellan's leaning against the kitchen counter, his arms crossed over his chest.

"Why did *you* leave last night?"

"I was tired."

"Really?" He raises his eyebrows, amused. "So you say. However, I got a different impression. You feel a strong need to run from me."

"Who's running? I'm not." I jut my chin out and regard him through narrowed eyes. "I could have asked Mandy to take me with her, you know?"

"But you didn't."

"No, I didn't. I chose to stay." I grimace, doubting the sanity of my decision.

A smile lights up his face. "I wonder why?"

Yeah, why indeed?

My traitorous stomach growls.

"Someone's hungry," Kellan says. "Come on, I'll make you a real breakfast, even though I shouldn't because I liked you better with only your bra on." He points at my clean shirt.

"I can make my own breakfast." I turn my back to him, suddenly nervous as realization dawns on me.

We are alone. In his house.

"Let me. I'm the host." Before I can protest, Kellan's standing next to me, arms on either side of me as he begins to fumble around for stuff, his hard body brushing against me at every opportunity.

Oh, for crying out loud!

It's his kitchen. Unless he's just suffered from a major case of amnesia, there's no way he doesn't know where he's placed all the stuff he apparently needs.

Mandy's barely been gone a few minutes, and I'm already caught between a kitchen counter and this statue of a man, his breath on my neck.

"You know what, I think I'll just grab some cookies on my way out," I say.

"What kind?"

Kellan laughs, the sound low and so erotic, it travels all the way down and settles between my legs.

Turning around, I press my hands against his hard abs and push, but he doesn't budge from the spot.

Now I'm really stuck.

"What do you want?" I whisper, my voice too low, too hoarse for my liking.

"You. All to myself." He doesn't even need to think. His words come out fast and casual, and completely take me off guard.

I peer all the way up into his green gaze, lost for words.

"You want me. I want you. We're both consenting adults. We're all alone on a big farm. What's the harm?" Kellan continues.

Yes, what's the harm indeed?

He's so gorgeous it takes my breath away.

The kind you fuck, and then discard.

I'm a successful, mature woman who can handle a bit of sex without getting her feelings involved.

"Let me guess, no strings attached?" I can't believe I'm even considering this when I should be smacking him.

"No strings attached." His eyes bore into me. His gaze is so penetrating, I can almost feel him inside my core, and he isn't even touching me. "That's all I'll ever be able to give you."

"I don't even know you," I say stupidly, like people only sleep with people after having read their résumé. "I shouldn't be staying here alone with you."

"You knew me well enough to let me go down on you," Kellan remarks.

My jaw drops.

"The way I see it, you don't need to know me to fuck me," Kellan says. "So, what do you say? You get the vacation you wanted, and I get to teach you all about sex. Good sex."

I have no doubt about that. Like my mother once said, guys like him are the building blocks of the fond memories that keep us all wet and writhing through years of doomed marriages and monotony.

I sigh.

If I'm to enter something I've never experienced before, I need to do it on my own terms.

"Tell me something about you," I say.

"What do you want to know, Ava?"

"Are you dating anyone?"

"I told you I'm single. I'm a lot of things, but not a cheater," Kellan says.

I stare at him as I try to read his features. His expression is honest. Suddenly, the million obstacles in my head seem to evaporate. "Good. Because I don't condone cheating."

"Because of the ex you told me about?"

I shrug, as though it's not a big deal when it is. A huge one. "It's the past. A long time ago. Doesn't matter. There were others since. Nothing serious though."

His eyes narrow slightly, but he doesn't press the issue, for which I'm grateful. My demons are mine to exorcize.

"Anything else you want to know?" Kellan prompts.

I shrug and look away, as though I'm pondering over possibilities and choices, when in fact I know exactly what I want to know. "What were you doing in New York?"

I could have asked anything in the world, and yet the one question he evaded before is the one I need answered.

Because to fuck him, I need to trust him. I need to trust that he's open and honest.

His stance changes instantly. His shoulders are tense as he turns away from me. "Business."

"What kind of business?" I persist.

"Ava." His tone is clipped, betraying his hesitation and inner turmoil. I know it's not my place to ask, and it's most certainly none of my business, but I can't just *not* know anything about him. I can't be detached like that. My body might not mind, but my head doesn't work that way.

Our gazes meet in a fierce but silent battle. For a split second, his eyes shimmer with stubbornness. Irritation. Even animosity.

I speak first. "I need to be able to trust you."

He blows out a breath and rakes his fingers through his hair, the tension in his shoulders magnifying. "Let's just say bad interpersonal decisions. Relationships are great as long as they don't turn bad. And in the end, all turn to dust."

Marriage?

Imminent divorce?

I wait for him to elaborate, but he doesn't.

I guess that's all the answer I'll get.

"So, what do we do about that guy who hurt you?" A lazy smile creeps up his face, and just like that, all the tension seems to evaporate from him.

God, I love it when he smiles. It's like we're the only two people in the world and his smile is only for me.

"You can't beat up a guy, Kellan. But thank you for the offer."

His arms wrap around my waist, and he pulls me a little closer to him. My breasts are pressed against his chest, my nipples instantly beading at contact. My world begins to spin just a little bit from the way he looks at me—all heat and want and carefreeness.

This doesn't mean anything.

We don't mean anything.

The thought is strangely arousing. Just being with him—not for who he is, but for his body, for having my needs fulfilled—is exciting.

Kellan's lips come closer to mine. His breath smells of mint and coffee as he brushes his lips over mine ever so gently.

"Want me to make you come again?" he whispers against them. "I could do it right here, right now. I know it wasn't nearly enough last night."

"Now?" I'm so up for it, my breath catches in my chest. All I can do is press my lips against his, my mouth opening slightly to grant him access.

"Yes, now. Your lessons start today."

His mouth comes crashing down on me instantly, his tongue forcing its way into my mouth slowly but decisively. Pressed against him, I can feel his body with every fiber of my being.

He's hard for me, and possessive—just like his kiss.

His length is pressing into my abdomen, reminding me of what I've been missing for over a year. My nerve endings are on fire; my body's instantly awake.

My moan is stifled by his exploring mouth.

His hands slide around from the small of my back to my hips, and in one swift motion, he lifts me up until I'm seated on the kitchen counter. I open my legs for him and wrap them around his hips, mentally swearing at the fact that I'm wearing jeans.

"You know your friend could change her mind about her trip, right?" Kellan says, drawing back just a little bit. The edges of his mouth tug up in a half smile.

Of course, I know that.

"But she won't," I say. "She loves anything

resembling a city way too much. Why do you care?"

He shrugs, grinning. "I don't. But you might."

That's my reason to back off, and yet I bury my fingers in his hair and arch my back.

"You're damn hot when you do that."

"Do what?" I run my tongue over his lower lip, the way I've envisioned doing ever since meeting him.

He groans and tightens his grip on my hips. His hardness jerks slightly against my abdomen, tenting the fabric of his jeans. Its warmth seeping through my clothes is like an electric current, searing wherever it touches me, gathering in that slow pulsating sensation in my clit.

"Did you make yourself come again last night?" he asks in that drawl of his that screams sex.

"No." The word comes out too breathy, too fast. I can tell from the way he looks at me that he doesn't believe me. "No," I say more slowly, avoiding his gaze.

"Why not?"

Because for some reason, it wouldn't have felt like you were doing it to me.

I shrug. "Didn't feel like it."

"We both know you're lying."

Without any forewarning, Kellan pulls back and

helps me down from the counter, his eyes roaming my body, drinking me in. His hair is a disheveled mess, but it looks good on him. His lips are slightly swollen from our kiss. I bet I look just as affected, but the disheveled look probably doesn't suit me as much as him.

"What?" My hands shoot up to straighten my clothes.

"I'm considering where to fuck you. Right now, I'm thinking it's either against the kitchen counter or on the table." His fingers begin to fumble with the zipper on my jeans. "Or I could do both."

My breath catches in my throat as I watch him walk over to the door and lock up, then sit down on a chair.

Holy shit!

Who the fuck has a lock on the door in the kitchen?

Someone who isn't doing this for the first time.

"Take off all your clothes. I want to see you naked."

I stare at him, unsure if I've heard him right. "It's the middle of the day, Kellan."

Think light streaming in through the window, bathing the kitchen in glaring brightness. I'm not usually the self-conscious type, but this is way too much light for presenting yourself naked to a man like him.

"Strip, Ava." His tone is sharp, demanding. "I'm not expecting a lap dance." His eyes glint, and the corners of his lips curl upward. "Not yet anyway. But I want you to do as I say when I say it."

I shouldn't be letting a guy tell me what to do, particularly not when I'm uncomfortable with his demand. But his charge is strangely arousing. Slowly, I unbutton my shirt and slide out of it, letting it fall into a bundle at my feet. Holding my breath, I pull my jeans down my hips and remove my bra. My breasts spill out, my nipples already beaded, ready to be sucked into his mouth.

I don't remove my panties. Fighting the urge to cover my breasts with my hands, I just stand there a few feet from Kellan, waiting for his reaction.

He takes a sharp breath and moistens his lips.

"Damn." That's all he says.

Damn good? Damn bad? Damn nice weather?

I raise my brows. "Care to be more specific?"

He doesn't.

"The panties." He gestures at my lace panties impatiently. "Take them off."

Sighing, I strip out of them and let them fall to my feet. Now I'm completely naked, exposed to his ardent scrutiny.

He takes his time running his gaze over my body, taking in every inch of me. His breathing is raspy.

"Come here," he says eventually, and I amble over, stopping right in front of him.

He stands, towering over me as he leans forward to whisper in my ear while his leg moves to part my knees, "Show me how wet you are."

It's not a question; it's a statement, as though he knows just how eager I am to have him inside me. As though he'd expect nothing else from me.

His fingers send shivers down my spine as they trail down my abdomen and settle at my entrance. My breath hitches, caught in my chest like a trapped bird. Holding my breath, I spread my legs a little wider to grant him easy access.

"You're dripping. So ready." Slowly, he dips the tip of one finger into me and then lifts it to his mouth and licks my moisture off it. "I like the way you taste and smell. I'll like your slickness even more around my cock."

Oh, God.

No one's ever talked like this to me before.

I don't know how to react to it, so I just stare at him while he strips off his shirt, jeans, and underwear—all in a matter of seconds. The motion is so skillful, I can't help but wonder how many times he's practiced it and with how many women.

The pang of jealousy is ridiculous when I'm not interested in him emotionally whatsoever.

Instead of following the irritating thought, I look down and almost choke on my breath.

Holy crap!

He's huge. Way bigger than I remember. And so hard, I almost come from just looking at him. No wonder he only does casual. With a cock like that, he's most certainly not short of eager women lining up at his door to get a good tumble between the sheets.

Hell, I've just turned into one of them.

I have to force my eyes away. Looking anywhere else but his hardness is good, and yet I keep stealing glances.

The tip is engorged, glistening with moisture. I watch him slide his hand up and down its length.

"You keep looking at me, Ava. And you should. This is how hard you make me, baby."

I avert my eyes instantly, my already flushed cheeks catching fire.

He caught me staring. Again.

"No," I say, but the lie's so obvious it's embarrassing.

"Look at me," he commands as he begins to stroke himself, up and down, the gesture both intimate and familiar.

My tongue flicks across my lips.

"I want to help," I whisper.

He groans but doesn't take me up on the offer. "Say you want me to fill you up."

I shake my head. Maybe other women talk to him like that, but I can't.

"Tell me how much you want me inside you," Kellan orders and lets go of his shaft. He inches closer, and his fingers brush the inside of my legs. His palm presses against my clitoris, the pressure unbearably hard and frustrating. I arch my hips forward, silently begging him to enter me.

I draw a sharp breath as two fingers move between my legs, settling against my mound.

"Is this what you want?" His fingers slide into me, filling me up like they did last night. I nod and tilt my head back, closing my eyes in the process. The pleasure is all consuming, frustratingly so because I won't come from it. I need more.

"It's not enough." My words are barely more than a whisper.

"Then say you want me to fill you." His voice is rough, the demand harsher than before. Through the lust-induced fog inside my brain, I can recognize a pattern. Just like stripping for him, this is an order he expects me to obey.

"I want you to fill me up," I whisper.

"Tell me you want my cock inside you, fucking you so deep you'll feel it for a week," Kellan says. "Now, look at me." His fingers leave my pussy and settle beneath my chin, forcing me to meet his heated gaze. "Say it."

Without his fingers inside me, I feel empty. I'm eager to please him so we can finally get to the action. "I want to feel you for a week."

"Good girl." He smiles, seemingly pleased.

For a moment, he releases me and fumbles with his jeans. I look away, but the noise of a tearing foil wrapper is unmistakable. There's something dirty about the way I just stand there, bathed in glowing brightness, waiting for a guy I barely know to pull on a condom.

I feel dirty. Surreal. Cheap.

And yet, I'm so turned on, I could make myself come within seconds.

Kellan's hand slides across my ass, cupping it, lifting me up.

He takes my lip between his teeth and sucks it into his mouth a moment before his cock plunges into me—all the way in. I flinch at the jolt of pain that's instantly replaced by a long wave of pleasure.

He's too big. I don't think I can take it.

"Kellan." His name erupts from my lips in a moan.

"Yes, baby. We'll take it slow."

But there's nothing slow about the way he thrusts deeper inside me.

Another moan escapes my lips. I've never been so stretched. The pleasure is almost unbearable. I should be moving my hips in unison with his, but all I can do is claw at his shoulders, holding on for dear life.

Electric jolts course through me, bringing me higher and higher to the edge.

"You're so wet and tight," Kellan growls, the sound almost feral, strained.

He's close. I can feel it from the way he twitches inside me.

"I've been picturing me fucking you like this for months," he says.

That makes two of us.

His hand moves between my legs again and begins to caress my clitoris in quick, circular strokes, the motion rough, demanding.

"Yes," I gasp. My legs begin to shake from the

effort of having him inside me when he puts more pressure on my clitoris, the motion sending me over the edge.

Kellan's mouth stifles my cry before it can erupt out of my chest while his cock continues to pump inside me, his heavy balls brushing my entrance.

"Oh, God." I reach that peak and close my eyes, my head rolling backward. From the periphery of my mind, I can feel his one last thrust and hear his own cry of release. At some point, he slides out of me, and his arms wrap around my waist, pulling me close to him.

We remain silent as he's holding me while my heartbeat barely slows down.

CHAPTER
TWENTY-THREE

SITTING DOWN, I draw the sunhat deeper over my face, not to protect me against the warm sunrays, but to stop the wind from whipping my hair against my skin.

"Is it always this windy?" I ask.

I've been in Montana for six days. The wind stopped only once.

"No." Kellan lets himself fall next to me. "It can also get very cold. Winter's always drawn out. Why? Do you miss the city already?" He pulls his hat back and looks at me, a blade of grass between his teeth.

I look at the way he plays with it, the way he chews it between his teeth, letting his tongue slide along the blade. The same tongue that tortured and teased me. The same teeth that tugged at my earlobe. The same mouth that aroused and turned my world from gray into an array of colors.

It's been a nice vacation so far, probably the best in years.

Correction.

It was the best I ever had.

He's been inside me so many times I'm not sure I can walk straight anymore. It's surprising we managed to get as far as the lake.

Taking in the scenery before my eyes, I realize the walk was worth it. The lake is vast; the water is silent and deep—much like Kellan. I dread the moment I'll have to go. That one last moment together when it'll be clear I'll never see him again. Ever since Mandy left, I've been counting the days, the hours, the minutes.

She'll be back tomorrow.

My vacation's drawing to an end.

"No," I say slowly. "I don't miss the city at all. I sure don't miss the stress."

"Your job?"

"What?" I laugh and shake my head. "No."

"What about your home?"

"God, no. My bedroom's as small as a closet. It's seriously crammed. But if you're talking about my family..." I shrug. "They're constantly traveling, barely calling. I rarely see them. I think it's safe to say that I'm closer to my neighbors. You?"

"Me?" His lips twitch. "What about me?"

"Do you miss the city?"

"Nah." He shakes his head, turning his eyes back to the lake. "Not at all."

"Not even your car?"

He shrugs. "Money can't buy you everything."

I nod and let out a small sigh. "Maybe, but money can make your life easier. A *lot* easier."

He remains silent for a while.

"That's true," he says at last. "But it doesn't buy you happiness, nor does it make your life less complicated, or less of a mess. It sure hasn't made mine."

And here it is again—a hint of his past without revealing too much.

But his tone is different, as though he wants to talk but just can't. As though opening up to someone doesn't come easily to him, but maybe, just maybe, he feels as though opening up to me may be a possibility in the future.

The past few days, I've been wondering what's happening to him. It's hard to believe that Kellan Boyd is the same man I met three months ago. The arrogance is still here, and the confidence, and as before, he exudes raw sex, but something is missing.

I cannot pinpoint what it is.

It's as if one part of him died. But what part?

There is the cowboy, wild at heart, loving the country and his family.

And there is the rich, superficial guy with the expensive car, who is more concerned with sex and appearance than with human relationships.

Who is he?

It's the one question that keeps haunting me. Kellan keeps denying that he's involved with Club 69. He's adamant that he's a silent shareholder and nothing more. I want to believe him, and yet I cannot. Because I have no idea what he really does.

Sure, he seems to know how to take care of a farm, but I'm not stupid enough to believe that a bit of livestock can earn him enough money to buy a Lamborghini and wear tailored clothes.

Just like the lake in front of me, Kellan is still as much of a mystery to me as the day I arrived, and I have no idea how to get to the truth without being pushy.

I have tried to get him to open up by confiding things I would never have told a stranger, like about my parents and their expectations of me. I have tried to be patient—all to no avail.

He is a closed book, revealing little, if anything, while asking questions about my life.

"What are you thinking?" he asks.

I grow silent as I pry my eyes away from his stunning lips. "Just life, you know. What you said about happiness."

"It's the country," he whispers. "That's why I love it here. Everything is still. It's as if time has stopped. Don't you think?"

I turn to him, eyeing him again. "Yeah. It's probably the part I'll miss the most." I didn't mean to be so honest, but the words are out before I can stop them.

"Not me?" he asks, brows raised.

"No, not you." I scowl and slap his arm playfully. "Obviously, you're a jerk."

"Still?"

"Very much." I nod. "Big time. I have yet to forgive you for embarrassing me in front of your brother."

He lets out a laugh. "Relax. Ryder told me you

had a nice body. That's good feedback."

"It's still embarrassing."

"Not around here, it isn't. We're like one huge family."

Maybe that part's true, but I still don't want my family to walk in on me having the time of my life with a guy.

"You know what I don't get?" I say, changing the subject. "Back in NY, you were this huge pain in the ass, and here you're this Texan cowboy."

"I'm a Montana cowboy. Don't compare us." He winks at me. It's hard to say whether he's joking or really taking something so trivial seriously.

"Why not?"

"Because we differ in too many ways. We talk differently. We fuck differently. The weather around here is different. Don't even get me started on attitude and culture."

This is the longest he's talked. I don't even care what we're talking about. I just like his sudden openness; the fact that he lets me glimpse into his soul.

"Give me an example," I say, eager to prolong our conversation for as long as I can.

"Let me think." Kellan pauses for a moment, thinking. "You can legally toke up in Montana, but if you try that in Texas, you'll get your ass thrown in jail."

"That's about the most useless piece of information I've ever heard." I grin at him. "What else?"

"People don't seem to care about keeping up with the Joneses. They just keep to themselves. You'll notice the pace here is slower. We're a close-knit community. We stick together. People are more down to earth. In so many ways, I think Texas has lost what Montana still has."

"Is that the reason why you're back?" I ask gently.

He peers at me, brows raised. "What makes you think I ever lived elsewhere?"

I shrug. "Your chick magnet sports car?"

He stays silent for a few moments, then shrugs. "That doesn't say anything."

He's evading giving me an answer again.

"This is where I was born; where I grew up. It's hard to get the same feeling elsewhere," Kellan says.

"What feeling?" I follow his line of vision. He's staring out at the lake now. It's so serene and quiet. Except for the birds and the soft rustling of leaves, nothing stirs.

"Home," he says. "The vast space. The air. The people. My happiest memories are here." He turns to regard me again, his green gaze dark and hooded, filled with a past I wish I experienced with him. "Fun fact about Montana: we have plenty of cowboys here, but most of them ride bikes instead of horses."

"Except you." I smile.

"I prefer the old-fashioned way in everything."

He's drifting off again, expertly maneuvering my questions so he avoids answering any of them. But I've never been one to give up easily.

"Because your family goes back generations?" I ask.

"You might be onto something." He pulls me to him, and I know in that moment that he's done talking about himself. "Tell me, how are you feeling?"

"Good," I say, wondering where he's heading.

He frowns. "Just good?"

"Yeah, good. I couldn't be better." I smile at him to convey that yes, I like both his home and his company. "You've been asking me this question every morning."

"Because I like to know I've left my woman satisfied."

I laugh again. "You do. You're a good host, but..."

"But what?"

"You promised to teach me to ride and you

haven't."

"As far as I remember, we did plenty of riding."

"Except horses." In spite of the relaxed conversation, I can't help but feel a little melancholy. "All in all, I'm happy and satisfied."

"Good." Kellan moves his arm around me and pulls me to his chest. "I've turned you into a country girl, then?"

"Fat chance. I still have a lot to learn."

"Yeah? Like what."

Like how to be what he wants and needs.

I shrug, as though my thoughts don't matter. As though it doesn't matter that I wish we met under different circumstances, in a different lifetime, with both of us ready for more than just a fling. "You still haven't shown me around," I say, implementing my own change in subject.

"I'd be happy to give you the tour."

Except I'm leaving tomorrow.

That reminds me we have less than twenty-four hours left. We've barely spent a week together, and yet it feels like an eternity has passed between us. Mandy was right. It feels like we're an old couple. There's chemistry, and yet there's no safety net.

I'm falling with no safety net.

I don't know what's worse. Falling in love with a

beautiful cowboy I'll never see again or falling in love with a jerk I know will break my heart.

In the end, it doesn't matter. Both outcomes suck big time.

We stay silent for a few minutes.

Kellan resumes the conversation first. "Why don't you move here?"

His question takes me by surprise. I look up to search his green eyes. He averts his gaze as though he doesn't mind saying the words but he doesn't want me to look into his soul while he says them.

"We could escape the madness of the past. Leave everything behind," he adds. "We'd have all the time in the world. I could teach you everything you want to know."

I straighten, my heart thumping harder in my chest. "Do you want me to stay?"

He shrugs. "I don't think it's bad here. And frankly, I think there's a country girl somewhere inside you. I think deep down you want to help me with the farm."

He must be joking.

Stupid, crazy hope.

For a moment, I really thought—

I shake my head, my mood suddenly plummeting to a new low in my life. "You wouldn't pay me for my hard work."

"Probably not. That's because I already pay people to do most of the farm work." He sighs. "But I'm a great cook, can offer you a warm bed, and let's not forget, I'll always make sure you come first."

"Wow." I grin at him. "You're extremely generous."

"Or a good host," he says, his expression sober.

I give him a little shove. He laughs and lies back, squeezing his hands beneath his head. For a moment, I consider snuggling against his chest, but decide against it.

We stay silent.

The sky above us is a clear blue. Not a single cloud. Lying back, I close my eyes and relax, soaking in the warm rays, the wind softly caressing my skin.

"Will you miss me?"

His question knocks all air out of my lungs.

I turn my head to him and find that he's pulled his cowboy hat over his face. The corner of his mouth tugs up. It's only thing I can make out, the only thing that gives away this isn't as serious to him as it is to me.

"I guess so." A hint of sadness seeps into my voice.

"Good." His lips twitch. "When you leave me, I

want to be in your mind for a long time."

You're already in my mind and I haven't even left yet.

There's no way we can feel so much attraction and have worlds separate us, and yet it's happening.

Kellan draws his hat back. "You're awfully silent."

I avoid his eyes as my glance turns back to the lake.

"I'm just thinking how beautiful this place is. That's all."

That isn't even a lie. This place is beautiful, but it wouldn't hold my heart if it weren't for him.

He props up on his elbow, towering over me and shielding my face from the sun. And then he leans into me to steal the kind of kiss that makes me rip off his clothes, the kind that makes me forget we're not a couple.

We'll never be.

CHAPTER
TWENTY-FOUR

"KELLAN," I DRAW out the word as I drop the hayfork. "There's something wrong with the horse. It looks sick."

"Which one?" his voice bellows a moment before he storms into the barn.

"That one." I point my finger to a huge, black animal with the most bloated tummy I've ever seen. The poor thing's so bloated, I wouldn't be surprised if people could smell it within a five-mile radius.

Kellan's hand brushes over the horse's head soothingly. "That's a she. The mare's about to give birth."

I stare at the horse, completely dumbstruck.

"What?" Kellan laughs. "You thought she was

overweight, didn't you?"

"I don't want to lie, but yes, I thought she was." Which is a lie. But I'd rather let him think I thought the poor animal lacked physical activity than admit that I thought she was bloated. My hands fly to my throat, suddenly nervous and in fear of the animal's wellbeing. "Shouldn't you be calling the vet?"

"We're in Montana. She'll be done before he arrives." Laughing, Kellan shakes his head and plants a kiss on my cheek. "You're adorable, you know that?"

More like stupid.

"I'm glad you think that because I definitely feel more like a fool," I say dryly.

"You're a fool for thinking that." His gaze shoots to the mare. "We'll get started soon. I need you to stay here and help."

My eyes widen. I've never been a fan of blood or pain. I want to run and wait this one out, but instead find myself asking faintly, "How?"

"Keep talking to her, sing to her. She likes that. If she can't manage on her own, I'll intervene, but that rarely happens."

I stare at him. "You're not going to be here?"

"I'll be outside, finishing up." He squeezes my hand at my horrified expression. "Don't worry. Just tell her everything will be fine. Giving life is such a beautiful thing. I want you to be there for her."

***

He's right. It is a beautiful thing. The whole birthing only lasts about fifteen minutes, but it feels like a whole new life experience. I expected it to be gross, but it isn't. It's everything but ugly.

The mare doesn't writhe in agony. As I keep stroking her head, she remains silent, graceful. I laugh as the tiny legs of the foal squeeze out of her, followed by the rest of its body. I'm crying as the baby slides to the floor, wrapped in a gleaming membrane.

I'm crying buckets and I don't even know why.

Scratch that.

I know exactly why. I've never been so happy in my life. I've never felt so much in awe. For a long time, I just stand there and watch the tiny creature struggle to get to its feet.

"You okay?" Kellan asks from somewhere behind me. His voice is soft.

I nod and sniff. My hands wipe at my face to get rid of the annoying tears, but let's face it. What's the point when I probably look like a puffy fish anyway?

"I just had no idea it would be like this."

"After watching this my whole life, it still surprises me every single time." His arms wrap around me, hugging my back to his strong chest. "It's okay to cry. You did great. I'm really proud of you." He kisses the top of my head, and then spins me around to look at me. His thumb brushes over my cheek to wipe away the moisture. "Come on, we need to celebrate."

Shaking my head, I peel myself away from him and head for the huge doors.

Kellan follows after me. "Where are you going?"

"Home." I cringe at the word. What is happening to me? I shouldn't be taking his attention when two poor animals might be in need of his assistance. "I mean your home."

"As long as you're my guest, my home is your home, and you haven't seen a lot of it." He points over our heads. "I promised to give you the tour. Well, now's the right time. You haven't yet seen my personal space."

I peer up at the high ceiling. "Your personal space?"

"It's up there. I hope you're good at climbing up ladders."

I suck at climbing up ladders, but that's irrelevant

right now. I'd climb up a ladder to the moon and back for a chance to see his personal space.

Peering back up, I realize I should have known. This place is so huge, there has to be a top floor. I saw the windows outside.

Kellan leads us to a narrow staircase, which I didn't even notice until now.

He climbs up hastily, his enthusiasm palpable in his swift strides.

I follow him through a trapdoor and let him help me to my feet. As my gaze sweeps over the space, I'm struck speechless.

The top floor is huge. Like an entire apartment huge.

And way more modern than I would have anticipated. There's a leather couch, a television set, even a small kitchen, with modern appliances.

"Wow," I say stunned.

"This is my tiny abode," Kellan explains.

"Tiny?" I laugh. "Kellan, this is huge. And I'm not even thinking by NYC standards."

"When I was fifteen, my father decided that it was time my brothers and I got our own space. I think he did it to get rid of us. We were quite the noisy bunch."

I spin in a slow circle, taking in the guitar and

musical instruments set up in a corner. Even I know this isn't the usual stuff you get in the shops. It's way too polished and huge, and there's other stuff, like amplifiers and other black boxes, I think are for recording, but I'm not sure.

"Is one of your brothers a musician?"

"All of us were," Kellan says. "We had our very own band. We called ourselves The Boyd Brothers, until we grew too old and developed other interests as well." He winks. "Think girls and panties."

Yeah, that's exactly the kind of story I don't want to hear.

I pick up the guitar. "Is this yours?"

He steps behind me. I expect him to reach out and take it out of my hands, but he doesn't. "How did you know?"

My fingers travel over the initials engraved on it. "It says K.B."

"My sister bought it for me. It was my first guitar." He hesitates. There's something there. I know it. I can feel his unease, so I put the guitar back and turn to look at him.

"Sounds like she's great," I say softly.

He nods. "When we were young, this was our thing. Friends used to hang out here all the time. The place was packed each weekend. There were parties." He catches my glance. "Not that kind. The kind where you sit outside, in front of a huge fire, and everyone's singing and having a great time. God, that was such a long time ago." His voice is melancholic, his eyes distant, focused on a past far away. "Then, life happened. We grew up. Everyone went their separate ways."

I nod, envying him because at least he *had* all those experiences.

"And by everyone you mean—" I prompt.

"Ryder, whom you've already met, and Cash."

"And your sister?"

He falls silent, and something flashes across his face.

I cannot bear it anymore.

"Who's the blond woman in the picture on the fireplace?" I ask, even though I asked the same question before and he's already given an answer.

He doesn't blink. "I already told you. That's my sister. At least...was." There is a short silence. His face distorts to...something, and then he walks away without another word.

I give him a minute before I follow after him.

I find him sitting outside the barn. I kneel down next to him, making sure not to touch him. His posture is rigid, his shoulders tense.

"I'm sorry I asked," I start, unsure what else to say.

"It's okay." His voice drops to a whisper. He looks up at the sky, his eyes dark and hooded, but, oh my god—the sadness.

"What happened to her?" I ask, fighting the urge to touch him.

There is a short pause, then, "She's dead, Ava."

I turn to him, even though I know he probably doesn't want my presence. "I'm sorry."

"Yeah, me too. She died five weeks ago."

I stare at him, shocked. It makes so much sense. The pain is fresh. He's struggling to come to terms with such a great loss.

I don't want to impose, and yet I find myself asking, "What happened? Do you want to talk about it?"

He takes his time replying. "She died in a bomb blast."

"She was the best friend you told me about."

He nods. "She was the best of everything you can have. Clara was..." He sighs, and a soft, sad smile tugs at his lips. "She was a good person. Her heart was in the right place. Ever since I can remember, she wanted to help others. If she set her mind to it, she went all the way. When she told our family she wanted to join the military, no one wanted her to. They were all afraid she'd get hurt." Another pause. He clears his throat, and I sense something huge is coming. "Except me. I told her to go after her dreams, that I'd be proud of her. Back then, I was so sure she'd be okay, because she was strong and she wasn't scared to get in a fight." He takes a deep breath and lets it out slowly. His eyes are cast downward now, focused on a spot at his feet. "I've been regretting that for the last five weeks, day and night, even in my dreams. There's not a single thing I can do to take those words back. If it weren't for me, she'd still be here. She'd be alive."

His eyes are shimmering with moisture. A tear slides down my cheek. His pain radiates from him, every word true and coming from the heart.

"Kellan," I whisper his name because I don't know what else to say.

He shakes his head. "Don't. You have no idea what my family went through." He looks up at me, meeting my glance. "My mother died when I was young. It was my sister who took care of all of us. She wasn't just the eldest, she was also the one who made sure that my dad didn't let himself go. She was amazing. I mean it when I say you would have liked her."

I can feel his anger. He's not past that stage in the grieving process yet. Whatever I say won't help. But I know keeping him talking is good for him.

"Why do you think that?"

"I don't know," Kellan says. "You're alike. When Sniper saw you, I knew it. It's the way he reacts, and the way you talk to him." He sighs. "She was fierce and stubborn. Always had her own mind about things."

"It must have been nice to grow up with brothers," I say softly.

"Well, I think it influenced her decision to join the forces." His eyes go distant again. "I hadn't seen her in almost a year. Then, out of the blue came, the call she'd be back home the following weekend. I was so happy. I tried to cancel everything, but work came first." He grimaces, and a nerve begins to pulse beneath his eye. "I told her I couldn't see her. I didn't come back home when I had the chance because other things seemed more important. It's the biggest regret I have. She spent that one last weekend here, and I didn't come to see her. She told me she was fine, that she'd be back home for Thanksgiving, but she died within a week."

"I'm so sorry," I whisper, wiping at the tears gathering in my eyes.

He just nods.

My fingers gingerly reach out to touch his, and he lets me. His fingers intertwine with mine, and I give them a light squeeze in the hope the simple gesture can convey a little bit of just how much my heart is bleeding for him.

CHAPTER TWENTY-FIVE

I DON'T KNOW how long we've been sitting here, our hands locked, the world around us heavy and hopeless.

Loss is a strange thing. It comes without a warning. It rips your heart to shreds and lets you learn to live with the pieces. It never lets you heal, but eventually, the memories you carry will help you learn to live with the pain of knowing that you will never see your loved one again.

So many words unsaid.

So many smiles turned to tears.

So many future memories unlived.

I look at Kellan and I see his pain etched into his features. His green gaze is turned toward the sky, hooded by long, dark eyelashes that cast soft shadows across his cheeks.

He's beautiful when he smiles, but he's even more beautiful when he's lost in his thoughts, his heart open, his emotions raw.

"Days have passed. Soon the weeks will turn into years. I'll always remember you with silent tears." His words are barely more than a whisper, his voice slightly humming, as though his pain has become a song that needs to rip through his chest.

Leaning into him, I rest my head against his shoulder and look up. His gaze meets mine, and then he smiles.

That glorious smile of his that catches the day and the night. That makes my heart both rise and sink.

The world around us stops for a moment.

Slowly, his mouth nears mine and his lips brush my lips in a kiss that's as soft as the beating wings of a butterfly.

"I want to show you the lake," he says and pulls me to my feet.

"What?" I laugh and throw a dubious glance at the shimmering water within walking distance. There's an old paddleboat secured at a pier that looks just as decrepit. I thought it was just décor.

"Water and I aren't exactly friends. Unless it's a pool and there's a bar nearby."

"Come on, city girl. You'll like it," he says with a wink.

"Two adults balancing on a bit of old wood? Hmm."

I very much doubt the sanity of the idea, but I follow him down the path to the lake. Kellan holds the boat for me as I climb inside—actually, make that *crawl* inside, because there's no way I can keep my balance while standing in this thing—and sit down.

It's actually much larger than I thought.

He grabs the paddles and expertly maneuvers the boat across the lake in long strokes, stopping in the middle of the water. From here, we can see both the barn and the woods.

I close my eyes and lose myself into the moment. The silence. The warm rays of sun on my face. His presence.

"You like it," Kellan remarks.

I nod and smile.

When I open my eyes, his gaze is on me. Slowly, he leans forward and presses a kiss on my lips.

My fingers intertwine at the back of his neck as I lie down on the blanket, the hard wood of the boat pushing into my back. But I've never been more comfortable.

I've never felt safer.

Kellan's lips are probing mine, his emotions slipping into me.

I feel the change when his tongue parts my lips to explore the cave of my mouth. His touch is gentle but determined. It's clear what he wants, and I'm more than willing to give it to him.

Slowly, I pull my shirt up and unhook my bra. His hands slide up over my breasts, his fingers lingering over my beaded nipples. His eyes drink me in. I can see the hunger in his eyes. I can see his self-restraint, his need to make this special.

But today, it's not about stilling that carnal need in us. He's so much more to me. He's the one thorn in my rose garden. He's the one mistake that has ruined me for everyone else.

I want to kiss him like I've never kissed anyone else before.

I want to let him claim my body like it's his to possess.

Come tomorrow, I'll be his sweet memory, and he'll be my one scar that will never heal.

"Kellan." I unbutton his jeans and help him do the same to mine.

"Ava." His tone matches mine, heavy and meaningful.

Our clothes are on the floor of the boat within seconds. His skin is bare against mine. The breeze makes my burning skin shiver.

He levers himself between my legs, his shaft hard, ready for me. His fingertips brush down my abdomen, between my wet folds, and his breath catches, the air trapped in his heaving chest.

His desire for me is my ruin.

"I need you inside me. Now," I whisper, my gaze locked with his, my eyes silently speaking all the words I cannot say.

"Are you sure? I don't want to—"

"Hurt me? You won't." Smiling, I push up to press a gentle kiss on his mouth in the hope that it'll scatter his worries.

I need this.

I need us.

Raw.

Our bodies and souls bare.

His mouth descends upon mine. His kiss takes my heart, sucks it inside his until his breathing becomes mine. I feel him rubbing his hardness in the dampness between my legs a moment before his erection fills me, his movements controlled. Gentle.

I lay my hand against his chest, where the muscles are flexing beneath his taut skin.

"Are you okay?" Kellan's voice against my mouth makes me smile.

"I've never been better."

Which is a lie. I was better when he wasn't in my life. But back then, I didn't know what I was missing.

I didn't know that the way he'd touch me would change my world.

My legs lock at his back, pulling him deeper inside me. His shaft is filling me, rendering me breathless. He begins to move again and his thumb rubs that one spot that intensifies the fire within.

His hands grab my waist to direct me, and I embrace his cadence. The first burn is gone, replaced by waves of intensity that rock my core. His thrusts deepen, his breath on my mouth hot and heavy. The pressure inside me is growing, racing through my veins.

The light of the sun slowly fades behind my closed lids, and my moans become choked—lost—as the pleasure he causes me rides up to new heights.

His name is on my lips as I come with our mouths locked in a kiss. I can feel him stirring inside me a moment before he finds his own release.

Afterwards, we lay still. Kellan's eyes are shut, his

ragged breathing slowly coming down. I watch him, enchanted and strangely nostalgic.

This is it.

I got what I wanted the first time I set my eyes upon him. A night with him. Only, our night together turned into a week and more moments that I ever dreamed of.

And nowhere near enough.

Even though we're barely inches away, I know Kellan's beyond my reach.

His arms pull me close, until my head rests in the hollow of his shoulder. With the sun on my face, I close my eyes, enjoying the moment together, not knowing how many more we might have left.

CHAPTER
TWENTY-SIX

A FEW MINUTES later, after I've come down from my orgasm, the world seems a little less surreal. Beautiful with the lake around us, but still less surreal. We're not the only people in the world, but for a few moments, it sure felt like it.

"I'll need to take care of some business. Will you be okay on your own?" Kellan says and disentangles himself from our embrace. I don't look at him getting dressed while I squeeze into my own clothes.

"Sure," I say, infusing as much casualness into my voice as I can muster. "When will you be back?"

"Probably after the weekend."

My heart drops.

Today is Friday. He'll return on Monday, and I'm

leaving tomorrow. Our little fuck didn't mean anything. He made that clear right from the beginning. What I didn't expect was for him to want to leave so abruptly.

A little warning would have been nice.

"So... I won't see you again, will I?" I ask breathlessly.

He says nothing, but he doesn't have to.

What is there to say?

A wave of disappointment—fast and all-consuming—sweeps through me, and a strange pang of pain settles in my chest.

That's it.

The end of my vacation.

The end of us.

We're not going to spend the last night together. Nor the day after.

I'll leave and I'll go back to my boring, old life, and he'll remain the mystery he is. We'll both move on. I didn't expect it to be over so soon, and yet it is.

"Feel free to stay as long as you want. When you're ready to leave, just leave the keys under the flowerpot on the porch," Kellan continues, oblivious to my thoughts. It seems so easy for him, as if he's talking about a short trip, not the fact that he won't ever see me again. "The mechanic finished all repairs on your car early this morning. You have new headlights, the engine's running, and he's even done a paint job. You'll get back home safely."

He's paying me off.

I can't believe it.

What he's done is so much worse than throwing a pity check at me.

I swallow the lump in my throat.

"You didn't have to," I say, my voice strangely choked.

He shrugs. "I wanted to. It's the least I can do after bumping your car."

God.

That feels like an eternity ago.

"Mandy should be back tomorrow, right?" Kellan asks, breaking the awkward silence.

"Yeah. I'll be busy packing up tonight." I let out a forced laugh, the effort making my chest hurt. Everything makes me hurt. My entire body feels like a truck slammed into it. "She has so much stuff, and because her suitcase was too small, she crammed it all in mine."

His hands trail around my waist, and there's another short, awkward silence. "I enjoyed my time with you very much."

His words sound so final, detached and resolute.

He might as well have said, "I enjoyed fucking you," and it would have made no difference.

"So did I," I whisper and look up to meet his questioning gaze. I know I shouldn't ask, and yet I have to know. "Will you visit me in New York?"

He regards me, hesitating. "I don't think I'll leave Montana for a while, but when I do, I'll make sure you're the first on my list."

His list.

Yeah, the stupid list of women he's fucked and wouldn't mind a second helping of.

My eyes feel moist. I break off his embrace and avert my gaze so that he won't see the turmoil that I'm sure is written across my face.

I've always hated saying goodbye. It feels too final, too heavy. But I knew this day would come after all. Kellan never made a secret out of it. I just didn't expect it so soon. I just never expected that I'd enjoy my time with him so much.

Kellan's lips brush my neck, and as he kisses me, he whispers against my skin, "I'll see you soon."

I want to believe him, but I can't because I'm not stupid. All men say the same thing to make leaving easier. Maybe they believe it'll soften the blow that it's over.

Or maybe they're just liars and would rather feed

a woman's hope than deal with the drama that often accompanies honesty.

Well, there won't be any drama.

"Yeah." My body goes rigid as I force a cold smile to my lips. "We'll stay in touch."

I close my eyes. He kisses my cheek before he turns and leaves. I don't follow him back to the house. Instead, I lie down and close my eyes, barely able to hold back the tears I cannot allow myself to shed.

When I head back inside, the house is depressingly empty and quiet.

Kellan's gone.

Gone from my life, with no intention of coming back.

Leaving behind memories that I know will hurt for a long time.

***

"Ava!"

Mandy's screech reaches me through the fog inside my brain. I look up from washing the dishes and flinch at the pain shooting up my back. I'm so not used to working on the farm. My arms ache and my legs feel like they're about to fall off.

Kellan left last night.

I was so immersed in my work and dark thoughts that I completely forgot the time.

"In here!" I yell.

The door bursts open and Mandy's head pops in, a huge smile on her lips.

"Howdy!" Dressed in a blue shirt and brown cowboy boots, she looks like she's just stepped out of a western movie. Her hair's curled into waves, which can only mean one thing: she's found a hair stylist and shops.

"What are you doing here?" I wipe my wet hands on a towel before Mandy engulfs me in a tight hug.

"That's exactly the question I thought I'd hear." Mandy laughs and lets go of me. "I can tell you guys had a great time and didn't miss me one bit."

"No, I'm just surprised. I didn't expect you back so early. What happened?"

"Plans change," she says and her cheeks flush.

There's definitely reason to press her for details, but I don't get a chance because her gaze falls on the dishes in the sink. "What are you doing?"

"House chores."

"You hardly ever do chores." She makes it sound like I've just committed a major crime. "You must really love the guy."

I take a deep, shaky breath. "I don't—"

"Hmm." As though she doesn't believe me, she cuts me off and waves her hand. "Come on, let's get you dressed."

I look down at myself. Last time I checked, I *wasn't* naked. Maybe my brain switched off and I forgot to put on some pants?

"I mean something nice and sexy," Mandy says, as though reading my thoughts. "And hurry up. We need to leave."

"Why?" I eye her, amused. "What's going on? Is someone chasing you?"

"No." She rolls her eyes, grinning. "I have good news and good news. Which one do you want to hear first?"

I close my eyes and groan inwardly. "Please don't tell me it's about the concert."

"It is." Mandy lets out an excited squeal. "Mile High are performing tonight." She jumps up and down like a child. "God. I'm so excited."

"That part's obvious. What's the other good news?"

"I thought you'd never ask." She pauses for effect. "Get this. We got first-class tickets. The best of the best view."

"Swell." I fight the urge to bail. "How do you

know?"

"As soon as Josh drove me to Helena, I called the concert venue. Josh introduced me to someone who met someone who knows someone who's friends with someone—"

"Get to the point," I cut her off.

"And that someone knows where they're staying." She wiggles her eyebrows at me.

I frown because I really can't follow. "Who?"

"Mile High."

Oh, God.

"Please don't tell me you're planning on stalking them," I say. "For God's sake, you're a lawyer."

"No," she says in that defensive tone of hers that tells me she's guilty as charged. "I'm talking about knocking on their door and asking for an autograph after the concert. What's the harm?"

I stare at her. "What's the harm? Mandy, you sound like a frigging groupie."

She shrugs. "So what? They're awesome. Getting their phone number is a major accomplishment, which I intend to fulfill."

"Oh, God." I shake my head. At least she's not hell-bent on hooking up with them. But I might be wrong on that one.

"Apparently, they've been here all along." She

leans closer and lowers her voice conspiratorially. "They're keeping a low profile, you know, small venue and all."

"Ah." Now that makes sense. At some point, even the greatest egomaniac will get sick and tired of having cameras shoved in their face and screaming groupies running down their hotel room door. And the band hasn't met Mandy yet. She's as obsessive as a fan can be. I wouldn't be surprised at all if the evening ended with a restraining order.

"I still have no idea why you want to see them," I say with the enthusiasm of a grumpy turtle. "They're not even singing live. Everyone knows that."

"Because it's my opportunity to get to meet them," Mandy says. "Hello? Did you hear a word I said? Good tickets. Small venue. I know where they're staying. This is a once in a lifetime opportunity, and you're coming with me. I want to find out everything about them."

I glare at her.

Apparently, everything about those guys is a huge secret, starting with their identities and the heavy eye makeup that makes them look like a badass copycat version of Green Day.

"But first, you really need to change." Mandy takes a deep breath and lets it out slowly, her annoyance with me obvious. "They'll never invite us backstage if I'm being accompanied by—"

"The not-so-hot friend?" I raise my brows, amused.

"No. I'd never say that." She looks appalled. "I was going to say 'frumpy'."

"Frumpy? As in dowdy, dull, homely?" I laugh out loud and almost choke on my laughter at the mortified expression on her face.

"I didn't mean—"

Oh, I'm going to hold this one against her for the rest of her life. She's always excelled at putting her foot in her mouth. "I know. Just stop."

"Are you going to make an effort?" She squeezes my hand imploringly. "Please. Just once in your life show a little bit of enthusiasm for Mile High, even if it's fake. Please."

"Gee, I didn't realize this means so much to you." I heave an exaggerated sigh. "Fine. I'll see what I can do."

"And you'll pretend you're a fan?"

"Now you're pushing it."

"Thanks." She ignores my annoyed look as she heads for the door, then stops as soon as she's reached it. "By the way, where's our hot host?"

"Who?"

"Um. The guy you fucked all week."

How does she even know that?

"If you're talking about Kellan, he left," I remark dryly. "He said something about business."

"Oh." She purses her lips and eyes me for a moment. "You'll have to tell me everything...after the gig, of course."

"Of course," I mumble.

CHAPTER
TWENTY-SEVEN

WHEN I MAKE my way downstairs, I find Mandy in the kitchen, head lowered over a cup of coffee and the magazine in her hands. From the doorway, I have a few seconds to take in her outfit her before she notices me. She's wearing a short leather skirt, high-heel boots that almost reach her knees, and a top that leaves very little to the imagination. I'm dressed in jeans, an off-shoulder top that isn't too snug, and flat boots. I don't know how long gigs usually last, but I'm pretty sure I won't get blisters, which is my top priority.

"Ready?" I ask with more enthusiasm than I actually feel.

Mandy turns and her gaze swipes over me. Her

thoughts are visible in the frown across her forehead, and she opens her mouth before I can stop her. "That's your version of sexy?"

"It's my version of being interested enough to listen. God. You just can't help yourself."

Her shoulders are tense with something.

"What's wrong?"

She hesitates, her back still turned on me. "I just—"

She sniffles.

"Mandy? Oh, my God." I wrap my arm around her shoulder and pull her in a hug. "Are you crying?"

She shakes her head even though two tears are trickling down her cheek.

"Is something wrong? Are you okay?"

Now I'm worried sick. Something's wrong with her, I just know it.

"It's happening," Mandy whispers.

"What's happening?" I frown.

Is a hurricane hitting Montana after all and we're going to die?

"Mile High," she speaks between sniffles. "I've been trying to get tickets for ages, but they were always sold out. Tonight we're finally going to see them. I cannot believe it's *that* day."

Oh. My. God.

I stare at her, dumbfounded. She must have gone ape-shit crazy because no grown-up woman in her right mind would cry at the prospect of seeing some dudes wail into a microphone, no matter how talented they are. I mean, seriously, that's so Europe in the Dark Ages, when people had no television and the Internet to entertain them.

"God, you scared me. I thought you were sick or something." I slap her shoulder playfully. "You're a lawyer, for fuck's sake. You're clever and educated. Get a grip, or you're going alone."

"Thank you." She smiles and nods.

I stare at her, expecting more drama. When none comes, I heave a sigh.

"Don't mention it. You know I'll always be here to talk some sense into you. That's what friends are for," I say and let go of her.

"No. Thank you for winning the tickets," Mandy says. "Now, if you could get changed..."

I shake my head in disbelief, hold up a hand, annoyed, and leave the kitchen, not in the least interested if she's following.

"What did I say?" Mandy calls after me.

"Where do I even start?" I yell back. "The answer is no. I won't be bullied into wearing a slutty outfit just because you want to meet the band."

I sling my handbag over my shoulder and grab my jacket. I most certainly won't be freezing my ass off out there, not even for the likes of Mile High.

The clicking sound of heels echoes down the hall a moment before Mandy reaches me.

I peer down at her shoes doubtfully. The heels are so high, at some point, I know, her feet will hurt so much she'll either want to swap or I'll have to carry her. Usually, I end up giving her my shoes. But today I'll let her pay the price of beauty just because she's inflicting this kind of torture upon me.

"Where's this gig?" I ask.

"Josh knows. He's driving us."

As if on cue, a car honks outside.

"Josh? Your most recent conquest?" I can't help but ask.

"Yes. So?" Mandy shoots me a frown.

"What about my car?"

"We'll get it after the gig."

"I can't believe you asked him to trudge along." I brush my hair out of my eyes, barely able to contain my laughter. "He'll be so into you when you start squealing in his ear."

"I don't squeal."

"You so do when Mile High's on."

"So what?" She glares at me. "He told me he's a

fan himself."

God, no!

Not another fan.

I'd rather be stuck with a zombie and the danger of being eaten alive than with a complete snooze fest of a rendition of Mile High's lyrics.

I open the door and head out to the waiting pickup truck, settling in the back seat. Mandy takes the front seat a few moments later, ignoring me as she leans into Josh to place a soft kiss on his cheek.

It's so obvious they have a fling, I turn away to give them privacy.

"Are you ladies excited?" Josh asks.

"Hell, yeah." Mandy giggles.

"Hell, no," I mumble.

Josh laughs and meets my gaze in the rearview mirror. His dark blue eyes shimmer with unspoken understanding. Or maybe that's what I want to see in them because they're warm and friendly and the complete opposite of Kellan's, with his brooding looks and evasiveness. Josh's hand travels to touch Mandy's arm as he's saying something to her. I turn away again, feeling just a little bit sorry for myself at the idea she's found someone so nice and easygoing while I seem to have caught the attention of Mr. Complicated-I-don't-do-relationships-aloof.

"Josh, do we have any plans after the gig?" Mandy asks.

"I have a surprise in store for you." He winks at her.

"Now we're talking," Mandy says.

Let me guess!

It involves his bedroom and handcuffs, which I'm sure he has stacked somewhere in there. All guys do.

"Thanks for driving us," Mandy says.

He smiles at her for a second before his gaze focuses back on the dark street. "Anything for you."

I lean back against the seat and try to blend in with the upholstery to give them privacy.

But in secret, I wish I was back home—my real home in NYC—with a bowl of popcorn or double fudge ice cream, watching a good movie while downing an entire bottle of wine.

Get drunk.

Anything to help me forget the taste of his lips on mine. Forget the heady scent of his aftershave and the sound of his laughter. Stop the echo of his name inside my mind and all the silly wishes and hopes that he's thinking of me the way I'm thinking of him.

I'm losing myself. That's not something I envisioned happening because I know that soon enough, maybe even today, maybe tomorrow, he'll be chasing the next girl. Someone who won't be me.

I'll become a blurred memory.

CHAPTER TWENTY-EIGHT

WE DRIVE FOR at least half an hour before I spy the huge tent adorned by hundreds of lights that sparkle like tiny fireflies in the evening sky. We seem to be in the middle of a field. There are countless cars parked to either side, and people are gathered in groups, chatting excitedly while they're waiting.

"What's everybody waiting for?" I ask and crane my neck to get a better look at what's happening around us.

"The customary pat down." Josh pulls the truck into an empty spot and points at a police officer, who's standing near what I assume is the entrance. I don't understand what he's doing there, until he moves aside. That's when I see the two huge, beefy guys looking into every purse and patting down everyone before they get a wristband and are ushered inside.

"There isn't much to pat," I say, eyeing the short skirts and snug tank tops that leave little to the imagination. Some have skipped the tank top part altogether and have gone straight for the underwear look.

"I've never seen so many women gathered in one place, unless there's a sale," Mandy says.

"That's Mile High," Josh says, as though that explains everything.

We exit the car, and Josh leads us around the tent toward a closed-off area with two security guys blocking the way. I suspect this is the private entrance for the artists. The guys' expressions are so grim I wouldn't be surprised to find them ready to break a few bones if we come too close.

"You can't be here," one of the guys says.

"Josh Boyd," Josh says. "The ladies are with me."

"Of course, Mr. Boyd," the other one says and hands us three guest passes. I peer down, and to my surprise, find my name on it.

Without so much as a blink, the security guy opens the door. I peer at Josh, who just shrugs and ushers me inside.

"We're backstage," Mandy whispers. "I can't believe it."

Me neither.

And why are our names on the passes?

"Mandy," I whisper. "How did they know our names?"

She shrugs. "You won tickets, didn't you?"

"Yes, but as you probably noticed, they're still in my handbag." I point to Josh. "What did you tell him?"

"Let's talk later, okay? Enjoy this."

"Fine." In spite of my repulsion for anything Mile High stands for, a tiny bit of excitement runs through me. From where we're standing, we can see the entire stage. Roadies are rushing past us, setting up various pieces of music equipment, while a band is tuning up, completely oblivious to the commotion around them. To the far end, people are flooding in and the first squeals of excitement carry over.

"The soundcheck's almost over. They're opening for Mile High," Mandy says, pointing to the guys on the stage.

Even though this is strangely exhilarating, I feel like an impostor. "I don't think we should be here."

"Relax," Josh says. "We're guests. Of course we're supposed to be here. You guys want anything to drink?" He points at a table with various refreshments.

I shake my head as a sign that I don't want anything. "How are we guests? We only won tickets."

Josh helps himself to a chilled can of soda and hands one to Mandy. "I know someone who knows someone," he says matter-of-factly.

"Told you." Mandy shoots me a warning look. "And we're not going to be ungrateful brats, are we, Ava?"

"Of course not," I mumble.

The place begins to fill with people. Spotlights begin to go off, bathing the entire place in a dim glow. The first lights of cameras and smartphones flash all around us.

"Come on. I think they're getting started," Josh says.

We follow him down the stairs to a lower level, where several security guys are standing guard, all sporting the same intimidating expression. We take our place in front of the barriers just in time before the opening act starts the show.

The crowd goes wild as the lights go on. It's all so bright I think I need sunglasses.

"TAYLOR! TAYLOR! TAYLOR!"

"Taylor, I'll give you a BJ."

"Take me, Taylor. Take me."

"K. TAYLOR! I LOVE YOU!"

I've never heard so much shrieking in my life.

I've never seen so many cameras flashing.

And then Mile High hits the stage, and the crowd erupts in cheers. Even Mandy's shrieking in my ears.

Damn. I wish I had thought of packing some earplugs before I go deaf.

I stare at the four guys in snug blue jeans and black T-shirts. Their faces are painted white; black traces their eyes; their features are hidden behind beautiful carnival masks that build a dramatic contrast to the simulated fire burning in huge baskets scattered across the stage. I have to admit that they look like living art, which I'm sure is the image they've been going for.

The guitarist strums the guitar in what I recognize as a slow, modern rock version of Mozart's Magic Flute, while the vocalist stands rooted to the spot, head lowered over the mic, his dark hair swaying in a simulated breeze.

He's hot.

Mandy got that part right.

He's *really* hot. Even though the moving shadows cast by the fires make it hard to see much of him, I can tell by his muscular body.

With the mask, he's like a fantasy.

No wonder women all over the world are going bat-shit crazy over him.

They probably think he lives up to their fantasies even without the mask.

"I wonder what would happen if he took it off, you know, the mask, the makeup, " I say, amused, unable to keep back a snort. "He's probably some old dude with a good body and nothing else going for him."

A guy's walking past, handing out drinks to the VIP guests, AKA us.

"He isn't that old," Josh shouts and passes me a Pepsi can.

"How can you tell?" I ask.

"I just know."

"They always play some part of the Magic Flute at the beginning of each gig," Mandy shouts. "It's their anthem or something."

I don't want to point out that Mozart wrote it because, while I'm not a fan of classical music, the guitarist really rocks it.

A few moments later, the music fades in the background, and the vocalist looks up, and the shrieking starts again.

"That's K. Taylor," Mandy shouts. Apparently,

she's taken on the role of narrator tonight.

"Thanks. I figured that part out," I say and go about opening my can and taking a long sip, hoping it's not spiked.

My nerves are so frazzled from all the shouting and screaming, I can barely even hear Mandy. I peer around us. Almost everyone's wearing fan merchandise. There are countless banners with things like 'Taylor No 1 girl' or 'This girl has Taylor Fever.'

Some messages are quite rude and graphic. Apparently, plenty of people want K. Taylor's baby. Or to take care of his sexual needs.

My attention flips back to the stage as the vocalist looks up from his microphone. A shiver runs down my spine.

He *is* frigging hot.

But there is no way I'd ever go for a guy in a mask. It's just one of those creepy things you usually see in a movie adaptation of a Stephen King novel.

"Hey, guys," the vocalist says into the microphone, his voice deep and sexy. "Thanks for being here tonight. It means a lot to us. You've probably been wondering why we're playing such a small venue. Montana is where it all started. It's a place that'll always be in our hearts. It's a place of new beginnings, which is why I'm dedicating our newest song, Behind This Shell, to a very special lady. Babe, come on up."

Oh, God.

My body freezes, and not because of his words.

I know that voice.

I've heard it whispering into my ear. I've felt it across my skin.

But it can't possibly be.

The singer's gaze sweeps over the front row and settles on us.

"You." He points a long index finger, beckoning me over. "Come on up."

I'm so shocked I spill my drink over my top, not even feeling it.

I stare at him, speechless, feeling the blood draining from my body, every drop of it, and yet my heart continues to race to reach what I'd guess would be a new record in the Guinness Book of Records. I've never felt so faint in my life, so frozen and surreal, as if I'm in a dream.

Holy shit!

He's looking at me.

He's talking to me.

"Ava," Mandy hisses.

"What?" I turn to her, confused.

"I think he means you." Even Mandy sounds awestruck. I notice she's awfully pale.

"She can't believe her luck," the guitarist says, which earns him laughter from the audience.

"Come on, people," the vocalist says. "Give this city girl a cheer before she decides to run and misses this awesome new song."

City girl.

Oh. My. God.

His name is K. Taylor.

The K can't possibly stand for Kellan, can it?

It's about time I visited my therapist and asked for a mental health check because there's no way...no way...that's Kellan up there.

I mean, I've bitched about this band. Not only to Mandy, but to *him*.

I must have it all wrong.

It's probably the mask that's having this effect on me. Some weird fantasy fetish to which no woman's immune—not even me.

People are turning to stare at me...their eyes are countless daggers that pierce my back.

"Up you go, Ava," Josh says, grinning, and pushes me forward toward one of the security guys, who takes it from there. With his hand clamped around my upper arm, I have no choice but to climb the few stairs up.

The crowd shrieks, intermingled with a few boos here and there.

"TAYLOR! TAYLOR!"

I barely register them though. All I hear is the pulse pounding in my ears. I'm so certain I'm going to die because no heart can pump so fast and not explode from the sheer effort.

The vocalist's hand wraps around mine, his fingers like butterfly wings against my skin. I look down and then up into his eyes. Suddenly, the lights fall on us, illuminating his face, his beautiful green eyes.

And in that moment, I know.

It's him.

Good heaven.

Those are the same green eyes.

The same devilish grin.

The same broad shoulders I grabbed onto while he pounded into me, taking me to pleasure heaven.

The same narrow hips, hard muscles, and delicious lips.

"Holy crap," I whisper.

My mouth is dry, my heartbeat strangely elated. I don't know what to make of this, and yet I know.

It's Kellan.

K. Taylor is Kellan Boyd—the guy I've been getting down and dirty with.

The guy I told I hated Mile High.

The mask makes it impossible to recognize him, and yet I know.

My legs threaten to buckle beneath me.

"Hello, City Girl." He smiles at me. And then he turns to the crowd, holding my hand, and I realize what he's about to do. But it's too late to run. I've never felt so exposed in my life. Everyone seems to be scrutinizing me, and there's a stain on my shirt.

The spotlights above us go off and on, and the background behind us changes to one showing city lights.

The guitarist strums the guitar, and the percussion joins in.

I stare into Kellan's eyes as he lifts the mic to his gorgeous lips and begins to sing, the voice beautiful, raw and sexy, each verse sending shivers down my spine as I just stand there, mesmerized—enthralled by the words and his beautiful voice.

You're the reason I stay
You're the reason I wait
Behind this shell, you set me free
In your smile, I come undone

You become a mystery
To me

You twist and tear this life apart
These walls that were there from the start
You cast a light into the night
You break it up, this breathless heart
Under the starry night, I didn't mean to fall
Time passes by and now you're gone
You become a mystery
To me

This man of yours is going down
This man of yours is rising up
Behind this shell, there's only you
Life's looking up, but I'm going down
In the webs of love, in the traps of life
One day I'll get caught
There is no doubt
But if I fall, I want to fall
With you

I hold my breath as Kellan lets go off my hand and walks around me until he's standing behind my back, his lips and the microphone so close, my skin begins to prickle.

I'm drowning in the ocean of your body
I'm lost in the beating of your heart
I'm falling as you laugh
And yet, you walk away from me
You walk away from me
Under the starry night
You walk away from me

Days have passed
Soon the weeks will turn into years
I'll always remember you with silent tears
With a prayer on my lips that I'll see you again
Kiss your lips, hold you tight
Coz you're the one I want to know
You're the one I don't want gone

The percussion takes center stage, and the melody changes. My heart slams in my chest. The sudden change in rhythm is more truculent, and it's throwing me off.

Yoooou said...
I'm not interested in you
Not now. Not ever
But I know you're lying

A liar spots a liar....
Behind this shell, you set me free

Sheeeeee said...
I'm not interested in you
Not now. Not ever.
But I know she's lying
A liar spots a liar....
Behind this shell, she sets me free

Yoooou said...
I'm not interested in you
Not now. Not ever
I know you're lying
A liar spots a liar
Behind this shell, you set me free

Sheeeeee said...
I'm not interested in you
Not now. Not ever
But I know she's lying
A liar spots a liar
A liar spots a liar
Behind this shell, she sets me free

As Kellan continues to sing the last line, the

crowd chimes in. I don't know when the song was released, but he must have sung it before because people know the lyrics; they're familiar with the rhythm. He stops singing, but the guitarist continues to play.

The crowd starts to chant, "TAYLOR! TAYLOR! TAYLOR!"

But instead of turning to the crowd, he turns to me and cocks a sexy eyebrow.

A smile tugs at his lips. And then he leans forward and clasps my chin between his fingers as he kisses me on the lips in front of the audience.

My breath hitches.

My head's swirling.

My heart's pounding.

At some point, the song ends. Kellan lets go of me and says something into the microphone. But I can't make out his words. It's like the world around us has dissolved into nothingness. From the periphery of my mind, I know that a security guy is ushering me back to my spot, while all I can do is focus on making it down the stage without taking a tumble.

I feel Mandy's shock a moment before she whispers in my ear, "What the hell, Ava? Why didn't you tell me?"

I open my mouth to explain that I had no idea,

but the words remain trapped on my tongue.

I need to get away.

Numb from the shock, I take off, squeezing through the crowd, until I've reached the back of the tent. I need the distance and for Mandy to stop her questions.

The band continues their set. I get an hour of watching him. Of listening to his magnificent voice while he sings one song after another. An hour during which my shock is slowly subsiding, making room for a throbbing sense of suspicion and anger.

Once or twice, I think I see his eyes roaming over the crowd, probably in search of me, but I can't be sure. I hide in the shadows nonetheless, out of his view. I don't want him to call me up there again.

A cowboy turned rock star!

I shake my head.

What. The. Hell.

And I was stupid enough to fall for him.

That was about the worst move I could have made in my life.

CHAPTER
TWENTY-NINE

"ARE YOU OKAY?" Mandy asks for the umpteenth time, her concern growing with each second that passes. When I nod, she whispers, "You didn't know, did you?"

I shake my head and follow Josh to his truck.

I don't want to make a big fuss out of the fact that Kellan's a rock star but—

Holy shit!

He's a rock star.

I still can't believe it.

That's why he was so secretive. He probably thought I might sell his story to the tabloids.

What's wrong with me?

Why can't I show enthusiasm for the fact that the

cowboy I met is a famous rock star?

Josh says something about an after party, when all I want is to lock myself inside my bedroom and Google the life out of Mile High.

There must have been some indication, some clue, and I was too blind to catch it. But I know better than to believe that. I just wasn't interested. I might never be.

I blame my parents and their crazy obsession with the orchestra. They've ruined music for me, and now I just can't be like any normal woman and squeal and wear fan T-shirts.

"Please take me home," I say, my voice shaky.

"I've been instructed not to do that," Josh replies.

I don't need to ask who ordered that. "I'm not feeling very well."

Mandy shoots me a concerned look.

"In spite of what he's doing, he's a good guy, Ava," Josh says.

"I never doubted that," I lie.

"He likes you. That's why he went through all the trouble to arrange you winning the tickets."

My head snaps to him. "What?"

"Sorry. What was I thinking?" He slaps his forehead. "I should never have mentioned it. Let's forget what I just said." His mouth clamps shut. In the rearview mirror, I see his expression darkening, like he's already said too much.

"It's okay. You can tell me," I say, my voice faint.

He takes a sharp breath. "Look, I don't know what's happening between you two, but I can tell you he's never been like this. He's never done this for any woman. I think you need to talk. Just listen to him, and then make up your mind. Please."

"Listen to what?" I stare at Josh's back, waiting for him to elaborate. He just shrugs and keeps quiet.

Mandy's eyes are big and mirror my countless questions. But even she remains silent as Josh stops the truck. He gets out of the car, and she turns to me, whispering, "Look, I had no idea."

I glare at her. "How could you not know? You've been a fan for ages."

'Probably the biggest of them,' I want to add, but don't.

"They never take off the masks."

"What about in interviews?" I ask incredulously.

"They wear heavy makeup," Mandy says. "Besides, I don't follow their every move. I'm not obsessed with them."

"Still." I shake my head. "You should have recognized the voice." I'm so mad at Mandy. It's all her fault that we landed at Kellan's door.

Josh opens the door for us, waiting for me to get out. I glance out of the window and realize we're at the same bar we visited more than a week ago, surrounded by hundreds of girls and women, all waiting to get in.

My heart lurches.

Huge, angry bouncers are guarding the door.

"Are you coming?" Mandy asks.

I shake my head again. "I don't think that's a good idea."

"He's inside, waiting for you," Josh says. When I make no move to exit, he leans against the car, his dark expression betraying his determination. "Look, I promised him to bring you here. Can you just do me a favor and see him?"

I let out a sigh, then get out of the car. "Fine, but you owe me."

Just like before, Josh mentioning his name grants us instant entry. The bar is full with what I assume are mostly locals. I spy Kellan sitting with three other guys at a table near the back, his face turned to overlook the entrance. The mask and makeup are gone. The man I see is both familiar and a stranger to me.

My heart does a summersault. I realize it's been doing that ever since I met him.

But that can't be. Summersaults remind me of stories of people falling in love and happy endings. Before he left, I knew I was about to fall for him. Surely, it hasn't happened already.

My legs are frozen to the spot as I realize I loved my ex, and it hurt like hell when he cheated on me. But it was different.

Summersaults are new to me. I never had them before Kellan.

I can't be in love with him.

Right?

I turn on my heels, ready to bolt out the door, when Josh steps behind me, blocking my way.

"They're over there," he says. His hand goes around my upper arm to guide me, but I know he just wants to make sure I'm not trying to get away.

Which is the plan.

I wish I could run away from the man I thought was only a nightclub owner. And then only a cowboy.

I have all of three seconds before Kellan's sweeping gaze meets mine, and he stands a moment before we reach him.

"You came." He sounds surprised. I look into his impossibly green eyes. He leans into me, and his lips brush my cheek. He smells faintly of aftershave and warmth. A stunning smile tugs at his lips, but there's a strange glint in his eyes. As though he's nervous. As though he cares what I might think about him now that I know who he is.

I want to lean into him and tell him that I wish he weren't who he is because it matters to me.

I also want to tell him that I had no choice but to come here, whether I wanted to see him or not. It was either this or jump out of a moving car while praying I wouldn't break a few bones in the process.

I want to ask him the one question that's been pestering me. *Why didn't you tell me?*

But my mouth remains shut, all those unspoken words trapped inside my chest.

"You want anything to drink?" Kellan pulls up a chair and points at the countless bottles on the table.

I shake my head in response.

While I'm all for a little liquid courage in situations like these, I need to keep my head clear.

He sighs and sits down, his leg brushing mine. "These are my band mates, Casper, Derrick, and Rock. Guys, this is Ava."

I nod at the three pairs of eyes staring at me. They look like nice guys, maybe a bit worse for wear, but I guess that's what the rock star lifestyle does to you.

"Ava, huh?" Rock says. I can almost see the wheels of his mind working. His blue eyes seem slightly glossed over; his movements are a little bit slow. "*That* Ava?"

And then it dawns on me.

He's high on something.

Of course he is.

Most musicians are. My parents thought I'd follow in their footsteps and always warned me of the dangers of getting involved with someone in the music industry.

"Kellan made us play this gig just for you," Derrick says. "I hope you know how to thank him tonight."

His band mates begin to guffaw.

I peer at Kellan, who's watching me intently, analyzing my every move.

"The women just soak it up, huh?" Derrick says to Rock. "Remember that chick, Kellan's last girl? She kept stalking him."

The words sting. They only confirm that I was just another conquest in a long list of them. That I was only a good fuck.

Isn't that what he called me?

"I'm sorry. I should go." I get up and turn, dashing past tables, through the door, heedless of the people rushing to get out of my way, until I'm outside.

CHAPTER THIRTY

ABOVE ME, THE moon and billions of stars are shining, their presence my only company as I head down the dark road. I'm walking fast, feet pounding, trying hard not to think or analyze the last week of my life.

I need the solitude and the detachment to keep myself from going crazy.

I don't ever do crazy. I forbid myself from doing it.

It happened once, and it made me obsessive. It made me love and swear off relationships for good.

Fucking a rock star with all the fans, the drama, and the emotional entanglements that come with it—that's a whole new level of crazy.

It tops all the charts.

A cold gust of wind seeps through my clothes, sending a shudder through me. I wrap my jacket tighter around me, cursing the fact that Josh was nowhere to be found when I left the bar. I would have liked him to drive me to Kellan's place to get my car, but I couldn't wait for him. I couldn't ask around, go looking for him. The chance of bumping into Kellan was too great.

It was either risk having to face Kellan again or head back without Josh driving me.

I chose to walk.

Now, I'm freezing my butt off.

I'm far past the point where I even care if Mandy's joining me. She'll be fine with Josh. I know she will. She made it pretty clear when she left me alone with Kellan on his ranch.

It's all her fault.

If it weren't for Mandy, I wouldn't have to deal with my emotions.

If it were not for her, I would have sold the tickets and never met someone like Kellan. Someone so sexy, he's every woman's dream.

But that's exactly what he is.

A dream.

Not realistic.

The sooner I grasp the facts the better, before my

stupid heart wants to confess that I have fallen in love with him.

Somewhere in the distance, a car's approaching. I turn and see the headlights. For a moment, I consider signaling it to hitchhike to Kellan's place, then realize it's Kellan's truck.

Even though I know that I'm being ridiculous, I turn my back to it and hasten my steps.

The truck pulls up next to me, and the window rolls down.

"Ava?"

I continue walking, mumbling, "Leave me alone."

The truck speeds up, coming to a halt a few yards down the road. Leaving the engine running, Kellan jumps out and slams the door shut. I try to ignore him as he plants himself in front of me, until I have no choice but to look up into his face.

"What are you doing? You cannot walk out here all alone." His expression is a mixture of worry and anger.

"I'm an adult."

"And I'm your host, and I say you can't be here alone."

I shrug. "Why not? You said it was safe. What changed your mind?"

"I wasn't talking about the people, Ava. We have

wild animals, and they can be dangerous." He sighs. "Look. I know you're pissed."

"Pissed?" I scoff and stare at him, pointing to my face. "Does my face look pissed? I'm hurt, Kellan. Disappointed. You told me you wouldn't return before the weekend. I thought that was our goodbye. A really crappy one, by the way. And then I find out that the sole reason I'm here is because you arranged for me to win tickets." My anger's choking me, but I don't care. I have so much to say to him. "The past week, I told you everything about my life, and you barely fed me morsels of information about yours. You kept the fact that you're a famous rock star to yourself. How is that fair?"

"I know how that sounds."

"You do?" I ask, doubting it. "Why didn't you tell me?"

He hesitates. "I wasn't sure you'd understand."

I shake my head. "Of course. What else?" I move past him to resume walking, when his hand grips my upper arm to stop me.

"I mean it," Kellan says. "I thought you wouldn't understand."

"Why wouldn't I understand? It's not like you have to be embarrassed for your job." I try to look up into his eyes, which isn't possible. He's standing so close, I have to tilt my head back, and it hurts. "Fuck, everyone would want to be in your shoes."

"Exactly. That's why I kept it from you."

"I don't understand." I frown at him. "You thought I'd be jealous? That I might want to be a rock star?"

The assumption is so ridiculous, I find myself laughing.

"No, Ava," he says sharply, "I thought you would judge me."

"Why would I judge you?"

"Are you kidding me?" He pauses, hesitating, as though what he has to say is hard for him. "People change when they find out I'm K. Taylor. They go crazy, especially once they realize I have money. I can't risk telling someone I don't trust who I am, out of fear that they might go to the papers and seek their own five minutes of fame. People think because they know my name and read made-up stories about me, that they know me. They don't." He grimaces, and his expression contorts into one of disgust. From up close, in the bright lights of his truck, I can see every line on his face. The tiredness. The frustration. "You have absolutely no idea what fame does to people or how far they'd go to get it. I've reached a point where I can't trust anyone. It has nothing to do with you. I just can't trust people. Too many have betrayed my trust and invaded my privacy. The only people I can trust are the ones I grew up with, and they are here in this town. My brothers. A few close friends. Sharon."

That's not a lot.

I'm sorry for him.

At last, I draw a deep breath and let it out slowly before I say, "You still could have tried me. I would have understood."

"Yeah." He cringes. "Except you hate Mile High, and you're a journalist. That's a great combination."

"I don't hate Mile High," I protest weakly, ignoring the latter part.

"You said you did. Do you want me to reiterate your exact words?" He lets go off my arm. "You called us a boring, over the top, overrated, untalented bunch of idiots."

I did?

I cringe at my choice of words. "I'm sorry. I might have said all of that, and I admit it's horrible. The truth is, I think you have an amazing voice. I do. But I never really listened to any of your songs. My parents made me biased toward the music business and anything commercial. Toward music in general. But just because I'm not a fan doesn't mean I hate the band. I just didn't care to give you guys a try. That's all. And I'll be honest with you, just because you're the lead singer doesn't mean I'll change my opinion about what the music industry stands for." The words are out before I can stop them. I can feel the offense in the air, and I couldn't blame him if he turned around and left without a look back.

I expect Kellan to unleash his annoyance with me, but he just laughs.

"I know, and I would never expect you to," he says. "Look, it's hard for me, too."

I frown at his words. "What's hard for you?"

"To like the business. To be excited about it. I hate my job."

Unsure whether I've heard him right, I stare at him. "I don't understand. I thought it was your dream. You and your brothers had a band."

"There's a difference between a hobby and doing it for fun, and a job, which basically forces you to sell your soul and kills any creativity," Kellan says. "Now don't get me wrong. I'm grateful for what I've accomplished, but this job, this lifestyle—" he shakes his head "—it didn't turn out like I expected. I still enjoy making music. I love writing songs, but in the end, the label decides which songs are recorded. Most of them aren't even mine."

I remain quiet as he continues, "The pressure. The fame. The constant traveling. Being stuck on a tour bus. Not able to sing my own songs or play my own music. It gets to be too much. I kind of realized that being famous and under the wings of a huge record label isn't how I envisioned my life. My own songs being buried just because they wouldn't appeal to thirteen-year-old girls sucks." He sighs. I sense more is coming, so I remain silent out of fear that pushing him to open up might have the opposite effect. "Look, there's no denying that I love singing and playing the guitar, but I don't want to do it professionally. Everything you saw up there, on that stage...that's not me. Not the real me anyway. It never was. I just stumbled into it. Ask my brothers, and they'll tell you how I was discovered."

"How?" I ask softly.

"We used to play the weekend gig at the local bar. It was our way to connect with friends and family. Someone uploaded us on the Internet. One day, a scout saw us live, and he liked what he saw. The next thing I knew, I was offered the lead singer position in a band he was working on creating. I took him up on the offer, because—" he sighs again "—well, I was young, and vain, and yes, I wanted to be rich."

"That's not necessarily a bad thing," I say.

"You need to understand. My family's just ordinary folks. We weren't poor, but we weren't rich either. It was my opportunity to support my family and the people in this town. So it was a closed deal. Five days later, I moved to Los Angeles, where I met Casper, Derrick, and Rock. They became my new band members. From there, our whole image was created for us, and we were told what to do, who we could date, how we should dress. It's all part of branding and image building. We started six years ago, and now we have six studio albums, two remix albums, and I have a net worth of ninety-five million."

I almost choke on my breath, shocked that he'd just divulge that last piece of information so honestly. "Wow. That's a lot of money."

I don't know how to take that.

That *is* a lot of money. No wonder he doesn't trust anyone.

"Yeah, it is," Kellan says. "But it doesn't matter if it makes me miserable. I've come to a point where I realize there's so much more I want to do with my life, but I have so little time to explore my interests. I mean, Ryder loves his job. And Cash has built up an entire string of nightclubs from nothing and turned them into a huge success over night." He looks at me, his eyes meeting mine, and his expression softens. "That's one of the reasons I quit."

"You quit?" I ask, confused.

Did I miss something?

What did he quit?

Being a rock star?

It sounds too far-fetched, incredulous.

"I got out of my contract four weeks ago," he goes on to explain. "I'm not the lead singer of Mile High anymore."

"Four weeks ago?"

That was around the time I won the tickets.

"Today was my last gig. It all started here, and this is where it all ends."

"I don't know what to say." Wrapping my arms around my waist, I stare at him, my mind devoid of any thoughts. "Is that what you want?"

"Yes." His arms go around my waist, and he pulls me to his chest. "It's what I want."

The weak moonlight bathes his face in a golden glow. I take in his beautiful features, the soft smile on his lips, and can't help but wonder whether someone like him could really be content with the relatively boring life out here—compared to that of a rock star, of course.

"What brought on such a huge decision?"

He shrugs. "You know how people say fame and wealth change you? It's true. I grew up here; I'm rooted in this kind of life, and yet life on the road still changed me. Rock fell into a crack addiction. Derrick's eight-year marriage broke down because he couldn't keep it in his pants. And Casper's suicidal because he's gay and in love with our makeup artist, but his contract stipulates that he has to stay in the closet." Kellan shakes his head. "It changed us all for the worse. Even me. That night you met me? I was an asshole. I didn't get why you wouldn't throw yourself at my feet."

His honesty renders me speechless.

"My life consisted of groupies, parties, sex. There were drugs everywhere," Kellan continues.

"Sounds like every guy's dream come true," I mutter.

"In the beginning, it was," he says, his lips twitching but not with humor. "I grew sick of it pretty fast. However, the easy sex rubbed off on me. I thought every woman was the same."

I think of Mandy mentioning the groupies. I remember the banners at tonight's gig and can't help but feel jealous of all the women Kellan must have met—and fucked.

As if sensing my thoughts, he touches my cheek

gently. "None of them mattered, Ava."

I know that, otherwise he wouldn't be here with me, and yet—

"It's your life. What you do is none of my business," I say. His grip tightens around my waist. I can feel his gaze on me. He's looking at me. Through me. His eyes are penetrating every layer of my soul, settling somewhere deep inside me.

"You asked what made me quit," he says softly. "It was my sister's death. It was a wake-up call. If it weren't for that damn tour, I would have seen her before she died. I might have changed her mind about going back." A shaky breath escapes his lips. I reach out to touch his cheek the way he touched me a few minutes ago.

"I'm sorry."

His eyes shimmer in the weak light of the moon. "She was always worried about me. Yes, it was just a job, but if it weren't for her, I think I would have fallen into the usual drug crap. But she made sure to call whenever she could. And she always listened. I still remember the last time we Skyped. She begged me to quit."

Which couldn't have been easy. A contract with a label spans years and countless albums. It's hard to break out of, and even more so when a lot of money is involved.

"How did you get out?" I ask.

"It wasn't so hard," Kellan says, as though reading my thoughts. "The contract was for five albums. I just told them that I wouldn't do another. Countless lawyers were involved, but in the end, they realized they couldn't force me to stay."

"How did they take it?"

"Not well." His dark expression lights up. "But anyone can wear a mask, right? My manager found a replacement, so it's all final. The news will be out next month, as soon as the PR department's done coming up with whatever bullshit story they think will sell best. Until then, this is one huge secret no one's supposed to know about. Except my team, my family, and..." He points his thumb at me. "You."

"So... officially, you're still the lead singer of Mile High." He nods. "And privately, you're—"

"Only a cowboy."

I nod gravely and tilt my head back.

Only a cowboy.

I like the sound of that.

A soft smile tugs at his lips as his hands cup my face. "I'm getting older, Ava. In eighteen months, I'll be thirty. That's like a dinosaur in music years. It was about time I retired and went back to my roots.

To a time when things were simple. To the things I once took for granted." He draws a deep breath, hesitating. "Of course, it's scary to leave everything behind, but you know, it's another reason why I wanted you to get to know the real me, not the image that I've been feeding to the public. To most people out there, I'll always be K. Taylor. But to you, I want to be Kellan Boyd."

"I think I like the real Kellan Boyd," I whisper so low I doubt he can hear me.

"Come with me." Before I know what's happening, he leads me away from the street, through the meadow, to an old wooden fence.

Away from the lights, the stars are more prominent.

He takes my hand and helps me climb up the fence until I sit on top of it, then he joins me. We're sitting so close our arms almost brush, but his proximity feels right.

Everything about him feels right.

Except the fact that he's famous, and I'm just some ordinary girl from NYC.

"I love it here." My low voice sounds surprisingly alien, surreal.

In the silence around us, I can't stop thinking about his sister, about the dream of a real cowboy to support his family, and the risks he took to get there.

Kellan has an amazing voice, and music is his passion.

People out there deserve to hear his songs.

I want to hear his songs, but I also feel sad for the man who wanted to quit all along, and yet didn't, until it was too late and his sister had already died serving her country.

"I love it too. But I love it even more now that you're here," Kellan says.

CHAPTER THIRTY-ONE

"SO, WHAT DO you think?" Kellan asks.

He *is* nervous. His tone is less forceful than usual. Less sure of himself. "Here I am, famous and rich, and I'm going to throw it all away. Not the money, of course, but everything else. Does that sound sane to you?"

Sane?

What is sane?

Besides, who am I to judge what is sane for him, and what isn't?

"It think it sounds human." I smile at him. "You must be really sick of your job."

He lets out a laugh. "You have no idea."

"It's okay." I shrug. "What you're doing is

definitely better than planning to kill your boss. Take me, for example. I sure would kill mine, if I thought I'd get away with it."

Which is just a joke, obviously.

But TB *is* unbearable. The mere thought of her breathing down my neck has me covered in a cold sweat.

"I knew you'd get me." His voice is serious again. His foot is tapping against the wood. His whole posture is tense.

"Yep, kindred spirits and all."

"So, now that you know the truth, has your opinion about me changed?" he asks. "Are you disappointed?"

In the soft moonlight, I can see that he's still smiling, but his nervousness is obvious. He doesn't need to say why he's feeling this way. I understand.

Quitting his job and turning his back on a world he's lived in for years is unsettling. The future's unpredictable.

People won't know the exact circumstances. Rumors will soon spread. The tabloids will say that he failed, entered rehab, died. Soon, people will move on and forget him. He'll become a nobody to them.

As a journalist, I know. This business is cruel. It

doesn't care about one's feelings. It only cares about money and selling more copies than the competition.

"Disappointed? Hell, no. I'm actually glad." My fingers move to intertwine with his. "I don't know about you, but I don't like things to be complicated."

He stays silent for a long time.

"Those six days with you were amazing, Ava," he says at last. "Before, I didn't know if I could trust you, but you turned out to be exactly the woman I thought you were."

I don't know whether to take that as a compliment. I still haven't quite figured out *the* Kellan Boyd, but I'd like to dedicate my time to solve the mystery he is.

"And who do you think I am?" I ask.

"Someone who's amazing. Someone I want to get to know in depth."

My breath hitches in my throat.

This is my chance to tell him that's exactly what I want, too, and yet I keep quiet, letting him continue.

"The moment I met you, I knew you were different. You weren't dressed up to see some band greeting the crowd in a nightclub. You weren't even there to see the band." His gaze flicks around the meadows before it settles on my eyes and lips again.

"I liked that, so I remembered your license registration and found out your name, where you lived, basically everything I could find out about you. It helps that my brother's the deputy sheriff around here."

"Wow. That's creepy." I slap his thigh in mock annoyance, marveling how hard and sculpted his muscles are. "See, that's why I told Mandy about you. I knew you were a creep, albeit a hot one," I say, my voice low as I think back three months ago, give or take a week or two. "If Ryder found out my number, you could have called me."

"You would never have talked to me, Ava. You made it clear that you didn't like me." His gaze meets mine. The glint of candor in his eyes makes me flinch. "And I don't blame you. I was an ass. But I still needed to see you again. It wasn't until my sister died that I had the courage to change my life, so I came up with a plan. I persuaded my band mates to play a last, small gig in Montana and made sure that you were picked as the winner in a radio giveaway swoop."

In spite of the fact that he deceived me into seeing him again and omitted most of the details about his life, I can't help but feel touched. No one's ever done something remotely twisted for me.

Then again, it is quite the romantic story.

Definitely one I could tell my children—leaving out Kellan's obnoxious sexual innuendoes and the part where he went down on me in his brother's back yard.

And the week-long, non-stop sex.

And the part where he made himself cum, and I watched him, which probably makes me the bigger creep out of the two of us.

"I have to say, that's the nicest thing someone's ever done for me," I whisper.

Kellan nods. "I have to admit it's also the weirdest thing I've done for anyone."

"But why me?" I ask.

He jumps off the fence and shifts in front of me, settling between my legs. His arms wrap around my waist. I lean into him and clasp my hands at the nape of his neck.

"Remember the first moment I met you?"

I nod, my pulse racing. "Yes."

Each and every detail.

"I was hypnotized—and angry as hell," Kellan says, grinning. "When I got back to my brother's place, where I always stay when I'm in NYC, the first thing I did was call my sister and tell her everything. She said that I was an ass to you. Those words stuck."

"Two women offending your ego in the same night?" I let out a laugh. "How did you take it?"

He smirks. "Don't ask. I told her that you're a New Yorker, and that you bunch of folks aren't exactly friendly. That I had no choice but to be an ass because you weren't exactly the epitome of cordiality either."

I open my mouth to protest, when he presses a finger to my lips.

"Remember the first moment I saw you again? Completely soaked, with that tiny umbrella in your hand, ready to battle a storm? That's the first time I felt happy since Clara's death."

His words stop my world.

I can't believe it, and yet I know it's true. We both make each other happy. I can feel it in the way he seems to own my heart. In the way his eyes lock with mine when he's inside me, holding me, possessing me.

When did that happen?

"At first, I thought someone was pulling a prank." He grins. "When you knocked on my door, I assumed Josh was behind it. Or maybe Ryder. Maybe even Cash, even though he's in Boston right now, and I only mentioned you once or twice."

"Is that why you—"

He nods, interrupting me. "Why I was so mad?"

No...why you almost kicked me out, I want to say but don't.

"I thought Josh had arranged for you to arrive on my doorstep," Kellan continues. "I wasn't mad at you. I was mad at myself and at him. Then we got talking, and I realized it was all a coincidence. To be honest, I had you pinned down as this city girl, and I didn't know what you'd make of seeing me here. This is my life, Ava. The plan was to meet you at the hotel, then introduce you to the idea gradually and see what happened." He shakes his head, laughing. "But life has this tendency to kick you where it hurts at the most unfortunate of times. Mandy took a wrong turn, and you ended up here. That isn't just crappy luck. It's fate."

I stare at him in disbelief. "You could have sent flowers. An I'm-sorry-for-bumping-your-car card." I grasp for words. "You could have turned up at Starbucks."

He inclines his head, thinking. "And risk exposing myself to someone I couldn't yet trust? I don't think so. It's hard to get to know people in the city. I was convinced you'd suspect who I was, like so many others. That you'd recognize my voice. That you might be a fan and would want to be with me because of my image and everything it stands for. When I realized you really had no idea who I was and that you'd never want to date a rock star, I thought that you were an extraordinary woman. No one ever rejected me the way you did. It reminded me of the times before it all started, when I was still me."

"So it never bothered you in the slightest that I wasn't a fan of Mile High?" I ask.

"I have to admit, I was offended...at first." He catches my exasperated sigh and laughs. "What? I was an ass, okay? I really was. But..." He shakes his head, his laugh dying. "But my sister's death has made me rethink life, the choices I've made. I think I lost myself along the way. It's time that I change that." He shrugs and leans into me, his breath scorching my lips. "I wish you could have met her. She would have liked you."

It's the second time he's saying that.

"How do you know?" I ask softly.

"I just know," he whispers and lifts my hand to his mouth. Slowly, he kisses my fingers, each touch sending shivers through me.

"You're one in a million, Ava, and it was important that you know the real me, not the one you see in the media. I hope you understand that I needed you somewhere else. Somewhere outside of your comfort zone." His eyes meet mine—green as the meadows. Emeralds catching the light cast by the moon over our heads. "I needed you to see my home. To fall in love with it."

The moment is thick with meaning. I know letting someone into his private space is a huge deal for him. A rock star as famous as he is has no privacy. I understand his problem, his dilemma. He has to fight for what normal people take for granted.

"Every day I thought I would forget you, but the next morning broke, and then the next, and I couldn't get you out of my mind," he whispers. "So, here you are."

"Here I am," I reply.

"Are you mad?" He lifts his hand to stroke my cheek. The movement is gentle, the calluses on his fingers grating my skin.

"No. Not at all." My lips tug upward, but the smile is somewhat nostalgic. "I think you went a bit overboard, but all in all, it's nothing to be mad about."

"I'm still amazed you found this place. It's what people would call destiny."

"You believe in destiny?" I ask, amused.

"Yes." He cocks his head, catching my amused expression. "What? I believe that we earn what we reap. I believe in good sex. I believe in instant attraction. I also believe in love at first sight. And I believe that likes attract likes. I believe that we know when the right person comes along. That love doesn't need to be sought and found. It'll find you when it finds you."

"You had to squeeze the sex part in," I say, laughing. "You do realize that has nothing to do with destiny, right?"

"Fair enough." He helps me off the fence and kisses me gently. "I want you to move here."

That would require me to quit my job. Throw away all my future opportunities.

I feel faint as it hits me. The blood drains out of my body, and my knees turn weak until they feel like jelly.

"Please come back home with me," Kellan whispers, his voice slightly choked.

Back home.

Not house, but home.

Coming from him, the words sound so damn inviting, I flinch. He says it like he means it.

Dangerous.

That's what he is. To any woman's heart, not just

mine.

I know I'm in love with him. That's why his words are so damn enticing.

I look at him and realize that, ever since seeing Kellan again, I haven't missed my old life. I haven't missed my job or my tiny apartment. But after saying our goodbyes, I sure missed him.

Home isn't a place; it's a feeling; it's the people who make you feel that you belong.

I know that I belong here, with him, by his side.

But does he want me the way I want him? Is there even room for someone like me in his life? Can I throw away my job, my life, everything I've worked so hard for?

My mouth opens and closes. "You want me to quit my job?"

"I want you to move here. Live with me for a while. Enjoy the countryside, and see what happens."

"But you don't know me."

"That's not true, Ava. I know you perfectly. I know enough to be able to tell you that—" He stops abruptly, his expression darkening.

"What?"

He moistens his lips, taking his time. "I know enough to tell you that I want you to stay. In my life." He brushes a strand of hair out of my face, curling it around his finger. "It was hard enough to get you here. I'm not ready to let you go."

I stare at him in silence.

My throat closes up. Everything inside me is shaking.

"I'm not sure I can," I whisper, the voice soft, defeated. "I have a job in the city."

"So quit." He sighs.

"You know I can't."

"If it's about the money, I can pay you to work for me. I—"

"No." I shake my head. "I could never accept your money. You know that."

Besides, I'm pretty sure Montana has newspapers and magazines. I could even freelance if I wanted to.

"I know," he whispers, and we fall silent. "If you decide to leave, I want you to know that my offer still stands. You can come back anytime, no matter how long it takes for you to make that decision."

"You would wait for me?" I ask.

He nods. "I would be doing a lot more than that." He lifts my chin. "Can you promise that you'll think about it, Ava?"

I love the way he says my name in that rumble of his. As if I'm the only star in the sky.

I swallow the lump in my throat. "I can do that."

His breath is tickling my face as he kisses me. His scent is intoxicating. The thought of being away from him is unbearable.

I wasn't supposed to feel anything for him, and yet I'm doing exactly that.

I don't know how long we're standing frozen in time, our arms wrapped around each other. Breathing each other in, while building up the courage to let each other go.

But I know I cannot give up my life. It would be too crazy. Too insane. All the money and time spent for my education, my future, I would have to give up. For what? For a guy who rocked my world for all of six days?

And yet—

My heart is asking me to be with him. Not seeing him again would shatter me.

Moving on...it's what I'm supposed to do.

That's what everyone would advise me to do.

In my mind, I can hear my parents' voices and Mandy's and all their warnings about not giving up my life for a guy.

Saying goodbye will be hard. Harder than before, when I was clueless and Kellan a mystery.

But what if, for once, I break the rules, let my

heart lead the way?

What if Kellan is that one single chance at finding happiness and love?

What if staying is the right decision?

What if building memories throughout life is more important than a career or being famous?

"Kellan?" I lift my head from his chest and look up at him. My voice is shaking. My head is spinning from all the questions and the choices I have to make. My soul is split.

But the heart wants what it wants.

There is a short silence as he tries to read my expression. "Yeah?"

Just like before, I can feel he's nervous, or maybe I'm seeing my own reflection in his eyes.

I trail a shaky finger over his cheek, enjoying the chafing sensation of his evening stubble on my skin.

"I cannot believe what I'm about to say—" I swallow hard "—but I'm staying. I'm giving us a chance."

His lips curl into a perfect smile. "I want you to."

"It's crazy. You know it is."

"Yeah, it is." He laughs, the deep sound reverberating through his chest and penetrating every layer of me. "I know this is a hard decision for you. Will it help if I give you a good reason for it?"

"Maybe. Depends."

"Okay." He turns me around until my back is pressed against his chest. At first, I'm not sure what he's doing, until his arms go around my waist, embracing me from behind. I can feel his breath on me, hear him inhaling the scent of my hair, his nose nestling between my shoulder blade and neck.

"I love you, Ava," he whispers. "I don't know where things will lead us. I don't know what our friends will say, or what the future has in store for us, or if this is one big mistake. But there's one thing I'm absolutely certain of. I love you. I don't want you to go. I don't want to lose you before we've even begun."

I turn around, shocked. The magnitude of the moment dawns on me...and yet I'm not quite able to grasp it. "I thought you didn't like me."

He shakes his head. "No, I didn't like the fact that I fell in love with you. I couldn't think of anything else but you. You occupied my day and night, every moment, every breath. After months of thinking about you and six days together, I think it's about time that you know I love you. And that I'm absolutely certain..." He trails off.

He loves me?

I blink, then blink some more.

I love you too, I want to yell, but I can't with the rock lodged in my throat.

"You're absolutely certain that..." I prompt, barely able to breathe.

"That I want to marry you." His expression is deadpan.

I frown, unsure what he's talking about.

He can't possibly—

I stare at him, trying to catch a sign that he's joking. And then it hits me.

Holy shit.

Holy. Crap.

My hands begin to shake.

"Wait. Are you proposing to me?" I ask, feeling really stupid for even saying something like that out loud.

I must have misunderstood.

"Yes, Ava. I am," Kellan says slowly. "Or why else do you think I'd be talking about destiny and all that stuff?" He cocks his head, a naughty grin on his lips. "So, the answer is..."

"No." There is no doubt about it. I can't lie. "I love you, too, Kellan," I whisper. "I love you, but you can be a jerk. There's no way, absolutely no way, I'm getting married to you after six days. That's crazy. That's insane."

"I love crazy and insane." He laughs at my horrified expression. "In fact, this is such a great idea. That 'no' of yours—" he winks "—we'll see about that. I tricked you once, you know, when you didn't want to fuck me. I did it again when I persuaded you to stay. What are the chances the third time's a charm?"

"I'm pretty sure that's not how the saying goes, and it sure doesn't fit the context," I say, annoyed that, yes, he's been pretty good at persuading me, and I didn't even notice. "Kellan, we're not getting married just because you feel the need to get your way with me."

"Okay," he says, nodding.

I narrow my eyes because I don't trust him. He's never been one to give up easily. "Okay? Just like that?"

"Sure. Whatever you say, baby." His lips find mine in a sweet kiss that soon turns not so sweet after all, as his hands begin to roam over my ass and travel places.

EPILOGUE

Two years later

IF I HAD known that my first meeting with Kellan would be followed with the loss of his sister, I would have accepted his first offer sooner and ignored my mind harder, if only to join him faster. If only to ease his mourning. It's clear that her death made him face his own demons and question his own beliefs, that she is the reason for the immense change in his life.

It's a slow process. Healing can take time, but I'm patient and confident.

While he doesn't blame himself for her death anymore, I still sense his regret for not being home when she was here.

I would have loved to meet Clara. I think we would have bonded. And it's thanks to her that

Kellan's life is where he wants it to be.

He's different now compared to the first time we met. The arrogance is almost gone. Left behind is a caring, down-to-earth, and committed man. He says that's who he was before he became famous. I don't know if that's true. All I know is that I love him and I don't miss K. Taylor one bit.

Today marks the day we first met in front of Club 69. I might have only known him for two short years, but he and Mandy are the people I trust the most. He's closer to me than anyone's ever been.

More than my parents. Even more than my best friends.

If someone had told me Kellan would change my life for the better, I would have laughed. In so many ways, I changed too.

As it turned out, there was never a question of whether I wanted to quit my old life. Things would have turned out the way they have anyway:

The moment the lines were back on and I switched on my phone, I received a *nice* voicemail from my boss from Hell, in which TB declared me fired for switching off my phone. Apparently, by being caught in a storm, I was violating one of the clauses in my work contract, which stipulated that I was to be available to her at all times.

My parents didn't even notice I was away. They were too busy with their own lives and work at the orchestra, so they didn't even pretend to miss me when I told them about moving to Montana.

During their one-week vacation, Mandy had invited Josh to come to NYC and stay with us in our tiny apartment, as if it wasn't already too crowded. Apparently, it sort of clicked between them and they were dating. So, moving back there wasn't even an option. I mean, no one wants to be the third wheel, right?

Last but not least, after the hurricane alert, my landlord panicked and decided to double our rent, in spite of the fact that a pipe had burst during our vacation. So I paid my share, thanked TB for the work experience, sent my parents an email to inform them of my new address, then tied up all loose ends, packed my bags, and moved to Montana.

That's where I've now been for almost two years. Kellan's family and friends have become my home.

So, no, I don't regret the change. As it turns out, trust your heart because she knows better.

Kellan was the right decision, the right choice.

I love my new life.

While I still love to help Kellan with the farm every once in a while, he does have people who do most of the work. I've become a freelance journalist and earn good money. (You hear that, TB? You can shove that job up your tiny ass.)

I haven't been to NYC in a long time, and at first, I thought I would miss it, but I don't. I don't miss it at all. I had been so engrossed with my work that I forgot how to breathe, to live in the moment, to not take people around me for granted. Stripped bare of all the things that come with working for someone like TB, I recognize how stressful my life had been. It makes me wonder how much pressure Kellan was under when he was on tour. I have no doubt that sooner or later, he would have turned into an addict like Rock, or suicidal like Casper.

As to Kellan's previous life, his music company spun a sensational story that he was fired. Apparently something about him being hard to work with.

The lie annoys me to no end, but Kellan says it's okay.

Just as expected, the news that K. Taylor was no longer the lead singer of Mile High resulted in a mass panic among the female population. Rumors started to circulate that he had checked into rehab like Rock, that he had OD'ed, that he had disappeared from the surface of the earth—all not true, obviously.

Kellan didn't seem the least bothered about all the wild speculation. Maybe it was all pretense, or maybe he really didn't give a damn. He says his previous life is nothing but a past chapter in a long book.

He's probably right.

After five months, the rumors began to die down, and the tabloids moved on. The next big headline made its way to the front pages, and Kellan was forgotten.

Mile High hasn't achieved the same success. It's not because of the new lead singer—the replacement is almost as good as Kellan, but only almost. With the mask on, they even look a bit alike, and people have been claiming that the story of K. Taylor's dropout was nothing but a propaganda spin to get media coverage.

As it happens, Mile High has slowly been disappearing off the radar, maybe because the new lead singer doesn't quite have K. Taylor's allure.

To me, they don't look alike.

I would recognize Kellan's broad shoulders and magnetic green eyes anywhere.

It's a new band—a bunch of eighteen-year-olds from Mississippi—that has taken the world by storm. Including Mandy.

Talk about so not being loyal to her old band. She even had the nerve to ask me to go see them live, which, of course, I declined politely.

It's one of those little secrets I'll take with me to the grave because I'd never think of saying something to Kellan that might hurt him.

The only thing I regret is not having accepted his marriage proposal that night when I heard him sing for the first time. Back then, I convinced myself that it was just a joke, even though it had felt very real.

He hasn't mentioned it again, and I'm not going to raise the subject.

I guess he's forgotten. I guess, too, that at that time I wasn't ready.

But I am now. More so because I'm expecting.

Only, I have no idea how Kellan will react.

The thought of telling him makes me a little sick.

I still haven't told Mandy about it because she can never keep her mouth shut, and I'm afraid she'll drop not-so-subtle hints to Kellan at every opportunity. Part of me wants to pick up the phone and call her, while another part of me refrains from doing so. I've been torn about it every single time we talk on the phone, and that's almost daily.

Music is still a huge part of Kellan's life. It's

inside him, in his blood. It's his way to express his soul, much like a writer lives for pouring their heart out through words. He often lets me sit in a corner, out of his vision, listening to his beautiful, smoky voice when he's composing one of his songs, which he usually goes on to play at Sharon's bar on a Saturday night whenever he feels like it.

***

It's early evening, and Kellan's not back yet. I'm sitting on the couch in the living room, cradling my laptop on my lap, a mug of coffee on the side table, when I hear the door open. I look up from my notes to Sniper trotting toward me.

"Good boy, Sniper." My hand reaches out to pat him, when I notice there's something in his mouth. He lets it drop to my feet. I pick up the small piece of paper and laugh. "I hope you didn't dig this up from some grave."

The dog wags his tail in response.

I unfold the paper and realize it's a handwritten note that reads:

Take Brenna and come to the barn.

I put my laptop aside and rise from my sitting position quickly. Even though Kellan can be pretty monosyllabic at times, his note makes me worried. It's probably about one of his horses, and he needs me. It wouldn't be the first time he's asking for my help.

Sniper follows me outside.

The ride to the barn only takes me a few minutes. Brenna might be the quietest horse, but she's a real cannon. Thanks to all the riding lessons I've had with Kellan (not all have involved a horse), I'm not afraid of riding her. The only thing I still refuse to learn to ride is a bull, even though it's a tradition among the Boyd brothers. It took me a whole week to convince Kellan to give it up for the time being out of fear that he might break his neck.

As I'm nearing the barn, I can make out the horses in the meadows, but there is no sign of Kellan.

I dismount Brenna and bind her to a post.

"Kellan?" I call out and cock my head to listen.

There's no reply, which can only mean Kellan is either busy with a horse inside the barn and can't hear me, or he's writing a new song and has his headphones on.

I heave a little sigh and stroll through the open

doors of the barn, freezing in place.

The entire ceiling is covered in red, heart-shaped balloons. The walls have been painted off-white. LED light curtains bathe the entire place in a beautiful glow.

Pink confetti and rose petals litter the spread-out rug.

On the right side, tables and chairs have been set up, as though we're having a party. On the far end, people have gathered, among which I spy Mandy, my parents, Josh, and Kellan's brother Ryder. Even Cash is here, which must be a sure sign that someone has died because the guy's either glued to one of his clubs' décor or the back of a bull.

I stare, unsure what's going on, when my gaze catches Kellan's. He's dressed in a tailored suit that manages to emphasize his broad shoulders and narrow hips. And is that a haircut? Compared to his usual jeans and shirt and tousled hair, he looks so different I'm not sure this is the same person I'm dating.

People begin to follow his line of vision, and within seconds, everyone's staring at me.

What the heck?

Someone takes my hand. It's the neighbor's kid—a chubby five-year-old girl in a beautiful dress.

"What's going on?" I mumble.

The kid tugs at my hand, leading me through the crowd to Kellan.

He's standing on a makeshift platform, cradling a microphone in his hand. Behind him, Ryder and Cash arrange their guitar and bass.

Cash nods at me encouragingly, and Mandy smiles. I think I'm pretty good at reading faces, so I know something's going on, but for the life of me, I can't figure out what this is all about.

Why's everyone here?

Was I so involved in my work that I forgot about a birthday party?

I shoot Kellan a questioning look. He nods at his brothers, and they start playing.

His beautiful green eyes pierce me a moment before he starts to sing, his voice raw and gritty and breathtaking.

She chipped my car
No words she said
Left me behind with a scar
As she drove miles away
In a Ford as old as my pop
So I called Ryder, who's a cop

Who are you,
My check torn in two
My heart in a strange place
Don't know your name
Wish I could see you one more time
To tell you that I'll make you mine
To teach you how to make love on the floor
Make you plead and scream for more

City girl,
I'm only a cowboy
I know this will drive you insane
But when I say I want you to stay
I mean it for real and for life
Oh baby,
When you hear this song
Better listen
It's the song you don't wanna miss

Beautiful, sexy, hot and kind
Just a few words that come to mind
When I look at you
All I wanna do

Happy, joyful, excited, and mad in love
Pound, pulse, shudder, throbbing

Just a few words that come to mind
When I look at you
All I wanna do

Oh baby,
When you hear this song
Better listen
It's the song you don't wanna miss
When I look at you
All I wanna do

He kneels before me, grinning, and the music stops—in the middle of the refrain. The silence is heavy and thick, as though everyone's forgotten to breathe. I stare at Kellan, whose right hand is reaching for mine, while his left hand is still holding up the mic.

His magnetic eyes are on me, and I can tell he is shaking.

I feel faint.

The sudden silence is too much. Earthshattering.

My heart is slamming hard against my chest, and I realize tears have gathered in my eyes. I'm shaking too.

I know what he is about to do, but I can't grasp the meaning of it.

My dream is so close, I can almost taste it, and yet it feels so far out of reach, it might as well be just that—

Only a dream.

"Ava, I love you," Kellan says into the mic, his deep voice steady, beautiful, penetrating every layer of my soul. "That day you damaged my car, that's the night I first wanted you. When I asked you to stay, I thought that would be all I'd ever want. I thought what I felt for you would pass. But I was wrong. I want you more than ever. I want you with me, by my side. I want to wake up next to you every morning for the rest of my life. I asked our families to be here so they can witness the most important day of my life. It's the day I want to tell you that I belong to you, and you would make me the happiest man alive if you became mine."

Pausing, he reaches inside his pocket to retrieve a black velvet box and opens it.

My heart throbs. Metaphorically drops. If I looked down, I'm sure I would find it at my feet. The ring is so beautiful it takes my breath away. I look up from the sparkling diamond to his eyes. They're shimmering with emotion. Fear. Happiness. Anticipation.

This is his moment, our moment.

"Ava." His voice is slightly choked now. "Will you marry me?"

I'm happy and overwhelmed. I clasp my hand in front of my mouth. My heart screams yes, but I'm having trouble pushing that sound out of my lungs. I just nod before I finally croak out, "God, yes. Yes. Yes."

I keep repeating it. He's all that matters in my life.

He is my life.

Kellan rises to his feet and slides the ring on my finger. His arms wrap around my waist, and then he kisses me. His lips are sweet and warm, and feel like home. I don't know what to say.

I'm touched.

I'm emotional.

People are cheering. Congratulations are raining down on us, but I'm too lost in Kellan's eyes to hear them. I want to stay in his arms forever.

I won't ever let him go.

Before I know it, he steps back and flashes me a grin. The music starts again.

City girl,
I'm only a cowboy
I know this will drive you insane

But when I say I want you to stay
I mean it for real and for life

City girl,
I'm only a cowboy
I know this will drive you insane
But when I say I want to marry you
I mean it for real and for life

When I say I'll marry you
I mean it for real and for life

When the song finishes, he receives a loud ovation, and the hugging begins—first Mandy, then my parents, then Kellan's brothers, who are huge and strong like Kellan, and from up close scare the crap out of me.

Seriously, I hope they won't smother me.

The party begins. Food and drinks are being served. We chat. We tell stories. We laugh. But Kellan's eyes never let me go.

It's only later, when the engagement party's over, and everyone is gone, and there's only us in the barn, that I sit on Kellan's lap.

I cannot help but keep staring at my ring.

It's such a big rock.

"Are you sure?" he asks, catching me staring at my ring again. "And you're not saying yes just because everyone was here, and there was a lot of pressure on you?"

"I think that's why you called everyone for emotional support. Your ego couldn't take another 'no.'" I kiss his lips, my mouth lingering on his, breathing him in, indulging in his taste and scent. "I've been waiting for this moment for the past eighteen months. You sure took your time."

His brows shoot up. "Well, I had to make sure you wouldn't refuse me. I worked hard to change your mind."

"I never had to change my mind, Kellan," I whisper. "I already knew I wanted to be with you the moment I saw you. I just thought you were too good to be true. That you couldn't possibly be serious about us."

He frowns. "Why would you think that?"

I shrug. "You're still famous, Kellan. You have the looks and the talent, and could go back to the rock star life any time. You could have any woman in this world, and yet you chose me."

"I did, probably because I only like one type, and that's you." His voice is soft, his tone meaningful. "I love you, Ava."

"I love you, too." I smile at him, then look into his eyes, and think of how our future will soon change. My voice is slightly choked. "Kellan, will you still marry me if I tell you that I'm pregnant?"

His eyes widen, though I can't tell whether it's with shock or horror. "You're pregnant?"

I nod. I'm so happy, and yet I don't know whether I should feel this way.

What if he breaks up with me? He said he'd never commit to someone with kids.

Instead of anger or confusion, I find his lips breaking into a smile. His eyes shimmer with joy.

"All the more reason to get married then." His smile turns into a grin. He's about to say something to try and annoy me. "Except..."

"Except?"

"How far are you along?"

I know what he's doing. He's being a jerk for the sake of it.

"Five weeks, and yes, to answer any doubts you might have, it's your child." I laugh. "I can't believe you were about to ask me that. You're so insatiable, I barely have the energy to walk around the house, let alone fuck someone else."

"Sorry." He lets out a laugh. "Old habits die hard. I just needed you to acknowledge that last part. I've been dying to hear it. How come you didn't tell me sooner?"

"We never talked about kids," I say slowly.

"I wanted to broach the marriage subject first," Kellan says. "I know how I feel about kids. They're all going to be trouble, particularly if they carry the Boyd blood." His fingers trail down my neck gently. "You'll have your hands full. I cannot wait to start a family with you. I wish you had told me earlier."

"Why?"

"Because I would have insisted that we get married soon so I can have you all to myself before I have to share you with a brat." His smile softens, and I remember why I fell in love with him.

He's funny, witty, and a little bit outrageous, and that's exactly what I need in my life.

Someone who doesn't take himself too seriously.

Someone who can make me laugh and let me be myself.

"You'll be a great dad," I whisper.

"I hope so." His hand reaches for my fingers and gives them a light squeeze. "I'm going to spoil our kid to bits. And then there's also Uncle Cash and Ryder. And my dad. They'll go nuts when they hear this."

I have no doubt about that. They've already been

asking when we'd start a family.

"Come on." I jump up from his lap and try to pull him to his feet, which, given his height and weight, is an impossible task. "I have great plans for you. After the stunt you pulled, I have to reward you."

"I'll take my reward happily. We could do it right here, right now."

As his hands begin to roam my body, removing layers of clothes, until I'm naked and panting, his erection filling me, I see the strap of a handbag slung across one of the chairs.

Someone must have forgotten it.

It'll only be a matter of time before they come back to get it.

They'll catch us red-handed.

It wouldn't be the first time.

Damn.

"Kellan," I moan his name as wave after wave of pleasure rocks my body. "Let's go home."

"Home?" he asks, his voice hoarse, his smile naughty. I swear it's the most mischievous I've ever seen. "We're already home, Ava."

His lips descend upon mine again, and it's like the world stands still and everything around us is spinning. Our worlds crash, collide, blur in one single moment.

We couldn't be more different: Kellan Boyd, a famous singer, and me, a normal girl from NYC.

But love happens.

One crash.

One beautiful distraction.

A cowboy who meets a city girl.

That's how the ball started rolling. That's how it all began. How the biggest sacrifice ended in the greatest reward. I can't wait to become Ava Boyd.

Life out here might seem a bit boring, but there's nothing boring about my future husband.

There's something I need to tell him, but I can't remember what it is. All I can do is make a silent promise to be the greatest wife he could ever have, because Kellan Boyd is one in a million.

And he's mine.

----THE END----

Loved Ava and Kellan's story? It doesn't have to end!

Each one of the Boyd brothers will get his own story.

Cash Boyd ➡ *Wild For You*

Ryder Boyd ➡ **Yet untitled**

Don't miss their release. Subscribe to the J.C. Reed Mailing List to be notified on release day: http://www.jcreedauthor.com/mailinglist

Also, fans of An Indecent Proposal will be happy to hear that all subscribers will receive the free novella, *Half Truths*. It's available exclusively for readers who subscribe to my mailing list.

Watch out for

LOVE ADDICTS
ANONYMOUS

(A standalone NOVEL)

by J.C. Reed

COMING LATE SPRING 2016

Watch out for

WILD FOR YOU

(A standalone NOVEL)

by J.C. Reed

COMING SUMMER 2016

ACKNOWLEDGMENTS

First and foremost, thank you to my family for allowing me to follow my dreams. Your support through my writing journey has been amazing. You are my inspiration, my motivation, and my reward.

Thank you to my amazing friend Jackie. Your encouragement and funny comments throughout the book have been a journey in themselves. You make the unbearable part of writing bearable. I don't know what I'd do without you.

Thank you to Larissa for this awesome cover and for being with me since the very beginning of my writing career.

I hope you never retire, because I'll still need you for many years to come.

Thank you to Kim Bias. You've always been a good friend to me. Thank you for ensuring that my work is ready for the world to read.

My huge gratitude goes to my beta readers, reviewers and bloggers. I'm most grateful for all who have supported me.

Thank you to my cats and my dog who I swear thinks she's a cat. You have been most my patient and superb companions while writing late at night.

Most of all, thank you to all my readers.

Thank you for reading and enjoying my stories, and for loving my characters. I cannot wait to share my next book with you.

Xxx

Jessica

ABOUT THE AUTHOR

J.C. Reed is the multiple New York Times, Wall Street Journal and USA Today bestselling author of the SURRENDER YOUR LOVE, NO EXCEPTIONS and AN INDECENT PROPOSAL series. She writes steamy contemporary fiction with a touch of mystery. When she's not typing away on her keyboard, forgetting the world around her, she dreams of returning to the beautiful mountains of Wyoming. You can also find her chatting on Facebook with her readers or spending time with her children.

https://www.facebook.com/AuthorJCReed

http://www.jcreedauthor.co

BOOKS BY J.C. REED:

SURRENDER YOUR LOVE TRILOGY

SURRENDER YOUR LOVE
CONQUER YOUR LOVE
TREASURE YOUR LOVE

NO EXCEPTIONS SERIES

THE LOVER'S SECRET
THE LOVER'S GAME
THE LOVER'S PROMISE
THE LOVER'S SURRENDER

AN INDECENT PROPOSAL TRILOGY

AN INDECENT PROPOSAL: THE INTERVIEW
AN INDECENT PROPOSAL: THE AGREEMENT
AN INDECENT PROPOSAL: BAD BOY

STANDALONE BOOKS

BEAUTIFUL DISTRACTION

Printed in Great Britain
by Amazon